THE CUNDY

SULLIVAN CARTER SERIES | BOOK ONE

R. H. DIXON

CORVUS CORONE PRESS

Front cover by Carrion Crow Design.

A CIP catalogue record for this title is available from the British Library.

ISBN: 978-1-9997180-6-0

Corvus Corone Press.

For Derek

Other books by R. H. Dixon:

EMERGENCE
A STORYTELLING OF RAVENS
CRIBBINS

The Collins Dictionary's definition of cundy:

Cundy in British (Scottish dialect)

1. A drain or drain entrance
2. A tunnel or passage

"You must have chaos within you to give birth to a dancing star."
— **Friedrich Nietzsche**

R. H. DIXON

1

1996

It was just after one in the afternoon when Mrs Carlton the maths teacher got electrocuted in the storage cupboard. I was in Mr Dunn's physics class at the time, looking out the window at the rain and listening to it beating down on the roof of the science block. It was a heavy, constant sound, like dogs dancing on the corrugated steel; somewhat comforting in its persistence, in its tenacious effort to ruin the Sports Day training activities which were lined up for later that afternoon. I, for one, was quietly cheering it on. I could do without the indignity of multiple failed attempts at long jumping, shot putting and javelin throwing like I could do without a poke in the eye with a pointed stick.

Philip Grisdale, a Year Eleven pupil with beefy arms and a wisp of bumfluff on his top lip, burst into the science lab to announce Mrs Carlton's unfortunate mishap. His round face was flushed not only with the exertion of having run from wherever to broadcast the news, but with the exhilaration of the high drama associated with the maths teacher's incident.

'Get out of here, boy!' Mr Dunn, a boyish looking old man who always wore suits of varying shades of brown, marking some Year Nine essays on The Crucible at the time and had to be taken to hospital to be treated for concussion. Some of the girls had speculated that maybe the spirit of Abigail Williams was responsible. You know, as though it was totally plausible that a group of 20th Century thirteen-to-fourteen-year-olds in the UK, who'd been analysing the story of the partially fictionalised play as part of their English Lit. classes, might have evoked the actual ghost of Abigail Williams from the 17th century Salem Witch Trial in the US, who had in turn unleashed a teenage strop on Mr Scott. But, hey, that's teenage girls for you. They don't always make a great deal of sense, do they?

Just minutes after Philip Grisdale had left the classroom, a Year Ten prefect, whose name I didn't know, came to tell Mr Dunn that Miss Ward, the school receptionist, had arranged for two buses to come and collect those of us who lived in Horden. We were to be sent home early after all. The prefect had a spiral perm, startlingly white slouch socks which were bunched around her thick ankles and a mouth full of metal braces, which I imagined must snag the insides of her mouth when she talked. Mr Dunn didn't try to banish her as he had Philip Grisdale, he simply flung his tweed jacket with the brown elbow patches about his shoulders and told us all in no uncertain terms to 'clear your stuff away and get out.'

I took my time packing my things into my bag, then slow-walked my way towards the school gates. En route, I overheard three girls who were in my year dramatising the events of the afternoon. There was plenty of arm waving going on and delighted gasps of horror as one of the trio relayed information to the others about how an ambulance had taken Mrs Carlton away only fifteen minutes earlier and that, as the maths teacher's unconscious body had been stretchered out of the school by two burly paramedics, her skin had sizzled in the rain.

I wondered if by the following week, rumour would have it that Mrs Carlton had been possessed by Beelzebub himself; the validity of the claim strengthened by the sheer evilness of the algebra she'd unleashed on us all lately. Or perhaps gossip would suggest she'd been struck down by Thor's hammer of justice, Mjölnir, as punishment for dishing out long division homework every Friday morning without fail, which was always due to be handed in first thing Monday morning. Mrs Carlton was a renowned destroyer of Sunday evenings. And maybe *that* was the real reason for the lack of empathy displayed by my classmates upon hearing the news of her accident.

The sky showed no mercy to the outpouring of pupils now making their way home. My jacket didn't have a hood, so by the time I reached the two buses which Miss Ward had organised, I was soaked. Cold rainwater chilled my scalp and breached the collar of my shirt, sending cold trails of discomfort down my back, where it had no business being. My hair was plastered to my head and my trousers were stuck to my legs.

Both of the white buses, probably the oldest vehicles in the entire fleet owned by a local bus company, were parked up and idling at the kerbside. As I hopped up onto the first step of the closer one, I heard footsteps hurtling towards me from behind, then hands clutched at my jacket and pulled me back down to the pavement.

'Get out of the way, Carter, you total spaz.' It was Martyn Robson.

He shouldered me to the side and I clunked against the bus's wheel arch. As Robson clambered on board I heard Kevin England's bellowing voice somewhere inside shout, 'Oi, Robbo, is Sullivan Carter getting on here? Tell him I'm gonna fucking bray him!'

I'd already dodged England's fists earlier that day, so I

turned and made my way to the other bus instead. Ever since England's head had got in the way of the football I'd booted towards the goal in Mr Hendrick's five-a-side tournament a few weeks earlier, he'd made it one of his top priorities in life to make my life a misery. The impact of the ball had knocked him onto his arse. He'd sat in the dirt for a couple of minutes in a state of total disbelief while he was laughed at by almost everyone else who was there. I must add, I didn't laugh; I wasn't feeling reckless enough to ignore the likely repercussions. But as it was, even though I'd apologised and hadn't laughed along with everyone else, I'd been the root cause of that ensuing laughter; the source of England's humiliation and dented ego. So the football faux pas had come with a hefty price which I continued to pay each day. The irony is that I bloody hate five-a-side and hadn't wanted to play in the first place.

As I approached the second bus, I saw that its door was shut. Its side windows were fogged with the condensation of however many warm, wet bodies were inside, so I couldn't tell if it was full or not. When I knocked on the door's glass panel, I didn't think the bus driver – an old, sour looking man with Bob Holness glasses and thin, tired-brown hair – was going to let me inside. I'd seen him before, many times, but didn't know his name. He always wore a fuzzy blue jumper, like muppet pelt, and an expression which conveyed his complete dislike of kids. That is, the utter pissed-off-ness of having to work in such close proximity to them. I imagined when he got home in the evening, his first grumbled words to his wife when she asked how his day had been would be 'little bastards.'

He must have seen something in me that day though, something he could identify with, because he opened the door and gestured me inside with a quick flick of his head. His eyes were narrowed, like he was letting me know he was throwing me a lifeline but that I had better not mess it up by giving him any backchat or hassle.

Muttering my thanks, I scurried on board.

The bus was crammed. It smelt of wet hair, dewberry perfume and too many hormonal bodies. And it didn't look like there were any spare seats. For an alarming moment I thought Bob Holness, the bus driver, might tell me to get off and go and get on the other bus instead. But then, like an epiphany, I saw an available seat, about ten rows back, next to Raymond Foster.

No one ever sat next to Raymond Foster, not if they could help it. Some days he smelt of ferrets and other days he smelt of old fishing bait. His fingers were covered with warts and ingrained dirt and the inside of his shirt collar was sweat-stained yellow. I didn't care though. I didn't care at all. At least Raymond Foster kept his fists to himself.

I took my backpack off and made my way down the aisle. Someone tripped me with their foot on the way past. Then someone else punched me on the arm and shouted, 'Yo, Carter, are you a fucking zombie or what?'

When I reached the vacant seat beside Raymond Foster, he turned and looked at me with vague mistrust. His blue eyes were especially cold for someone of our age. They radiated suspicion and guardedness. I expect he was prematurely cynical about people. Goodness knew what his home life was like. Raymond was one of about five or six kids. I'd heard that his folks had split up and his mam's new fella was an alcoholic layabout who wasn't shy with his fists. Let's just say, I imagined Raymond had it pretty rough. I felt sorry for him. Not that he needed pitying, just, I knew from first-hand experience that fate can be a total arsehole when dealing the cards of life. Mrs Resnor my old junior school teacher used to say that we're all born equal in this world, but that's utter bollocks. Let her try telling that to

Raymond Foster.

His clothes were mostly worn hand-me-downs, a few years out of fashion, and, as ever, his top lip was wet with snot. Some hankies or rolled up toilet paper in his pocket wouldn't have gone amiss, but he tended to use his sleeves instead. Most of the time his cuffs glistened like slug trail. His mousy brown hair was wet from the rain, but it hardly looked any different to usual. It curled down and around his ears in an unkempt sort of way. Not that I expect he particularly wanted it to in any stylistic sense. Rather, it was a few months overdue a decent trim and probably the only remedy was to let his mam take the kitchen scissors to it.

I offered him a smile which felt every bit as miserable as I was. He merely scowled at me in return. Then, because he was forced to drag his backpack off the spare seat next to him, he huffed to convey his annoyance at the inconvenience of having to put the wet bag in his lap, after which he mumbled something I didn't quite catch. Could have been, 'Fucking zombie twat.'

Well, fuck you too, Raymond Foster, I thought, as I sat down.

Across the aisle, directly opposite, a girl leant forward and caught my eye. She was all willowy and delicate. Long strawberry blonde hair, damp at the front. Her eyes were the colour of a speckled dolphin. And just as inquisitive. I'd seen her about, but didn't know her name. At a guess, I'd say she was in Year Eight.

'Hiya,' she said, smiling, her cheeks subtly colouring.

The bus pulled away from the kerb, jerking me forward. I wrapped my arms round my backpack to stop it from falling into the aisle.

'Hi,' I muttered in feeble response before turning to watch out of the window and feigning interest as we drove past the school gates, making out they were the most fascinating things in the whole damn world. I scolded myself for being so lame. But then, I'd always been awkward around girls, so I couldn't have expected any better from myself.

As soon as we left the school grounds someone at the back of the bus shouted, 'Cheers for the afternoon off, Mrs Carlton!'

A subsequent uproar of laughter spurred Bob Holness to call back from his driver seat position, 'Oi, less it, you lot!' But much like Mr Dunn's failed efforts to control his unruly pupils, no one paid the least bit of attention to the bus driver. I imagined him cursing under his breath, *little bastards.*

The journey to Horden was mostly soggy and uncomfortable. Raymond Foster was emitting a hugely unpleasant musky smell, which I concluded was made even worse by his dampness. The girl to the other side of me, Strawberry Blonde, the one with the dolphin-grey eyes, kept glancing over. I could see her out the corner of my eye. It made me anxious to think that she might think Raymond Foster's smell belonged to me. Scrunching my feet inside my shoes, I willed the journey to be over already.

When the bus pulled up on Sunderland Road to let the Crossroads lot out, one of the Year Eleven lads, who was called Skunk (because of his recreational drug use, not his smell), yanked Strawberry Blonde's hair on his way past. Crying out in pain, she leapt forward and struck out with her fist, hitting him in the middle of the back.

Twirling round, Skunk got right in her face and said, 'I've seen your sister's tits.'

Everyone round about sucked in a collective breath.

Strawberry Blonde's eyes turned stony – Medusa stony – and her jaw tensed as she sat back down in her seat. After a few moments of killing him with her eyes, she said, 'Piss off, dick breath.' The way her anger simmered, she reminded me of a cat who was warning her tormentor that if he didn't back off, she'd rip his face off.

Skunk laughed and made his way off the bus with an arrogant swagger. Once outside, he pointed at Strawberry Blonde through the window and shouted, 'Your sister's tits are better than yours, Ginny!'

Ginny.

I took her name into my head and explored how it looked and sounded there. It was a purple name, I thought. Like Blue Moon roses and Parma violets. Pretty and delicate, with a sherbet tang. I caught her gaze and gave her a sympathetic look. She was massaging her head, where Skunk had pulled her hair. Her scowl seemed to soften when her eyes met mine. I didn't presume to know the right thing to say to her, so I didn't say anything at all. I turned my head and looked past Raymond Foster to the grey streets beyond the rain-smeared window.

The bus continued on, passing the Methodist church and Memorial Park, till it was snaking around parked cars on Cotsford Lane bank. The way the rain was coming down, pummelling the windscreen, making everything completely wet, and the way Bob Holness handled the bus, it felt like we were being swept along on river rapids. Standing up in preparation to get off at the next stop, I hoped I wouldn't lose my balance and fall.

The two girls who were sitting in the seat in front turned to look at me. One of them whispered to the other, then they both giggled. The one nearest to the window, whose hairsprayed fringe was like a cast iron sculpture, said, 'You're Sullivan Carter, aren't you?'

I shrugged, like, *so what if I am?*

'You're so dead,' she crooned. 'Kevin England's waiting at your stop. He's totally gonna deck you when you get off.'

My face flashed cold. Looking ahead through the bus's stippled front window, where the windscreen wipers thrashed back and forth, I saw that what she said was true. In matching black Naff Co. 54 jackets, probably rip-offs from Peterlee market, Kevin England, Martyn Robson, Ian Watson and Keith Hake were leaning against the wall of Ellwood's gym, waiting for me.

Shit!

Taking a step back, I contemplated ducking behind some empty seats, to hide out of view, but then I saw Ginny looking up at me. There was an unreadable expression on her face. She was about to find out what sort of person I was based on whatever I decided to do next, I thought.

Shitting hell!

If she'd liked me even in the least bit before, I figured this was about to turn into the part where she didn't anymore. Because, in my head, each of my options equated to the same thing: deep humiliation.

Did I get off the bus so as not to look like a total chicken in front of her, but get my head kicked in while she watched? Hardly impressive. Or did I just sit back down and miss my stop, knowing full well she'd know the reason why? I decided rather quickly that I'd look like the biggest wuss to have ever walked the planet if I was to do that.

So, what will you do, Sully?

Deep humiliation option A? Or deep humiliation option B?

It was decision time.

Tick tock.

Ginny was still looking at me. Those big grey eyes.

Fight or flight?

Swinging my backpack over my shoulder, I breathed in deeply and marched to the front of the bus, like a condemned boy. All the while my innards melted into a big gloop of jelly and my head was suddenly filled with lightning thoughts: *She's watching. They'll kill me. It might not hurt. She's watching. It WILL hurt. Knuckles. Rain. Blood. She's watching. Cold. Wet. Pain. Everyone's watching. I'm going to die…*

The bus pulled up at the kerb.

Oh God.

'Are they waiting for you, son?' Bob Holness grabbed a fistful of my jacket and pulled me backwards, away from the door that he hadn't yet opened.

I didn't answer, but he must have seen the sheer despair on my face and deciphered that the answer was yes. He pushed me onto the empty seat behind him and said, 'Nuh-uh, you're not getting out here, lad, sorry. You can get off at the next stop. Jumped up little pricks, hanging round in the rain like that, waiting to jump on someone littler than them. You'd do well to keep away from that lot.' He steered out of the bus stop then, and I watched as Kevin England lurched away from the wall as though he might chase after us.

'I'm gonna kill you, Carter!' he shouted. His hair was hanging down on either side of his forehead like a pair of wet curtains and his squinty eyes were livid.

Everyone on the bus behind me fell silent, each person absorbing and examining the wrath of the school bully's words. I imagine they must all have decided pretty quickly how very pleased they were not to be me.

'You wanna get that one on his own, lad,' Bob Holness said to me. 'Mouthy bastard would probably shit his pants. He's got one of them faces you wouldn't tire of punching, hasn't he? Deserves a good kicking to knock him down a peg or two, do you hear what I'm saying, son?'

Loud and clear. And I loved the idea, even the vote of confidence that the bus driver thought I might be able to do it. However, his words did nothing but concrete my misery, because I knew that it would be *me* who'd end up getting a good kicking.

When I got off the bus, opposite Kingy's coal yard on Cotsford Lane, I already had in mind that I'd head towards Paradise Street via Acacia Avenue, head down the bank then cut up Third Street to get to Murray Street. It was a longer route home, but I knew that in all likelihood Kevin England and his mates would already be heading my way along the main road.

Affixing my backpack to my shoulders, I was about to start running when someone called my name. Turning, I saw Mrs Baxter, an elderly lady who lived three doors down from me. She was wearing a pink anorak and had a determined expression on her face as she battled through the wind and rain with a floral brolly, as though it was some sort of shield that might deflect bullets if put to the test. In her left hand was a plastic carrier bag with what looked like a two-pint bottle of milk inside. In hindsight, Mrs Baxter probably wasn't as old as I'd thought her to be. Her short, grey, granny-permed hair was often hidden beneath a headscarf and she always wore pleated skirts with elasticated waistbands which ran the range from dowdy draylon couch to gaudy wallpaper design. At the time she'd looked pretty ancient, but was probably only about sixty.

'Is your dad at work, pet?' She drew close and held her brolly over my head.

'Er, yeah,' I said, itching to be away. Already I anticipated the feel of England's fist in my face.

'Thought so.' Beneath the cover of the brolly, Mrs Baxter's breath smelt of soured milky tea laced with Rich Tea biscuits and was too much in my face. 'In which case I should probably let you know that I've just seen Colton heading down there, towards the beach road.'

'What?'

'I know.' She shook her head and pulled a face of pure exasperation. 'Walking about in this weather like he didn't have a care in the bloody world, he was. I shouted to him, but he either didn't hear or pretended not to.'

'Are you sure it was him?' I glanced towards the beach road, the opposite way to home, suddenly feeling conflicted. Worried. Scared.

'Oh aye, it was definitely Colton alright. He had his red raincoat on.'

My heart quickened. My stomach sank. 'How long ago was it?'

Mrs Baxter sucked rainwater off her bottom lip while she thought. 'Hmmm. About ten minutes ago? Maybe fifteen.'

Shit, fuck, shit, Colton!

Taking off at a sprint towards the beach road, I left Mrs Baxter to stare after me.

2

The Cosmic Kids

Mam used to call me and Colton the Cosmic Kids. She was whimsical like that. I was born during a solar eclipse – which is why, she said, my eyes are such light blue. She reckoned the moon replaced all of the melanin in them with part of its own luminescent soul. Apparently, I came into the world at the exact moment of daytime darkness, which I'm not sure is wholly true since she always did love to embellish details in order to make a good story even better. She was a natural born storyteller, see. We used to love listening to her grandiose tales, encouraged them, in fact – me especially – because they made life that little bit better.

According to Mam, because of my personal attachment with the moon I have supernormal vision and can see through the night sky and into the Great Beyond. Perhaps even to the end of absolutely everything there is. Again, I can't say with any amount of certainty that what she said was definitely true, since I still don't know how far the boundaries of the universe stretch nor all that it keeps within itself. To go into too much of that right now, though, would be to get ahead of myself and go off on a huge tangent. So I won't. Not yet. That'll come later. Much later.

Mam said Colton was born when the stars were aligned just right for him. His eyes are darkest blue and she used to reckon that if you look closely enough into them you can see meteorite storms raging. He has the constellation of Orion on his chest, each star represented by a freckle. All seven freckles, which make up Betelgeuse, Bellatrix, Saiph, Regel and Orion's Belt, are proportionately set out. Colton has verified this precision many times throughout the years. He is very thorough with his calculations. Very thorough with many things, in fact. He also has a not quite so accurate depiction of Ursa Major on his inner right thigh and a sloppy version of Cassiopeia on his left bicep.

During the four years before Colton was born, I was simply nicknamed Moon Boy. Then when Colton came along we were known, collectively, as the Cosmic Kids.

When Mam died, so did both nicknames.

We've always been close, me and Colton. Nobody understands his foibles quite like me. Not even Dad. For example, the fact that Colton's favourite colour in the whole world is red, and that he must always wear an item of red clothing somewhere about his body each day – otherwise the Earth will stop spinning and we'll all fly off – is relatively straight forward, right? But if you put anything red on his dinner plate, then…oh boy! It's probably best we don't even go there. Let's just say it's an explosive quirk of his that's better avoided.

Dad does of course know about Colton's aversion to red food, but he doesn't understand it. That's not to say I pretend to understand the logic behind any of Colton's many anxieties, but I do acknowledge the fact that certain things make him particularly fretful. That's just the way he is. Therefore, I've always thought it unfair to get overly frustrated with him about any of his idiosyncrasies, especially since he always makes it clear when something makes him unhappy. Dad, on the other hand, in those early days, often displayed the odd mild to moderate bout of irritation at what he deemed to be 'trying behaviour'. He reckoned Colton was pandered to by Mam too much. It's a matter we both still agree to disagree on.

Colton just likes things to be the way he likes things to be. That's all. He's relatively simple in his needs, so long as you take the time to learn what they are. He's loving and thoughtful, for the most part, but he also has a fiery streak. One hell of a fiery streak. So anyone who wants to try touching his kneecaps or feet should bear that in mind.

He's my kid brother, what can I say? I look out for him. I love him.

So, on that rainy afternoon, after Mrs Carlton had fallen prey to the electrics in the storage cupboard, I ran and ran and ran, ignoring the burn in my lungs from each furious inhalation which would have crippled me easily if I'd let it. I didn't have time for physical pain. I had to find Colton and get him home before Dad finished work. Colton was on a final warning. There was to be no more bunking off school. The penalty had already been laid out: a full summer at Aunt Julie's house. Which, of course, by default meant that if Colton was to be sent there, then so was I.

Dad had been struggling since Mam passed away six months earlier. We all had, in our own ways. It was tough seeing Dad, the male figurehead of the house who had always been emotionally constipated anyway, having to become mother as well as father. Having to adapt his role to try and fill both pairs of parental shoes. No matter how hard he tried to make them fit him, Mam's never did.

All of us bottled stuff up too much, it's easy to see that now. Each of us reacted in our own way to the hand we'd been dealt, tragically not knowing how to interact with each other. We didn't know how to look to the future either without the soul-crushing grief, which had consumed us since Mam's diagnosis, dashing any small hope of easier times ahead. The future was a dark cloud of abject misery and hopelessness. Life was finite. Death was known. And this inescapable combination, which always lingered at the forefront of my thoughts, was enough to prompt a maelstrom of panic and terror in me so strong I had regular bouts of physical nausea in the months and years after Mam's passing. That life's light only stretches so far, with limited tendrils of opportunity, and that death's darkness is ready to swallow us into its vacuous maw at any given moment was just about the scariest thing I could imagine. It still makes me feel sick now.

As well as working full time, Dad soon discovered there were endless chores to take care of in order to maintain a fully functioning household. He became short tempered whenever he made a mess of doing something simple, like heating lasagne in the oven or ironing school uniforms. Prior to Mam's death, these were the sort of tasks he simply hadn't got involved with. In a way, though, I guess it was all of these newfound responsibilities and routines that kept him from sinking and drowning in his black sea of mourning. If not for me and Colton simply being there, as in, Dad taking care of us in a general day-to-day sense rather than in any emotional capacity, I'm not sure Dad would have made it through the worst of those days. He'd lost too much of his spark. Without Mam, he was running on autopilot most of the time and that function was threatening to breakdown at any moment. They were intensely difficult days.

As for Colton, he started doing things without any thought to what repercussions there might be for his actions. Typically, he tended to do this anyway, but Mam's death seemed to have amplified this problematic trait of his. If he was feeling sad or angry at school, for example, he'd just walk right out of those school gates and not tell anyone where he was going. He's another of life's deep thinkers, and in those turbulent instances where he found himself sucked into the vortex of such uncontrollable melancholy or rage, I suspect Mam was right, that if you looked closely enough you'd be able to see meteorites crashing and storming in his eyes.

Over time I came to learn that Colton's grief was a complex, fragile thing which could move harshly between sadness and anger in a heartbeat, and was almost always directed at Mam for having left us. Whereas Dad's grief was way deeper than I could fully comprehend – at that age anyhow. It was something which I think he consciously tried to keep internalised, possibly for mine and Colton's sake, but also because he's as deep as the ocean and doesn't give his emotions free reign – unless the dominant emotion is anger, of course. But his stewing emotions seeped from him in a black fog of depression, nonetheless, and a lot of the time he wasn't particularly approachable. That's not to say he would have turned us away had we wanted to talk, it was just a matter of confused expectations. Expectations which challenged us all; mine and Colton's expectations of Dad and life, and Dad's own expectations of himself.

Does that even make sense?

I'll try to explain a little better.

Mine and Colton's definition of Dad was that he was supposed to be this strong, burly man who could protect his family no matter what. I mean, in the eyes of kids, that's what all great dads do, isn't it? And I truly think Dad had believed that too. Only, he hadn't, had he? He hadn't been able to protect us from what had happened.

He hadn't been able to save Mam. So, in a way, he'd let us all down. He'd allowed catastrophe to infiltrate our family home.

I think that's one of the main reasons why Dad retreated into himself. Why he fell into a dark, wallowing funk. Because his grief was further complicated by feelings of guilt – unwarranted guilt, but guilt all the same – because of the unnecessary pressure he'd put on himself to be some sort of alpha male. After Mam had gone, it seemed like Dad was in a permanent state of simmering anger and resentfulness. It wasn't a malignant rage specifically directed at me and Colton – unless we'd been misbehaving, of course – but it was enough to deter us from bothering him too much. He had a lot of emotional healing and figuring out to do. That much was obvious.

Me and Colton knew, even if only on some subconscious level, that we would have to set about re-evaluating not only what life meant to us, but what the new definition of Dad was. Right then it was too soon to draw any conclusions though. He was much too raw. And to do so would have been to slap another grossly unfair definition on his head. Parents aren't superheroes, after all. They don't have special powers that will shield us from everything that hurts. Which was life's first (and most awful) lesson that we ever learnt.

So, what about me? How did I cope in the aftermath of Mam?

Well, I clung to the memory of her in the most ferociously personal way. I kept all of her in a painted black shoebox inside my head, which I wouldn't let her out of – or anyone else into, for that matter. I didn't like to talk about what had happened or acknowledge the fact she was no longer around. Most days I'd pretend that she was still alive, that she'd just popped out to go to the shops and would be back any minute. But some days she was entirely unreachable. Gone. No matter how much I tried to lift the lid of the black shoe box, I couldn't. And it was on those days I couldn't help but feel that perhaps she'd been no more than a character from a favourite book of mine, which had since been misplaced and therefore couldn't be reread. As a coping mechanism I lied to myself as often and massively as I could. This meant that the days when I couldn't open the box that contained her were the hardest of all. They were the longest, blackest of days, where it took all of my effort simply to breathe. I had to keep telling myself: *in…out…in…out…in…out.*

After Mam, all three of us – me, Dad and Colton – set out on our own individual paths of mourning, each of us doing our own thing in order to move along one step at a time. Which, in hindsight, was a mistake. I'm sure Dad would agree. We should have set out on the same path together. Even knowing that we wouldn't walk at the same pace, we should have drawn strength from each other and shone a light whenever one of us strayed off course or lagged behind. But no one knows quite what to do when, suddenly and irreversibly, they're thrown into the hellish pit of grief that's caused by death, do they? Especially when they've never been in it before. I guess it's like being commanded to climb the highest mountain without any climbing equipment. Or being forced at gunpoint to walk a tightrope across a vast chasm that's at least a thousand feet high when you've never walked a tightrope before in your life. It's a terrifying ordeal. Surreal in its sheer awfulness.

Our waking lives descended into a nightmare dreamscape; a strange reality that we couldn't escape. We were amateurs, totally winging it, and even after months had passed, when the raw agony became a dull ache, I doubt any of us expected that we'd ever be experts at coping with our loss, because every single day had a way of kicking up something new and unexpected. Something we hadn't yet dealt with. An emotion. A memory. A dashed hope.

For Dad, he was left juggling work and two kids while trying to adjust to the bleak continuity of heartache. It must have been brutal for him. And as if home life wasn't difficult enough, his boss, James McGregor of McGregor's Funeral Home, hinted that redundancy was on the cards. Dad hadn't told me this himself, but I'd overheard him talking to Aunt Julie on the phone. McGregor's grandson, Stewart, who had just turned eighteen, was looking likely to replace Dad at the funeral home. McGregor was looking after his own in a dog eat dog world, that was all, and Dad reckoned McGregor was waiting for the perfect opportunity to lay him off. This meant Dad couldn't take any time out over the school holidays to look after me and Colton, otherwise this would have given McGregor the excuse he needed to get Dad's P45 in the post sooner rather than later. Not that Dad would have had the luxury to take time out financially, even if his job had been secure. So that's why the decision to ship us off to Aunt Julie's had been made.

I thought I'd pretty much convinced Dad that I could take care of Colton and myself without the need for us to go anywhere. At first it was a firm 'no', but after I continued to explain to him how we wouldn't stray beyond the back lane and that if adult supervision was required, for whatever reason, then Mrs Baxter was only three doors away. And Granny Carter was less than five minutes walk away. The fact that Dad wasn't outright saying 'no' anymore had given me hope. I felt like he was valuing me as a trustworthy young adult and that maybe I'd get to prove myself after all. But Colton's recent spate of truancy was now looking likely to scupper summer. His skiving looked set to undo all I'd done to sway Dad's decision about sending us away. Because lately Dad had started to complain that Colton couldn't be trusted to behave himself. Dad said I wasn't really old enough to look after him for hours on end. And that, in any case, it wouldn't be right of him to expect me to.

I could tell he was stressed about the situation. Torn because he wanted to do right by us as minors, but also because he wanted to do right by us in an emotional sense. Even so, at the time, I didn't think he could feel nearly half as stressed as I did with the situation. I *seriously* didn't want to go and stay with Aunt Julie.

She lived in a three-bedroom terraced house in Wingate with her three teenage sons: Andy, a shifty as fuck nineteen-year-old who may or may not have had Tourette's; Davey, a moody fifteen-year-old who slammed doors and punched walls a lot and had too many posters of Take That's Robbie Williams above his bed; and Micky, a hyperactive twelve-year-old who probably went way off the ADHD spectrum and had a penchant for tormenting next door's dog. Suffice to say, I wasn't keen on any of them. Not even Aunt Julie. She was hard-faced and had all the sensibilities of a feral pit bull. I imagined she'd offered to have me and Colton over the summer for two reasons: one, because Dad would pay her, albeit minimally, to do so; and two, because it would mean she'd have two extra skivvies at her beck and call.

I was angry at Colton for undoing all of my efforts and I was angry at Dad for thinking that Aunt Julie was even an option. I was also angry at Mam for leaving us, for not fighting harder to stay.

My eyes were blurred with rain and tears, and my breaths came out as long, harrowing moans, each of which frightened me. The sky was a swollen grey thing which I imagined had lungs and was able to breathe. It hung over Horden and extended way out over the North Sea, perhaps reaching as far as Denmark, Sweden and Norway. I thought it might flop to the ground and flatten everything beneath it on land and cause a tidal wave in the sea that would then wash everything away. I wished more than anything that it would.

I was in a bad mood and cursed myself, because I knew the target of my anger was wrongly assigned. It wasn't Dad's or Mam's or Colton's or even my own fault that life was so shit. We hadn't asked for any of what had happened to us. And most importantly, none of us had set out to hurt each other. So, as I ran on, I cursed the world and every bad thing that had ever happened in it instead, as well as the sky for not falling and flattening everything.

By the time I got to the end of the beach road, where it tapers into a single track that leads down to the tank blocks and onto the beach itself, I slowed to a canter. My insides were screaming and my limbs felt three times heavier than usual. The rain had eased to a substantial drizzle, but by that point there wasn't an inch of me that wasn't wet to some degree. I'd gone way beyond the discomfort of simply being soaked, my sodden clothes now felt like they were part of me.

Raising my arm, I sniffled and used my jacket sleeve, Raymond Foster style, to wipe away the snot that was pouring from my nose like rainwater. I looked ahead to the grey North Sea, which was crashing onto the shale shore with what seemed like incensed provocation. I imagined I'd successfully channelled myself there. That I was the waves. The sea-salt turbulence.

Then I saw Colton in the distance.

His red raincoat was standing out against the greyness of everything else. A small beacon of hope. He looked so small and vulnerable in such a bleak and lonely setting, my heart swelled with fear and love and something like vexation.

I'll bloody kill him.

My legs started sprinting again, despite my body's protests, and I waved my arms in the air. 'Colton, wait!'

3

Bloody Rain

The soles of my shoes slipped on every smooth-surfaced, rain-slicked rock as I scampered across the beach towards Colton. The wind buffeted me about, trying to knock me over, but I held my arms out at both sides for balance and managed to stay upright.

'What are you doing?' I called to Colton. The words scraped up my scorched windpipe, making me want to double over and cough up every last fiery breath from my lungs. 'Why aren't you at school?'

Colton stopped walking and waited for me to reach him. Beneath the red vinyl hood of his raincoat, the blue parts of his eyes looked purple.

'I didn't want to be there.'

'You realise Dad's gonna kill you, right?' I clutched my side, as if to squeeze out the stitch that seared muscle and tissue there.

Colton frowned. 'So what if he does?'

'You won't be saying that later when he goes off on one.'

Shrugging, he said, 'I don't care.'

'You bloody well will when he sends us to Aunt Julie's next month.' My tone conveyed my downright unhappiness on the matter. I kicked up a spray of pebbles, sending them flying.

Colton looked to the floor. The wind caught his hood and blew it back. He snatched it with quick hands and pulled it onto his head again. His fair hair, I saw, was mostly dry.

Sniffling loudly, he said, 'Sorry, Sully. I just didn't want to be at school, that's all.' He dipped his hand into his pocket and pulled something out. 'Look what I found.'

In his palm was a large, flat piece of white sea glass which had a blueish tinge to it.

'Cool,' I said, managing to sound every bit as enthusiastic as I was – too cold and wet by far to give a shit.

'I kept it because it reminds me of you.'

Bemused, I glanced at the sea glass again. 'Why would a piece of glass remind you of me?'

'It's the same colour as your eyes,' he pointed out.

I suppose it was.

'Maybe it's a piece of the moon that got chipped off by a massive meteor,' he went on. 'Then fell all the way down to Earth and landed here. On the beach.'

'Hmmm.' I squared my shoulders against the wind. 'Maybe.'

A gull swooped overhead, travelling seawards. I wondered if that meant the storm was almost done.

Doubtful.

I watched for a few moments as the bird glided over the shallows of the shoreline, its white plumage brilliant against the contrasting dark grey seascape. The sky over the North Sea looked full of hell, like it was nowhere near finished bestowing its bad mood on Horden.

'Let's go home, bot sniff, and get dry before Dad gets in,' I said, almost unable to remember what it was like to feel dry. 'Mrs Harper might not have noticed you were missing from class. You might not get busted.' I knew this was bullshit, but I had to say something to give us both incentive for the long walk home. The wind was slicing through my sopping clothes and the water that they'd retained added extra chill. My hands had turned a blotchy pink colour like corned beef. I could barely feel them.

We turned and started back towards the four tank blocks in the distance; the large concrete cubes which had been there since World War II. Their purpose had been to prevent land attacks by German tanks during any beach invasions. As far as I knew, there hadn't been any.

'Why did you come here anyway?' I asked Colton.

He stooped to pick up another piece of sea glass. This one was green; rare compared to the many white pieces that were scattered about. I watched as he inspected it. His small fingers held it up to the sky, force of habit, as if he might see better. But it looked exactly the same; a dull emerald that had lost its sparkle under a sunless sky, in the pissing down rain. I wasn't sure what Colton would do with it, since green is a tricky colour at the best of times. I was surprised he'd even picked it up. He rubbed wet sand particles off with his fingers, then put it in his coat pocket alongside the piece of moon he'd already claimed.

'Uranus is green,' he said, as if that was reason enough to explain why he considered the fragment of green sea glass acceptable.

'I know,' I said. 'Green's cool. So's Uranus. But are you gonna tell me why you came here or what?'

'I like the sea.'

'I know you do, but it's raining.'

'I know. I like the rain as well. Other people stay indoors when it's raining.'

Even though I fully appreciated the sentiment of what he'd said, because I like walking in the rain for the exact same reason – though not necessarily on that particular day, I might add – I shook my head and made a face of disapproval. I was his big brother, after all, and had to be seen as the sensible one. I had a duty of care to keep him in check. *Do as I say, not as I do* kind of thing. 'You can't just go wandering off like this.'

'But…I did.'

'You know what I bloody well mean.' I flashed him a warning glare. Cupping my hands, I blew into them. 'You'll catch your death being out in this.'

'Ha!' Colton looked at me, his eyes glinting with humour. 'You sound like Gran.'

I grinned and cuffed him playfully across the back of the head. 'Come on, shithead, I'll race you to the beach road.'

Colton tore off ahead, hollering with glee, apparently not at all bothered about the likely bollocking that awaited us at home. It didn't take much effort for me to catch up, but I kept a slower pace than usual so he could keep up. The soles of our shoes slapped noisily on the wet shale and my backpack flapped up and down behind me like a piece of dead skin. At least, that's how I imagined it. Each time it slapped against my back a penetrating coldness reached right through to my kidneys with a closed-fisted punch, hurting so much it knocked the air from my lungs. I gritted my teeth and pulled the bag's straps tighter against my shoulders to restrict its movement.

Already I was dreading seeing how my physics and geography workbooks had fared; the canvas material of my backpack wasn't waterproof. I hoped the warmth of the house might salvage the pages from watery ruin, as long as the ink hadn't run. If not, I decided I was probably in deep shit with Mr Dunn and Mrs Dennis. On the plus side, I'd left my Walkman at home that day. I could just about cope with redoing a write up on protons and neutrons, but saving up the funds to replace my Walkman would have taken just about forever.

The sky pulsed pink like a blip of migraine and seconds later thunder rumbled. Out in the open the sheer bass of it sounded like a monster tunnelling up from the pit of the Earth. As we left the beach and passed through the gap between the two middle tank blocks, something hit me on the side of the head with a skull-thudding thump. Whatever it was was hard enough to knock me onto my arse. Dazed, I barely had time to register what was happening when I heard bellows of laughter coming at me from all sides.

'You think you're so fucking clever don't you, Carter?' It was Kevin England. He'd been hiding behind one of the tank blocks, waiting. Must have seen me heading towards the beach road and followed.

Shit!

Revealing themselves from their own hiding places around the graffitied, rain-saturated tank blocks, Martyn Robson, Ian Watson and Keith Hake came to stand next to England.

Four onto one.

I was as good as dead meat.

'Leave me alone, England,' I said, miserably. Rain-soaked dirt seeped into the seat of my trousers and I wished the thunder monster would break through to the surface right beneath me and swallow me whole.

England pulsed his fists and stooped down in front of me, so close I could feel and smell the heat of his Refresher lollipop breath on my face. His fair hair had been darkened by the rain and was flattened to his head. His weasly eyes were more hateful than I think I'd ever seen them before. I knew then that things would get particularly bad.

'Leave me alone, England,' he echoed, putting on a whiny voice of supposed mimicry.

'Yeah, leave him alone!' *Shit!* It was Colton.

'Shut up, you little goon.' England snorted snot from the back of his throat, straightened up and spat a mouthful of phlegm at Colton.

Colton jumped out of the way.

I made to stand up, thinking that if I was going to take a beating then I'd sooner get it out of the way. But England kicked my arm out from under me and I crashed down onto my back.

'Oi!' Colton cried, rushing to my side. 'Pack it in, you big knobhead!'

'Go home, Colton,' I told him. But he just stood there, as though he might protect me from four fourteen-year-olds. My heart was loud in my ears and already I worried about how far things would go: the four of them could beat me to a bloody pulp if they liked because there was no one else around. No one to intervene, to break things up. 'Please, Colton. Now.'

'Please, Colton,' England said, in his mocking voice. He reached out and grabbed Colton's coat and jerked him away from me. 'What kind of a name is that anyway? And *Sullivan*? Who the fuck do you think you are?' He slapped me hard across the side of the head. 'You and your poncey fucking name.' Jabbing a finger at Colton, he said, 'Do you think you're something special as well? Just like your faggot brother. *Huh?*'

Robson, Watson and Hake laughed.

'Shut up!' I felt a defensive rage ignite in me. 'He's only ten!'

A pink bolt of lightning lit up the sky directly above us.

'So?' England raised a fist and pretended he was going to lash out at Colton, probably intending to make him run away or cry or do both. But Colton stood his ground. He stayed where he was, glaring at England from beneath his red hood.

31

Thunder split the air and roared. I felt the ground beneath me quake.

Lurching upwards, I clambered to my feet. 'Leave him alone. It's me you have a problem with.'

'Who told you you could get off the floor, freak?'

My whole body became tense and I focussed all of my rage on England, as if I might be able to knock him off his feet without even touching him. Narrowing my eyes and lowering my voice, I said, 'Go to hell, dickhead.'

He came at me hard and fast then, his fists raining down on me. His knuckles cracked against my nose, cheekbones and jaw, again and again and again, till I could taste my own blood. I raised my arms to try and block some of the blows and managed to land a few punches of my own. But England was easily four inches taller than me and probably a good two stone heavier. I felt like a featherweight amateur being pummelled by a heavyweight pro. I could hear Robson, Watson and Hake laughing raucously, goading him on. And I could hear Colton screaming for England to stop. Which was the absolute worst of it: my own little brother helplessly watching as I got my arse kicked. The humiliation I felt because he had to bear witness to it hurt worse than the actual punches.

Sickened by the sound of England's fists pounding my skull, I wondered how much reverberation my brain could take before I blacked out. I backed up, trying to escape the relentless onslaught, but one of England's mates kicked the back of my legs, so I dropped to the floor on my knees. Then all four of them were on me, like a pack of rabid dogs; pulling and pushing, kicking and punching, tearing and tugging at me and my clothes. One of them tore my backpack off, then they all fell away from me, as if the bag was some prized possession that took precedence over beating the shit out of me.

'What've you got in here, gay boy?' England said,

ripping the zip open and peering inside. 'Your stash of gay porn?'

I stayed kneeling on the floor where they'd left me, bleeding and woozy. I felt lightheaded, like I might keel over onto my front and black out in the mud. There was an awful sound, a sort of wet snorting, which filled my head. I noticed how it coincided with my breathing, then realised it was the blood in my nose, bubbling and flowing. Cold air stole in through the gap where my shirt gaped open. My skin was taut with the icy sting of it and I remember being more aware than I probably should have been that my nipples had tightened so much they hurt. I was also aware of Colton next to me; the redness of his raincoat swirled in my peripheral vision. Then I felt his hands on my upper arms, trying to pull me to my feet. I could sense his urgency. And his terror. But I couldn't move. Didn't have the will.

Go home, Colton, I told him in the throbbing, swirling confines of my head. *Just go home now. Leave me.*

'Oh look,' England said, whipping the two workbooks from my backpack. 'His physics book has a big love heart on the front with 'I love Mr Dunn' written across it.'

Robson, Watson and Hake all guffawed at England's blatant lie as though he'd just cracked the funniest joke ever.

'I bet you wank off over your homework, don't you, Carter?' Robson said, putting his hand down the front of his trousers and grabbing his crotch. His dark brown hair looked black in the rain and the patches of wannabe moustache at both sides of his top lip appeared more prominent. His face was reddened, probably even sore, with pus-filled acne which covered his skin. It was easy to imagine he was filled with so much animosity that his body couldn't contain it. That it had bubbled to the surface, erupting from his pores in yellow badness.

'Because you're a total swot.'

When I failed to respond, England opened up my physics book and tore it in half, then threw it into the rivulet of water that was coursing down the bank at the side of the grassy verge. Some of the pages flittered down into the mud, the rest of it was swept off towards the beach.

'What are you gonna do about it?' England cajoled, baiting for a reaction – perhaps even an incentive, as if he needed one, to give me another beating. 'Are you gonna go crying to your dad?'

I stared at him. Unspeaking. Unmoving. Breathing through my mouth. Tasting the blood at the back of my throat. Hating him with all of my being.

'Your dad's an undertaker,' Robson said, as though he thought I might not know it already. He scooped a pile of mud onto the toe of his shoe and flicked it at me. It hit the side of my face, merging with blood and stinging the skin around the open wounds there.

I gritted my teeth. Determined not to show how much it hurt.

'Aye, he is, isn't he?' Watson said. 'He's creepy as owt. Proper weirdo. I've seen him in his funeral gear.' He bent and scraped a handful of mud off the floor, evidently inspired by Robson, then pelted me with it. It erupted on my chest in a dark explosion and sprayed up onto my chin. Watson hooted with laughter. He wasn't as tall as the others and looked a bit like Tintin. As in, harmless enough with a dodgy quiff. I'd seen him fighting in the schoolyard before though. I knew he was just as dangerous as the others.

'I bet he fucks dead bodies,' Hake said, with forced laughter. Hake was the wildcard of the group. He was the quietest of the four, edgy and unnerving. When he did speak you never knew what the hell to expect. 'I mean, Jesus, he looks like a frigging sex offender with that beard, doesn't he?'

They all fell about laughing then.

'I bet that's why you look like a zombie-eyed freak,' England said, throwing my geography workbook up onto the grassy embankment to the right of him. His own eyes blazed with a dangerousness which suggested he was daring me to challenge him. 'Because your dad likes to fuck dead people.'

When I still didn't rise to the bait, he hurled my backpack at me. Before I could dodge out of the way it hit me in the face with such force, my nose started to gush with more blood. The metallic-tasting thickness of it coated my teeth and poured onto the muddy floor in front of me, combining with the earth. Combining *me* with the earth. My blood and the Earth's mud.

Mud and blood.

Behind my eyes I saw reddy-brown.

'Come on, you lot,' England said, beckoning to Robson, Watson and Hake. 'I'm gannin' home now. I'm soaked to me nads and I'm bored of this shit.' He inspected his bloodied knuckles, then looked at me and grinned.

They all moved off then, a quartet of goons wearing fake Naff Co. 54 jackets. Making their way up the dirt track towards the beach road, they mouthed off to each other and were generally rowdy as they went. Their ascent was agonisingly slow. I half expected them to change their minds and come charging back to give me another pounding. Even so, I just knelt there. Unmoving. Feeling broken, inside and out, with Colton by my side like a crestfallen mascot.

My eyes were already beginning to swell and the rain felt like acid on my face. I tipped my head back and looked to the sky. It flashed pink in its entirety, but there was no forked lightning this time. None that I could see, anyhow. I guessed the storm was on the move. A subsequent grumble of thunder rolled around in the distance, the acoustics of it loud but its exact whereabouts distorted. Unclear. Still, the roar of it filled all the empty spaces within me with angst. I willed the storm to come back. To crackle and sizzle right above me, so that I could be at the very heart of it. Numbed.

When England, Robson, Watson and Hake reached the top of the bank, England called back, with a whoop of laughter, 'Hey, Carter!'

I groaned. *What now?*

'Next time,' he yelled, 'I swear I'm gonna punch you so hard, you'll get to see your mam again!'

I barely had time to register what he meant when I saw Colton stoop to pick up a rock that was twice as big as his hand. To this day I still don't know where he found the strength, or how he managed to aim it so well, but he drew back his arm and launched the rock, which then seemed to arc across the sky in slow motion before hitting England, a crashing blow, on the back of the head.

Oh fuck!

Despite my pain and dizziness, I was quick to my feet. My heart was in my mouth and blood roared inside my head, louder than thunder, as if it had reached boiling point. The wounds on my face throbbed with the heat of it. Already anticipating the backlash that Colton's rock-throwing would incite, I grabbed his arm, pushed him in the direction of the beach and screamed, *'RUN!'*

4

Run!

Colton seemed to understand the urgency of the situation and ran.

'The dene!' I cried. My words were snaffled away by a gust of wind and the memory of them was drowned out by the sound of raging surf way down across the beach. Making my voice louder in case Colton hadn't heard the first time, I said, 'Head towards the dene!'

Choosing not to reach my own top speed in order to put more distance between myself and England, I hung back to allow Colton to keep up. Colton was a pretty fast runner, but not compared to a group of physically fit boys who were over four years his senior. No matter what happened, I had to stick with him. He was my kid brother. We were in this together.

When we emerged onto the beach, I steered Colton to the right, towards the mouth of the dene, and told him to, 'Hurry up!' We kept close to the bank side and followed the dirt track till we rounded the bend and saw the trees of Castle Eden Dene ahead, alluringly close yet worryingly far. The red-brick viaduct, which spanned the width of the dene, looked like a colossal beast standing guard. We'd need to run beneath it, between two of its many legs. The viaduct always made me feel anxious because it seemed, to me, to be overly tall. Which instilled a feeling of mistrust. As a kid, I could never comprehend why a train track would need to be positioned so close to the sky. Suspended on stilts, way above the dene. And who the hell had built it? Which daredevil had masterfully positioned each and every brick at such a height? Standing beneath any of its arches and looking up always made my stomach flip upside down. It was so incredibly high.

According to Dad, who'd been told by his dad, the viaduct's nickname was Gregory's Leap. I'm not sure who Gregory was, because apparently Granda Carter's snippets of trivia hadn't covered those finer details. I can only guess that whoever he was Gregory had leapt from the top of the arches at some point in time – as had many others over the years.

As a direct result of the dene's suicide-related history, I always imagined it must be a haunted place; the trees having become home to the spirits of all the tormented departed ones. Under different circumstances, I'd have felt spooked about venturing into the vast but secluded lair of trees on such a dark day, just me and Colton. Alone. But going into the dene was our only choice. And, let's be honest, I knew I'd rather take my chances facing its many ghosts than Kevin England and his mates.

The rain had picked up to a steady downpour again, which seemed to threaten in its persistence never to stop. The dirt track we followed was slick with mud and every crater along the way was filled to the top with dirty rainwater. We had little choice but to plough straight through these ankle-deep pools. Dad would go mental when he saw the state of our socks and shoes, I reckoned. But the stern ticking off we'd get from him was massively more favourable than the horrific beating we'd get from England, Robson, Watson and Hake if we were to slow to dodge puddles.

The blood had begun to congeal in my nose, making it difficult to breathe as I ran. I gasped through my mouth, trying to keep up with my lungs' harsh demands for a rapid air supply. Every ragged inhalation and exhalation was a struggle that burnt my windpipe and I considered that each one might sound just as loud and terrible outside as it did within the confines of my own head. I also considered that the exertion of my heart might cause my nose to unplug and for blood to spurt everywhere. My entire head was a mass of bloody, throbbing hurt.

A jagged white thunderbolt split the bruised sky directly ahead of us like a flash of anaesthetic. The storm was returning and we were running straight into it. Somehow this felt right, because the situation was totally out of control and absolutely terrifying. The earth beneath us shook with thunder. That, or Gregory's Leap was stamping its feet. Shaking off new ghosts, perhaps. I imagined a horde of spirits might be waiting to greet us beneath it; a ragtag crew of tortured souls.

I also imagined that England and his mates would be closing on us by now. But when I listened hard above the sound of blood thumping and roaring in my ears, all I could hear was the lingering snarl of thunder and rain beating down on everything.

My plan was to reach the shelter of the trees, where Colton and I would be less visible, then carry on till we reached the coast road. If we could pull that off, we'd be almost home and dry. If Colton struggled to keep a fast enough pace, however, we could hide in the trees till England and his gang had passed by, then double back along the beach. It would take ages to get home and Dad would go absolutely berserk. But it was a desperate situation. And we were shit out of luck.

I couldn't even begin to imagine how angry England

would be or, more to the point, how heavily his fists would pummel me next time around. He'd catch up with me sooner or later, I had no doubt about that. I just didn't want it to be right then, in a place so devoid of other people. If he gave me a beating at school, at least there'd be any amount of teachers close by to prise him off if things went too far. I'd dare say the handful of dinner nannies would gladly step in if the beating were to take place at dinner time. The dinner nannies were other people's grandmas who patrolled the schoolyard at break time like Rottweilers with permed hair. They had stern faces and a sadistic fondness for dishing out bollockings to anyone they considered to be 'acting the arse'. Perfect for my cause. But, of course, in Castle Eden Dene there was no one. No one to hear me scream.

The threat of such rage and aggression surely just moments behind us chilled the blood in my veins. I fully expected that if we got caught then at least one of us, me or Colton, would end up hospitalised, with fractured bones or worse. And because there was nothing I could do to safeguard Colton from such an eventuality, I found that my legs began to pump harder and I urged him to, 'Keep up!'

The rock that Colton had thrown had totally floored England. He'd hit the deck like a sack of potatoes. It was a mental image that played over and over in my head as we ran. A mental image that might have been funny if not for the terrifying consequences it forecast. I clung to a sliver of hope that England might have been knocked out cold, thus giving us a decent head start. But we'd only got another twenty paces, at most, when I heard his dreadful voice call out, 'Carter! You and your retard brother are fucking dead, do you hear me?'

Shit!

I chanced looking back and immediately wished I hadn't. England, Robson, Watson and Hake were a fair distance away, but they were charging full pelt as if into battle. Unless Colton was to speed up, I reckoned it wouldn't be long till they caught up with us.

'The trees,' I cried, wincing with the pain that each step brought with it. My heels were chafed and screamed with the promise of blisters. The backs of my shoes were biting into my ankles and I could feel the raw skin there being scoured by my wet socks every time my feet hit the ground. I wondered how long it would take for the leather and cotton to grind through tissue and tendon till they reached bone – if they hadn't already. 'Get to the trees. Quick!'

Colton yelped with terror and accelerated forwards, the proximity of the bullies fuelling his speed. As well as the loud blood that filled my head, my thoughts throbbed with some nonsensical chant which, in hindsight, was highly concentrated and heartfelt enough in its plea to reach celestial beings had any been listening. *Trees, trees, trees. The trees. Got. To. Get. To. The. Trees. Oh God. Please. The trees. Got. To. Get. To. The. Trees.*

I heard a thud somewhere behind and risked looking over my shoulder again. England had slipped in the mud and was lying on his belly, starfished. Watson and Hake both stopped to help him up, but Robson carried on and was hot on our tails. So close, in fact, I fancied I could feel the heat of his temper.

Another flash of lightning lit up the sky. White electric-charged fury. As Colton and I passed beneath one of the giant arches of Gregory's Leap, a roar of thunder echoed around the brickwork with deafening clamour. At the other side there were no ghosts waiting for us, but we'd reached the first of the trees.

'Follow me!' I told Colton. 'Hurry! Keep up!'

I left the path and plundered through nettles and undergrowth, wishing Colton was in front of me, so I could see him. But I needed to lead the way, to navigate us off-track through the dene. I could hear him right behind me. I could also hear Robson. Too close for comfort. Ivy and other foliage snagged at my feet and ankles as if deliberately trying to slow me. As if in allegiance with the bullies or trying to fulfil a dark agenda of its own. To harness me. To keep me there. I ploughed on, leading us around trees and bushes.

Rainwater splashed all around, falling from the leaves above our heads. The treetops were a dark green canopy of sound which allowed the rain and insipid daylight to infiltrate their leafy boughs. I couldn't imagine ever getting out of this situation. It was a never ending nightmare. On and on and on it went. Deeper and deeper. A labyrinth of hurt. I imagined this was our fate and that we'd be trapped here forever. Home was a distant, unreachable prospect.

I remembered the urban legend Mrs Resnor had recited in junior school about the windmill in Easington and the two kids who'd broken in and got trapped on the winding staircase in a perpetual state of up and down. No end to the steps, no matter which way they went. In some other dimension, to some other class, I imagined Mrs Resnor might be relaying the story about two kids who were trapped in Castle Eden Dene.

Sullivan and Colton Carter: urban legends.

As we wound our way through the densely wooded area, where roe deer and ghosts most likely coexisted, the sound of water became more prominent. It wasn't just rainfall now though, it was more of a determined, forceful gushing. A voluminous body of water. I knew then exactly where we were headed. The undeniable sound of the beck coursing towards the beach meant we were almost at the tunnel.

The cundy.

The cundy is a water conduit which passes beneath the coast road. It's been terrifying kids (and adults of a flighty disposition) probably ever since it was built.

Why?

Because inside, it's much darker than you'd ever expect it to be. Like, unnaturally black. Even on a sunny day. Once you venture into its midst it's impossible not to ponder what might dwell in all that blackness alongside you. It's hard not to imagine ghost fingers reaching out to touch you. To stroke your bare skin with phantom caresses which will also touch your sanity. There's a very real risk that they might then grab you and pull you further into their ghoulish abyss. To keep you there forever. In some space that exists beyond reality and logic. Where no one else can reach you.

Colton must have sensed where we were headed and eased up on his pace. I heard him yip and when I turned round, I saw that Martyn Robson had grabbed him by the shoulder.

'Come here, you little shit!' Robson spun Colton round so fast, Colton lost his footing and slammed into the trunk of a sycamore tree.

I gritted my teeth at the thunk his body made, as if I'd felt the impact myself.

'I'm gonna smash your teeth in, dickweed,' Robson said, holding Colton upright. 'Every single one of them.'

My heart just about leapt out of my mouth.

No!

Robson's threat, as well as the sight of Colton's red raincoat bunched up in his fist, sparked some sort of rage in me. The sky pulsed white beyond the heavy canopy of foliage above us. Without much thought to what I was doing, I flew back and punched Robson in the face. It was a satisfying blow, as hard as it was well aimed. Either the bone in my knuckle or the gristle in Robson's nose made a crunching sound. Then thunder crashed all about us. Robson let go of Colton. So I hit him again. A firm crack on the left temple which made his eyes glaze over.

Then we ran, me and Colton. Oh how we ran. I might even have laughed deliriously at the sheer danger of it all, at the exhilarating throb of my knuckles and the electric energy of the storm. For a few fleeting moments of insanity, I was beyond caring about myself. No, that's not exactly true. It's more like I had simply surpassed the limits of fear and had transcended into some realm of acceptance. The acceptance that some things in life can't be avoided. No matter what.

If not for Colton, in that moment of adrenaline fuelled madness, I think I might have turned round and gone back to meet Robson and the others head on. But onwards I scampered, leading Colton closer and closer towards the sound of rushing water. Towards the cundy.

Robson was no longer pursuing us. I could only presume he'd hung back to wait for England, Watson and Hake, his pride probably dented by the two punches I'd dealt him. I bet he hadn't expected me to retaliate. But that's the way with most bullies, isn't it? Get them on their own, away from the bravado of the group, as Bob Holness, the grumpy bus driver, had suggested I do with England, and more often than not they'll shit their pants when you fight back. Bullies, I think, are nothing but weakling sociopaths, after all. Too hung up on their own insecurities and not strong enough by far to overcome life's problems, which we all have. Therefore, they like to choose someone who they deem to be a weak link, someone they perceive to be in some way physically or mentally lesser than themselves, to humiliate and grind down to such a low level they can at least feel in control of something and better about their own shitty self-esteem.

The entrance to the cundy snuck up on us. It was like a vertical hole waiting to be fallen into. A concrete structure that imposed itself on the surrounding natural greenery with its manmade ugliness. The grey arch of the entranceway was decorated with colourful graffiti and the path leading inside was glittered with shards of clear glass from a broken vodka bottle. Hardly inviting. I could see the level of water that rushed through the tunnel was so high it lapped over the rim of the concrete channel, flooding the footpath inside. I don't think I'd ever seen that happen before. But then, it'd been raining so heavily that day it was hardly surprising. Colton's eyes grew wide and he skidded to a stop.

'Come on,' I urged. 'We have to go in.'

He shook his head. *No.*

'We don't have a choice.'

'I don't want to.'

'It's not up for discussion, mate.' I pointed at the blackness and commanded him to, 'Go on, get in.'

'Nuh-uh.' Again he shook his head. More adamantly this time. He gestured to the ground in front of the cundy's opening with his forefinger which was poking from the sleeve of his slick, red raincoat. He was wide-eyed and fearful. 'Look at that.'

At first I thought it was a mound of dirt next to the neck of the broken vodka bottle, but on closer inspection I saw that it wasn't. It was a large, dead rat. A gruesome heap of decomposition that was well underway. The rat's body was bloated, as if waterlogged, and its dark fur was matted. Its front feet were curled into tight, pink fists, which gave the impression that it had spent the last moments of its life clinging on to the unseen fabric of existence. Trailing behind it, the rat's tail was flesh-coloured, like a long, bloated earthworm sprouting bristly hairs. The most disturbing thing, however, was that the rat's head had been severed and was nowhere to be seen. It was a grisly sight, one which depicted all too well a horrible death. But we didn't have time to fuss. Didn't have time to be grossed out about the hows and the whys.

'It won't hurt you,' I told Colton. 'Just step over it.'

'No.'

'Come on,' I insisted. 'We need to go inside before England gets here. We have to hide.'

Colton still didn't budge. 'But…what happened to its head, Sully?' His eyes were still wide and he looked on the verge of one of his meltdowns.

Not now, Colton. Please, please, please not now.

'I dunno.' I regarded the open, gory wound of the rat's neck again. Exposed muscle and tissue glistened with rainwater. Maybe even maggots. I was saddened by a fleeting thought that just days ago, maybe even hours, it had been a living, breathing thing. Going about its business of finding food and shelter and trying to stay alive, which is all any of us do in the grand scheme of things. But now the rat didn't need to worry about any of that stuff. Its light had been snuffed out. I sincerely hoped it was in a better place. Somewhere less harsh.

'A fox might have eaten it,' I suggested, not at all convinced by this theory, but needing to move things along. I managed a blasé shrug as if to say *who cares anyway?* even though I did.

'But, why wouldn't the fox have eaten the rest of it?' Colton asked.

'God, I don't know,' I said, probably a little too harshly. We didn't have time for this though. I felt almost high on nervous energy and was all too aware of the valuable seconds that were passing us by. I ran my hands over my head, exasperated. 'Maybe rats taste like shit, you daft bugger. Just get inside, will you!'

'I can't,' he whined, tugging on the front of his hair.

The approaching voices of England and his mates resounded around the underside of the trees' dark awning. They were shouting and hollering. Close. So close. Almost upon us.

We were out of time.

Colton froze.

I grabbed the sleeve of his raincoat and dragged him into the cundy.

5

Inside The Cundy

Beyond the mutilated rat there was blackness; an all-encompassing wet blackness that I could remember all too clearly from the last time I'd walked through the cundy. It had been the previous summer, not yet a year since, when Mam had still had aspirations of growing old with Dad, watching me and Colton grow into adults and, perhaps one day, becoming a grandma. I'd been out walking with Dad and Colton. Mam had stayed home to do some chores around the house. At that time, we all thought she was well. Outwardly she looked fine. She'd complained that maybe she was coming down with something. Something minor like a summer cold, which she thought she'd be able to shake off with plenty of vitamin C and some paracetamol. None of us could have guessed what was really going on. What was really taking hold.

That last time Colton and I had passed through the cundy, both of us hollering, me daring him to go first, had been one of the very last days of contented family life we'd known before we were plunged headfirst into a void of fear, hopelessness and grief. What transpired in the days afterwards was to be the beginning of our ongoing nightmare.

I wondered, as I pulled Colton behind me, whether this time around, if we carried on walking till we were out the other side of the tunnel, everything would be reversed. Would Mam come back and be with us again?

Perhaps it was this last memory of being in the cundy – and not the headless rat – which made Colton reluctant to go inside. Maybe he was worried that there'd be terrible new consequences for revisiting such a dark place. That by re-entering we'd be picking at the scab of a wound that should have been left alone. We didn't have the luxury of time to stop and ponder whatever it was that gut instinct might have been trying to tell us, though. I had to coax Colton further onwards, into the cundy, into the blackness, otherwise we'd get our heads kicked in by England and his mates.

Our feet sloshed along the unseen footpath, which spanned the length of the tunnel on the right hand side. The sound of water flowing past us, to the left, was treacherously close. Amplified within the close confines of the concrete walls, it was dizzying in volume and disorientating because of the absolute blackness that kept it. Every now and then I could feel cold spray coming over the brim of the water channel, splashing my ankles and feet. The temperature inside the cundy was a couple of degrees cooler than outside and the air felt dank. Colton clung to me, his fingers biting into the tender skin of the underside of my arm. I could feel him shaking uncontrollably. It was impossible to tell who was shivering the hardest, me or him.

By now my swollen face was numb; no longer hot with the blood and bruising caused by England's fists. My heart pounded, but I imagined the blood it distributed was chilled; the heat of it spent from the chase. My top lip felt like it should belong to someone else. It was twice as big as usual and unfamiliar against my bottom lip. My left eye was swollen almost shut. Through it I could see only a slit of the cundy's blackness. And around the black, on the underside of my inflamed eyelid, I could see deepest red; the colour of my own promised agony, which I knew would come later when adrenalin and the numbness of the cold had worn off.

Groping along the damp, gritty wall with my right hand, I led Colton further and further inside. The other end of the tunnel was in sight, but the swatch of daylight offered no illumination other than marking where the exit was. It hung there like a circular grey canvas and seemed to suggest that the cundy was a dark portal which light from the outside world couldn't penetrate. When we were at the midway point, or thereabouts, I came to a halt.

Colton's fingertips pressed even deeper into my arm, nipping the skin and guaranteeing bruises. 'What's the matter?' he said, his voice an urgent hiss. 'Why have we stopped?'

'We have to wait,' I told him. 'To see if they followed us here.'

'And what if they did?'

'Let's just see.' I didn't know what we'd do next. I could only hope that the darkness of the cundy would keep us hidden and that England and his mates wouldn't venture inside. Or better still, that they'd bypass the cundy and go straight to the coast road to look for us there. We had no such luck though. Mere seconds later I heard England near the entrance.

'Reckon they're in there?' he shouted. His voice echoed all around the concrete walls, booming above the sound of water.

'Dunno,'someone, probably Robson, replied.

'Didn't you see which way they went?'

'Nah.'

'Fuck sake, man, Robbo, you useless tosser, what were you doing?'

'They lost me off.'

'Well go on then, get in there. See if they're hiding.'

There was a dull smacking sound, probably England shoving Robson towards the entrance.

Colton clutched me tighter. 'What shall we do?'

'Shhh.' My body was so tense, every muscle hurt. I put my arm across Colton's chest and forced him against the damp wall, then settled beside him, so that both of our backs were pressed against the cold, curved wall of concrete. Keeping my arm where it was, I held him in place. 'Don't move. Just stay still.'

The daylight at the entrance flickered brighter for a fraction of a second. Then a subsequent bellow of thunder made the cundy growl. It sounded as though we were in the belly of a beast. A prehistoric lizard, I thought, or a mythological giant. It didn't much matter which, either was bad enough. All I could think was that its digestive juices were flowing right beside us and getting out alive seemed like an impossible prospect because England, Robson, Watson and Hake were loitering around the arsehole like the great big turds they were and even if we managed to spew ourselves from the mouth, Colton and I would get caught. No doubt about it.

My bladder twinged and because of the sound of water echoing around the unholy black, I worried that it might be encouraged to let loose. I willed it not to. That would be a step too far. A step from which my dignity might not recover.

Sullivan Carter pissed his pants in the cundy.

How embarrassing?

Okay, so no one else would notice, since my trousers were already sopping wet, but I would. And that counted for a lot. *I'd* know that I pissed my pants.

I closed my eyes and counted to ten. A distraction technique.

Mam used to tell me to do this whenever I had a nightmare and was too scared to sleep. I had lots of nightmares when I was younger. I guess you could say I was ultra sensitive to the dark and all that might be in it. Everything that I couldn't see. This anxiety all too often manifested itself as ghosts and monsters in my subconscious, which would then gate-crash my dreams.

Sometimes, though not all that often, thankfully, I'd wake up and find an old woman pinning me to the bed. It was the same woman every time and I used to think she must have the ability to slip right out of my dreams and pop into actual existence whenever she pleased. She used to scare the absolute shit out of me. Her skin was mottled grey. It was like crinkled crepe paper, especially around her mean eyes – the irises of which were black in their entirety. Her teeth were white needles. Inhuman and impossibly sharp. She looked as though she'd spent days laid out on a mortuary slab but hadn't been made over by the mortician yet. A smell like camphor wood and mothballs clung to the black swathes of fabric that hung all about her bony body. It must have been a dress or a cloak, but I never could tell for sure. By simply pressing down on my chest with both of her gnarled hands, the old woman had the power to render me completely paralysed. And not only was she able to take away my ability to move, I found I couldn't find my voice during her visits either. No matter how much I wanted to shout and scream, I couldn't.

When I told Mam about these frightening experiences, she said the old woman was nothing but a night terror. My own fearfulness playing tricks on me. She said maybe I should give the old woman a name, which might make her seem less scary. I said I didn't think she could ever be any less scary and, besides, I couldn't think of a name that suited her. Mam suggested Edith. So I went with that.

Even with a name, I found Edith to be just as real and terrifying. In fact, by naming her I sort of felt like I'd accepted her into my life and okayed her visitations, like, 'Hey night terror, I love you so much I'm gonna call you Edith. In fact, now we're on first name terms, maybe you can visit more often.' I think things with Edith spiralled out of control for a while then.

Just before she got ill, Mam hung a dreamcatcher over my bed 'to catch any nasty dreams that tried to creep out'. By which, of course, she meant Edith. Funnily enough, I never saw Edith again after that.

I fully expected her to show up now, though. Her clawed, arthritic hands to press against my chest till my spine grated against the wall and I had to choke and wheeze for breath. Because if there are pockets of darkness in the world which store all of the bad things dreamcatchers capture, I expect the cundy is one of them.

Edith didn't appear, however.

Maybe counting to ten had worked to alleviate my anxieties somewhat. But no, I still felt like I might piss my pants.

If I ever got out of this situation, I knew I was in all kinds of trouble. In trouble with Dad for coming to the dene and getting into such a state. In trouble with Mr Dunn and Mrs Dennis for losing my physics and geography workbooks. And in trouble with Kevin England and his mates for simply daring to be. There was a time when I used to be able to slip past them unnoticed at school, but now that I was on their radar my mere existence seemed to rile their aggression. They saw me as easy pickings and took cruel delight in tormenting me daily. It totally sucked to be me.

'What's that smell?' Colton gripped the sleeve of my

jacket and shook my arm to ensure he had my attention.

'What smell?' But as soon as the words were out of my mouth I smelt it: an overpowering musky odour, like the sebaceous secretions of an animal. So sudden. So strong. So near. It made me feel dizzy.

'Is there a fox in here with us?' Colton asked, his voice high and tight.

'I doubt it.' But I wasn't sure. Foxes were shy creatures, as far as I knew, but what if one had wandered into the cundy seeking shelter from the rain before we'd arrived? What if it felt threatened about us being there? What if it was bold enough to attack?

I grasped Colton's fist, the one that was clutching my jacket, and squeezed; a signal for him to be quiet. Whether there was a fox nearby or not, there wasn't a great deal we could do about it. I looked back towards the entrance and saw that it was obscured by the silhouettes of England, Robson, Watson and Hake. *They* were a very real threat. And it looked like all four of them were about to come inside.

Shit!

What now?

We had to stay put and hope they'd pass us by without noticing – no easy feat, I realised. I glanced the other way, towards the exit. It seemed so far away. We were totally screwed. Even my body was against me, I thought, miserably. My bladder ached as if to remind me, *I'm gonna piss down your legs, Sully, whatcha gonna do about it?*

'What's that?' Colton gasped. He gripped my arm tighter to his chest.

Something moved in the dark. Right in front of us. It was a shape that I thought would have been impossible to see had I not seen it. Whatever it was was even blacker than the darkness itself. An impossible thing, and yet, there it was. A large, skulking, stealthy thing that was bigger than a fox. *Way* bigger than a fox. It slinked past us, so close my skin tightened as if in defence against the promise of sharp teeth to come. We pressed ourselves even closer to the wall behind us and held our breath.

The thing, whatever it was, moved silently, yet somehow its presence was greater than the sound of rushing water. And its smell – oh God, its smell. The musky stink from before had intensified to a heady stench, encouraging images to form in my mind of wiry fur, a snarling snout and carnivorous teeth that would easily rip flesh and grind bones. I had a distinct feeling that we'd entered a wild animal's lair and were not welcome. Not one bit. In fact, a new sense of danger had filled the tunnel with such power that I felt what I can only describe as being close to death. I know that sounds extreme, but I was overcome with a predominant awareness of having been exposed to something I couldn't yet hope to understand; I was too young and the danger was too deep and dark and preternatural. I felt threatened by the black form itself, which had crept past us, but I detected something much worse than an earthly animal there in the tunnel with us. I felt there must be an invasive extension of the creature which was even more terrible. And it lurked at the periphery of darkness, waiting to take us into it. Into the black.

England and his friends were now a secondary concern.

Me and Colton, we were in grave danger.

'Stay still,' I whispered. 'Don't move.'

'Did you see it?' Colton whimpered. 'What was it?'

'I don't know.'

I could see that England, Robson, Watson and Hake were still by the entrance. Their silhouettes were joined together. They looked like a shadowy mass of heads and legs against the grey strip of daylight. I scanned the rest of the tunnel, but couldn't see the creature. Couldn't see its blacker-than-black form.

'We shouldn't be here,' I heard Robson say.

'Why not?' England said.

'It's our Tony's hangout. He'll kill us if he finds us mooching about.'

'Why? What does he do down here?'

'I dunno. Comes with his mates to smoke and drink and do weird shit.'

'What weird shit?'

'I'm not sure.'

'Devil worshipping, I bet,' Hake said.

England barked with laughter. 'Piss off, man. Robbo's brother couldn't rouse his girlfriend never mind the fucking Devil.'

Watson and Hake bellowed with laughter.

'Let's just go,' Robson said.

'What's the matter, you poof?' England chided. 'Are you scared of the dark?'

'Ugh, look at that!' It was Hake's voice. 'A dead rat!'

There was a loud guffaw of nervous laughter and Watson shouted, 'Gross! It's got no head.'

'Hey, Robbo, that's what your Ruth's fanny looks like,' Hake said.

'Ah go and fuck yourself, shithead.'

'Ha! That's what she said.'

There was an uproar of laughter, then England said, 'Is that the sort of weird shit your Tony does down here, like, Robbo? Do him and his mates kill rats and eat their heads to summon the dark lord?'

'Piss off, you big wanker,' Robson retorted.

'Who're you calling a wanker, you goon?'

'It was probably Zombie Carter and his spazzy brother who did that to the rat,' Watson said. 'They're a right couple of weirdos.'

'Hardly surprising, having a dad like theirs,' Robson

said.

There was a throaty growl to my right. For a moment I was confused, then realised with dawning dread that the creature must have doubled back and stalked past me and Colton again without us having realised. Which meant we were now penned in. Stuck in the middle of the cundy; the bullies at one end and the creature blocking our way to the other.

Oh God.

I wanted to scream for it all to stop. For it all to end. I'd had enough. My nerves couldn't take anymore. But the creature snarled again. Louder this time. It was the type of warning growl that precedes an attack and was more bassy than the crashing water.

'What the fuck was that?' I heard England say. 'Did you hear it?'

'I told you we should go,' Robson whined.

Yes, just bloody well go! I screamed, inside my head.

I saw the massive black shape of the creature looming then. It moved so fast, me and Colton didn't have time to react, to move out of the way, before it ploughed straight into us. It hit me from the side, knocking all the air from my lungs. As I crashed against Colton, we were bowled clear from the wall. The creature's death-hot breath was right in my face and its coarse fur touched my skin. It was thick and wiry, just how I'd imagined. I felt Colton toppling away from me. I grasped the air, using frenzied snatching motions till my fingers found purchase on his raincoat. But the glossy vinyl slipped through my damp fingers and he began to fall again. His arms flailed in panic and, by chance, one of his hands caught in mine. I gripped it tight and jerked him towards me.

'What the hell's in there?' I heard England shout. 'A frigging lion? Did you hear it? Did you see it? Did you see the size of it?'

'Let's just get out of here,' Robson insisted.

'But did you see it?'

'*Yes, I fucking did.* Now let's just go!'

At least they had the option to leave, I thought. Me and Colton were as good as dead. The creature roared. It was right behind us. Instinct told me that this time it intended to go for the kill. Keeping tight hold of Colton's hand, I squeezed his fingers between mine so he couldn't let go and did the only thing I could. I leapt forward, taking him with me, into the rushing water. The black torrents of freezing cold knocked all the air from my lungs and my gasps of shock echoed around the cundy's walls. Colton and I landed upright in the concrete channel, precariously so. I waited to see if the creature would follow.

It didn't.

I could see its dark form pacing at the edge, no doubt watching us. Waiting to see if we would climb back out. The water pounded and frothed around my legs at upper thigh level, but I was steady enough on my feet for it not to drag me over. Colton, however, was in a state of panic. The water was up to his waist and he was struggling to stay upright. I worried that if he let go of my hand, the current would sweep him away, inevitably taking him right past England, Robson, Watson and Hake. Dragging him to me, like a slippery deadweight, I hugged him close. Then together we began to wade towards the exit, fighting against the flow of water. One steady step at a time. My teeth chattered with the cold and I watched as the black creature followed our progress.

The grey swatch of daylight at the exit was impossibly far away; a melancholic smear on the black which promised rain and all kinds of other trouble. But I didn't care. The creature from the cundy couldn't get us beyond the black, I thought. It couldn't tear us to shreds with its teeth once we were back out there in the real world.

All we had to do was make it to the grey.

6

Bad Dreams

Dad didn't go as mental as I thought he would when we got home. Instead, he retreated into a quiet, brooding sulk, which seemed far worse than if he had shouted at us. I saw disappointment in his eyes, as well as something else that I didn't like: despair. I think he'd reached a new level of hopelessness. It was as though he didn't know how to deal with us anymore. And judging by his silence, I wasn't sure he wanted to.

When he asked where we'd been, we lied and said we'd gone to a friend's house, making out that we'd got soaked to our underpants during the walk home in the rain. We knew we'd be in big trouble if we told the truth about going to the dene and taking a swim in the cundy, but we also knew that our made-up story reeked to high heaven of bullshit. Still, Dad didn't question us further or poke holes in the flimsiness of our tale. I got the distinct feeling that our fate had been sealed for the summer and that we'd be packed off to Aunt Julie's as soon as school was out.

When I stripped out of my wet clothes in the bathroom, Dad came and stood in the doorway. He looked much older, I realised, as though the past year with all of its bad news and hardship had served to hurtle him through the remainder of his youth, thus carrying him straight into a progressed state of middle-age. His dark blonde hair was scattered with more grey than I think I'd ever noticed before and he had more creases about his face, especially around his eyes. He wore a beard at a time when it was highly unfashionable and uncool to do so. I didn't hate or resent him for this, I felt only pity, because he was like the ghost of the man he'd once been. A beardy ghost who couldn't be bothered anymore. It was as though a large part of him had died when Mam had.

'Put them in the bathtub,' he said, indicating my wet clothes with a nod of his head. 'Don't leave them lying about on the floor. I'll sort them after tea.'

I nodded and kept my face downturned, to avoid eye contact. Dad hadn't yet mentioned my beaten up face, but I knew under the fluorescent strip lighting it must look pretty horrific. If he hadn't noticed my burst lip, swollen cheekbones and purpling eyelids before, he certainly would now. But then, of course he'd already noticed. How could he not? In fact, the real reason he'd come to the bathroom wasn't to badger me about where I should put my wet clothes, it was to find out who'd tried to rearrange my face.

'What happened?' he said.

Here we go.

Dad pointed at his own face, in case I might pretend not to know what he was talking about. He'd lowered his voice considerably, as if he didn't want Colton to overhear. Which seemed absurd, given that surely he realised Colton had seen what had happened to me or at the very least had spoken to me about it already.

I shrugged, feeling small and vulnerable under his scrutiny, while standing there in my underpants, shivering. 'Doesn't matter.'

Dad sighed and ran a hand over his face. I heard his beard bristle beneath his palm. 'This has got to stop, Sully. If you won't tell me their names, I'm going to the school tomorrow to talk to the headmaster about it.'

'No, Dad, you'll just make it worse.'

'*Worse?*' His dark blue eyes glinted dangerously. 'How can I make it worse? These kids, they need to stop picking on you.' He inhaled deeply. 'How many of them are there?'

'Four.'

He stayed at the doorway and studied my face some more. His breathing was loud through his flared nostrils. His hands were balled into fists. 'Is there a particular reason why they've singled you out, do you know?'

I shook my head, didn't want to go into any tale-telling specifics. Dad had enough on his plate without having to worry about me not being able to stand up for myself. 'No.'

'If you won't tell me, then the school needs to know.'

'Don't, Dad. *Please.*'

He closed his eyes and turned away from me. Resting his forehead against the doorframe, his shoulders sagged and all of the anger seemed to seep out of him. I thought for a moment he might cry. He looked so forlorn. Broken. It was one of those moments where we both needed Mam. She'd know what to do. Or at the very least, she'd tell Dad that she'd take care of things and then bundle me into a hug, which wouldn't feel at all awkward, and tell me that everything was going to be okay.

I grabbed a bath towel from the radiator and wrapped it around myself. It was the closest thing to a hug I'd get. The towel's warmth transferred to my skin, soothing most of my goosebumps, but it wasn't nearly enough to thaw the cold that had settled in my bones. I pulled the soft cotton tighter around my torso and was unable to help myself from wondering if I'd ever feel wholly warm again. To be dry and warm, I realised, was such taken-for-granted luxury.

When Dad looked at me again, his eyes were intense. Unreadable. We regarded each other for a couple of seconds, but it seemed like much longer. He appeared to have so much more to say to me. I willed him not to.

'Ten minutes till tea's ready,' he said, at last. He surprised me then by turning and walking away. And that was that.

Tea was tinned spaghetti on toast with Cheddar cheese grated on top. It hurt like a bitch to eat because my top lip was swollen and sore, but I was so hungry I demolished the entire plateful within five minutes. Colton had a more meagre meal of cheese on toast. The spaghetti sauce was too close to red for his current mood; usually it would be classed as an orange food and therefore safe, but not that evening. Dad hadn't even bothered to argue. Colton picked and poked at his plateful with his knife and fork till the cheese turned into a cold, solidified mass on top of the toast. By the time he left the dinner table, he'd hardly eaten any of it. I was surprised that Dad let him get away with it. But then, Dad seemed almost vacant. Like nothing else existed beyond whatever thoughts were sparring in his head at that time.

Later that night as I lay in bed, aching with physical affliction and emotional exhaustion, I had my own troubled thoughts to contend with. Mostly about school the next day. About what Kevin England and Martyn Robson would do when they saw me. Would the bruising and swelling on my face satisfy their egos enough to make them feel like they didn't need to give me too much more of a beating? Or would they do it anyway – and totally go for the kill? Gut instinct told me it would be the latter. It had been a hugely stressful, traumatic day and I was pleased it was over, but I dreaded to find out what new horrors lay in wait.

Long shadows stretched across the ceiling, caused by the weak moonlight which had crept around the curtains. I imagined they were nightmares trying to break free from Mam's dreamcatcher. As well as being anxious, I felt on edge. Spooked. The night had an eerie quality, as though life's mortal path and death's unknown one were running parallel to one another. Much too close. I imagined that anyone from either path could take a small step and cross the divide, thus entering territory in which they didn't belong.

Tipping my head back, I looked up at the wall above my headboard to make sure the dreamcatcher was there. It was the sort of night, I thought, in which Edith might pay me a visit. The insidious blackness of the cundy was still with me. It had been all evening. It haunted my waking self with its menacing ambiguity, making me consider and then reconsider all that it might hold within itself and all that it might conceal from the eyes of the living. No doubt it was also busy wreaking all kinds of havoc on my subconscious mind. I expected nightmares aplenty that night. The web-like silhouette of the dreamcatcher was there on the wall, just as it should be. On guard. Ready for action. Ready to snare otherworldly trespassers. It gave me some small comfort.

My thoughts soon drifted to the animal that had attacked me and Colton in the darkness. Its smell, the feel of its coarse fur and the feral threat of its anger were still all too clear in my mind. As much as I'd felt susceptible to some kind of preternatural attack, it must have been a stray dog, I reasoned. A German Shepherd, perhaps. At the time it had seemed much bigger. But then, it had been too dark to tell and I'd been wired on adrenalin. I hadn't exactly been thinking straight. It absolutely could have been a German Shepherd.

Probably a mistreated one that was scared of people. We'd gone in and frightened it, that was all.

Absolutely.

As I began to drift off, my subconscious startled me with the unwelcome image of the dead rat. I tried to convince myself that the stray dog must have killed it and eaten its head. But deep down I knew the rat had been killed, or at least mutilated after its death, by a person. The wound on its neck, where its head had been detached from its body, had been much too neat to have been caused by the rough serration of a dog's biting teeth. Its head, most likely, had been severed with a blade. Martyn Robson's words came back to me loud and clear: *It's our Tony's hangout. Comes with his mates to smoke and drink and do weird shit.*

But, what weird shit? Cutting heads off rats? Because that was certainly weird shit.

I'd heard that one of the signs to watch for when trying to determine if a person is a fledgling serial killer – you know, as a matter of general curiosity or perhaps in the interest of self-preservation, when someone you know is dodgy enough to make your gut instinct itch with paranoia – is the harming of animals for fun. Aside from being a total dickhead thing to do, it shows a complete lack of empathy. For that person then to extend their thrill-seeking pastime to a much riskier one of human torture would be, in a way, like natural progression. I wondered, therefore, if Martyn Robson's big brother, Tony, was a fledging serial killer.

Since certain types of behaviours are often hereditary, this also made me wonder if Martyn Robson might be more unhinged than I'd originally thought. Perhaps even worse than Kevin England. Because as much as Kevin England was a bona fide arsehole, I didn't for one minute think he would turn out to be a serial killer. He had a shaggy, sandy-coloured mongrel called Benny

Andersson, which I'd seen him out walking plenty of times. The dog always looked happy enough, in that tail-wagging, tongue-lolling manner dogs have. I'd also heard that Kevin England helped his dad to race pigeons and clean their crees out too. Gut instinct told me that as much as he was a bully, he was an animal person, not a wannabe serial killer. I wasn't yet sure what gut instinct was trying to tell me about the Robsons though.

I fell asleep feeling miserable and in pain. My dreams were a jumble of troubled nonsense, but at least nothing tried to kill me in them. When I awoke it was still dark. The duvet was pulled taut over my body, restricting my movement, and a black figure loomed over me.

Edith!

Trying to lurch away, I yelped. Terrified. Then realised it was just Colton.

'What the hell are you doing, shithead?' I was vexed that he'd managed to scare me so badly. My heart galloped.

'Sorry.'

I reached over and switched on my bedside lamp. The light was harsh and when I squinted against it the swollen, tender skin around my eyes stung. Sucking in air between my teeth, I made a harsh hissing sound.

Colton seemed to squirm with some embarrassment, but this was mostly overridden by fear. His brow was furrowed and his eyes were alert. 'I had a nightmare,' he said. 'And I couldn't get back to sleep.'

Rolling my eyes, I sank back down against my pillow, my heartbeat still erratic. 'Well what do you want me to do about it?' I'd never known Colton to seek refuge in my room during the night before. Not even in the days and weeks straight after Mam had passed away.

'I dunno.' He looked at me with wide, pleading eyes, as though he expected that by default, because I was his older brother, I should know. 'I'm scared.'

I presumed that the cundy's blackness must have got to him. That it had tainted his mind with its indelible darkness, as it had mine.

'It was just a dream,' I told him, feigning stoicism as though I hadn't been affected by the lurking horror myself. 'Think nice thoughts instead. You'll soon fall asleep again.'

'But what if I do and it's there again?'

'If what's there again?'

Colton seemed suddenly younger than he was, all small and vulnerable in his red pyjamas. 'I dreamt we were in the cundy,' he said, tugging at the front of his hair. 'The monster was there. It was waiting for us.'

'What monster?'

'The one we saw today.'

'That was just a dog,' I scoffed, wafting my hand dismissively. 'A stray dog. That's all.'

Colton didn't look at all convinced.

'There were voices in the water as well,' he told me. 'Lots of them. And all of them were speaking at the same time. They were trying to talk to me, I think. But I couldn't tell what any of them were saying.'

'I'll tell you what they were saying,' I said. 'They were saying: Stop bunking off school and buggering off down the beach on your own, shit stain, else you'll end up getting yourself and your big brother, who's already in more trouble than he needs, fast-track tickets straight to Aunt Julie's for the summer and maybe even Dad's belt across the arse.' I grinned, despite the elements of truth there, and play-punched him on the arm.

'But, Sully,' he whined. 'I think the voices were really real. When I woke up I could still hear the water.'

'That's because it's still raining, doofus, and the drainpipe is right outside your window.'

'But it wasn't that,' he insisted. 'I think it's coming for us.'

'What is?'

He gripped my duvet and leant closer. 'The monster from the cundy.'

'I told you, it's just a dog.'

'No it's not.'

'Yes it is.'

'When did you ever see a dog that big before?' he argued.

'How do you know how big it was?' I said this as though I hadn't considered the exact same thing myself. 'It was too dark to tell.'

'I couldn't see you and you were right next to me, but I could see the monster moving about. Whatever it was was even darker than the dark.' He moved his face away from me. I could see the absolute conviction in his eyes. He totally believed what he was saying. Lowering his voice to a whisper, he said, 'It wasn't a dog and you know it. And now it wants to come and get us because we were in its home. We disturbed it. We should never have gone in there, Sully.'

I made a clicking sound of big-brotherly reproach with my tongue. 'Go back to bed, bot sniff. Stop being silly. We're both gonna be way too tired for school tomorrow.'

'I don't want to go back to bed. What if it gets me?'

'It won't.'

'It might.'

'Well, what do you me want to do?'

'Let me sleep in here with you.'

A few seconds dragged out where I stared at him in utter bewilderment. He was being totally serious.

Groaning, I threw back the duvet and said, 'Get in, you goon. But no snoring, mind. And if you kick me, or touch me at all for that matter, you're going straight back to your own room, got it?'

'Okay.' He hurdled over me onto the bed, then lay on

his side facing me.

Before I turned the bedside lamp off, I saw in his eyes something besides the residual fear of whatever nightmares he'd had or whatever monster he thought waited for us inside the cundy. Intuitively, I could tell he was anxious about something else altogether. About getting into trouble at school, maybe?

Doubtful.

About being sent to Aunt Julie's for the summer?

Possible. But, nah. Unlikely.

He wasn't displaying the type of high-energy fretfulness he would if he couldn't find an item of red clothing to wear. This was more of a stewing unease. Something more serious was eating away at him. Something secret. Something I knew he wanted to tell me but wasn't yet ready to talk about.

I didn't press him. Happy to leave him to whatever troubles he harboured, because goodness knew I had enough of my own.

Colton fell asleep surprisingly quickly and even though his head was right next to my pillow and his breathing was heavy, I didn't mind at all. I lay there for a while listening to his rhythmic inhalations and exhalations, till eventually I fell asleep myself.

The same water that had haunted Colton's dreams flowed into mine. I heard the voices that he'd spoken of; an eerie chorus of watery, turbulent death that was loud in the dark. Head-hurtingly raucous, in fact. I could understand the words, but as soon as I tried to apply meaning to them it was lost to me. Forgotten. I was inside the cundy and I could hear the creature's silence there too. Its breathing was drowned out by the voices of the dead, but I could hear it loud in some defunct, untapped part of my mind as it watched and waited. When its black, hulking outline finally stepped into view, all of me cowered. If it was a dog it was gargantuan. This time I could see its eyes. They were fiery, luminescent almonds, so bright they should have cast light all about them, but didn't. It was as though all of the fire from the core of the world burned within the creature but couldn't pierce the darkness of the cundy. The blackness was absolute.

The creature began to pace back and forth like a caged animal. It was so close I could smell its musk; an invasive stink which clung to the back of my throat. The darkness covered my face like a mask, I could barely breathe. Its tendrils of nothingness smothered me. I wanted to escape, but there was no swatch of grey daylight at either end of the tunnel. Everything was black. Everything.

Shuffling to the edge of the footpath, where water sloshed over my bare feet, I peered down to the rush of water which was channelling through the tunnel. I couldn't see it, of course, but I could hear that it was filled with much torment. So many voices churned in the froth and frenzy of the rainwater deluge. I was overcome with an insurmountable feeling that the water wanted to pull me in. To add me to its collection of rolling souls. Leaping backwards, I flattened myself against the cold, damp wall and whimpered.

No, you can't have me. You can't.

Those voices. Those terrible, terrible voices.

The creature stopped pacing and fixed its burning eyes on me. Then it started to growl; a low, bassy noise which made my innards vibrate.

'Sully. Sully. Sullivan. *Sully.*' The voices in the water were calling to me by name. Trying to coax me back to the edge. Trying to draw me close. And I was almost tempted to obey, because the threat of the creature was even worse. I imagined its teeth tearing the flesh from my bones, the agony as it gorged on muscle and tissue.

'Sully. Sully. Sullivan. *Sully.*'

'Okay, I'm coming,' I said, taking a deep breath and stepping towards the water. *I'm coming.*

'Sullivan!' I woke up to find Dad standing over me, gripping my shoulders. 'Wake up.'

'The water,' I said, deliriously. My hairline and pyjama top were soaking with feverishness. 'I must have fallen in again. I didn't mean to.'

'Fallen in where? What water?'

'Where the voices are.' I was hot. Burning hot.

'You were having a bad dream,' Dad said, touching my forehead with the backs of his fingers.

I turned my head and saw Colton propped up next to me, his cheeks were red and his eyes were wide.

Was I hallucinating?

'By the looks of it,' Dad said, 'thanks to yesterday's escapades, the pair of you are running a bloody temperature. I'll have to call Gran to see if she can sit in with you while I'm at work.' He marched from the room, briefly stopping at the doorway to glance back. His own face looked flushed, but his colour was down to stress, not fever.

'You saw it, didn't you?' Colton whispered as soon as Dad had left.

'Saw what?'

'The monster.'

I closed my eyes against the morning light that was streaming in through the window like thick bleach, burning my retinas. Lying there with the sound of water still in my head, I shook my head and told him, 'No.'

7

Fever

Before he left for work Dad made Colton go back to his own bed. He said he didn't want us fuelling each other's fever, but I reckon it was more to do with him not wanting us carrying on and becoming a nuisance should we make a rapid recovery. The way I felt though, chance would have been a fine thing.

It was extremely rare that Dad would ask Gran for help. He had to be in a real panicking-like-mad situation before he would make that call. I think it actually pained him to do so. Whether this was to do with his sense of pride or something else altogether, I didn't know. He strove to be self-sufficient at all times, even when the shit hit the fan big style. Maybe it was too many years not feeling good enough in Gran's eyes. I mean, it didn't take a genius to see that Gran was all for Aunt Julie. That is, for whatever reason, she favoured her daughter over her son. She doted on Aunt Julie's three kids as well. Me and Colton were second class in comparison. Leper grandchildren because we'd been born of Hugh, not Julie.

Traditionally, Colton and I would each get ten pounds off Gran for Christmases and birthdays, but Aunt Julie's kids would each get fifty quid. Micky, Aunt Julie's youngest, took great delight in telling me this several times. I don't suppose I ever really cared about the financial aspect – hell, I'd have been happy with a fiver – but the principle of it stung nonetheless.

Dad hadn't really talked all that much about his mam over the years, yet he reminisced often about his dad. There were all kinds of rehashed stories about Grandda working down the pit, tending to his allotment and nursing lame animals back to health. My favourite story was about Flappy the magpie who'd decided to stick around well after his broken wing had mended and who went on to develop a mania for stealing the silver tops off all the milk bottles in the street. By the sounds of it, Flappy had caused merry old hell in Fifth Street in the late seventies.

Dad's stories about Grandda all seemed to have taken place impossibly long ago, in times when people, to me, were faded black and white and a bit dog-eared at the edges. Grandda had survived the D-Day landings during World War II, as well as an incident at the pit where a coal shaft had collapsed. These two stories in particular felt especially ungraspable and a little bit scary. Not overly scary though, because Grandda had lived to tell the tale. It was more like re-watching a favourite movie where the protagonist is in grave danger, but it's okay because you know how it all ends. You know that the character you're rooting for is going to make it out unscathed.

I always figured that Dad had a better relationship with Grandda than he did with Gran. And it was a shame I didn't really get to know Grandda Carter all that well. He died of a massive stroke the day before Colton was born. I have this vague memory of Gran standing by the buffet table at Mam's wake with her arms crossed saying to Dad, 'Now you know how I've felt these past few years.' I can't be sure that it's an actual memory or just something I dreamt up. You know, like some sort of mental dump as a result of dealing with too much grief and disappointment. Who knows. I'm about eighty percent certain that it did happen. And I liked Gran less for this thing that she might or might not have said.

I heard the diesel engine rumble of Gran's car pulling up outside. The metallic jangle of keys in Dad's hand and the opening of the front door was then followed by the familiar holler of Gran's nasally voice as she entered the house. No matter what the time or situation, Gran seemed incapable of speaking quietly. When I was much younger, I remember thinking she must be hard of hearing. Mam assured me this wasn't the case and that, in all likelihood, Gran had aspirations of being the town crier. At the time I didn't know what that meant, but it had sounded plausible. Mam had been straight-faced and seemed wholly serious when she told me. In hindsight I appreciate Mam's dry humour a whole lot more.

Not long after Gran had arrived, the front door opened then closed again. More loudly this time. The sound of it reverberated through the entire house, marking Dad's exit as well as his bad mood. I heard his car misfire a few times before he finally got it started, then he was off. It seemed like a whole hour passed by before Gran came up to see us. It wasn't really that long, it just took ages for her to climb the stairs. I could hear the tick of her walking stick on each step and her hand rubbing against the glossed wood of the bannister as she hauled herself upwards. If I hadn't known it was Gran, her slow progress would have creeped me out. It would have been too easy to imagine a ghoul with disjointed limbs, using slow, deliberate steps to taunt me. *I'm coming for you, Sullivan. I'm coming to get you.*

Gran was riddled with arthritis and her mobility was pretty restricted, or so she made out. I never doubted she was pained by her joints, but I had my suspicions as to how badly her movement was affected and just how much she played on it – I'd seen her move when she thought no one was watching. It seemed to me that if her neighbours were up to anything gossip worthy, she was like shit off a stick in getting to the window to see.

It was because of her arthritis she'd said that me and Colton couldn't stay with her during the summer holidays while Dad was at work. I'd promised – and practically begged – that we'd be good and wouldn't give her any cause to run around after us, but she was adamant that Aunt Julie was better equipped to have us.

In many ways I resented her decision, it felt too much like a rejection. After Mam, Gran was the next female figurehead in our lives, yet it seemed to me that she didn't have our backs. Unfairly of me or not, even though we weren't Aunt Julie's offspring, I still expected her to move mountains to make us happy. I dunno, I just thought that's what parents and grandparents did. Especially after all that me and Colton had been through. I thought grandparents were supposed to be on hand, no matter what, to snatch every opportunity to spend with their grandkids. Instead, I got the vague impression that Gran didn't want us disrupting her set-in-stone daily routine of sitting on her arse watching chat shows and home design programmes, taking the odd nap, doing the crossword in the morning paper, making a million cups of tea and spying on her neighbours. I think it was far more convenient for her to adopt Teflon shoulders and let us slide right off into the hellish realm of Aunt Julie's care, regardless of how we felt about it. Mentally documenting how often Maureen from across the road went to bingo and how many times a week Cynthia next door washed her bed sheets was obviously far more important to Gran than the happiness of her son's kids. She knew damn well how much we hated staying with Aunt Julie. But did she care? Did she fuck.

I guess some grans are utterly selfless. Ours wasn't. Not as far as we were concerned, anyway. And as a kid that insight left a bitter taste in my mouth. It made me re-evaluate life. It made me realise that there aren't many people you can truly rely upon, not even the ones you'd most expect to be able to. I'd already decided some time ago that I'd move mountains, however massive, for Colton and would always have his back. No matter what.

I heard Gran go to Colton's room first. Her voice was loud through the wall, but I couldn't make out exactly what she said. Then I heard her hobbling along the landing towards my room. I closed my eyes and pretended to be asleep.

'How're you feeling, sunshine?' If I really had been sleeping, she'd have woken me with the sheer timbre of her voice.

I opened my eyes and saw her at the door. Her mop of permed hair, which was dyed some weird sun-damaged brown colour, was the first thing I noticed. It looked as coarse as horse hair and a worthy home for any nesting bird or small mammal. Anyone who didn't know her might have been fooled into thinking that she hadn't had time to run a comb through it before leaving the house, since Dad had called on her at such short notice. But that simply wouldn't have been the case. This was Gran's usual look.

As for her clothes, it was a given that Gran would throw any old shit together for any occasion. That particular day she was wearing a nautical navy and white striped t-shirt, complete with old tea stains, over a pink floral skirt. Her clothes always looked too big. Like she'd lost weight but hadn't bothered buying new outfits in the correct size. This wasn't true though. Gran had always been scrawny and for whatever reason preferred to be swamped in ill-fitting clothes. On her feet were a pair of brown moccasins which looked stretched and worn. The flesh of her bare ankles was grey like whale skin and bloated with water retention; so much so, it spilled over the leather of her slippers. Gran's ankles were the largest part of her.

I remember Mam once asked Dad if his mother got dressed in the dark. Dad had seen the funny side and laughed. But that was in the time before he'd mislaid his sense of humour.

Gran had the same dark blue eyes as Dad and Colton, and right then they were just as steely and analytical. She was trying to determine if I was foxing.

'I feel awful,' I told her. *Bloody awful.*

She stayed at the doorway and regarded me with her most austere grandma-stare. Eventually she nodded and I got the distinct feeling I'd passed some sort of test. That somehow I'd authenticated my illness. I felt somewhat relieved.

'Well, it'll teach you to go mucking about in the rain, won't it?' she said, unable to resist giving me a ticking-off nonetheless.

'Hmmm.' She didn't know the half of it. But I couldn't be bothered to argue my case. I was feeling too ill to care. And besides, I'd probably get a cuff round the ear for what she'd perceive to be backchat, so I left it at that.

I suspect Dad must have told her about my beaten up face already, because she didn't mention it. That or she simply didn't care.

'I'll make you some chicken soup for dinner,' she said. 'About twelvish. I'll call up when it's ready. You'll have to come down for it because I can't be dealing with them sodding stairs again.' She stooped and gripped her left knee, wincing for effect. I imagine she'd given the same demonstration to Colton. 'They're bloody murder.'

I felt like telling her not to bother. Her attempt at

compulsory concern wasn't wanted. The fact she wasn't interested to know first-hand how I'd acquired two black eyes and a fat lip made my resentment run deeper. Some kind words and a grandmotherly hug wouldn't have gone amiss. But no, I figured she'd probably already missed too much of Eamonn Holmes on GMTV to waste any more time hanging around talking to me.

'If you want anything, give me a shout,' she said, turning to beat an as-hasty-as-she-dare retreat to the television. Her walking stick clattered off the skirting board on the landing, which unduly vexed me. 'But you'll have to come down for it yourself. Like I say, I can't cope with them swining stairs again. Once is enough.'

When she'd gone I stuck two fingers up at the empty doorway, then rolled over so my back was to the door. I buried my head beneath the duvet. What was the point in her even being there? I felt frustrated and angry. I was too young to be treated like an adult, but too old to be babysat. Life just felt so unfair.

I must have fallen asleep. When I woke again I could hear the sound of the television downstairs and Colton was sitting on the edge of my bed, watching me.

'What're you doing?' I complained, reaching up to rub the sleep from my eyes. I remembered just in time about the swollen, bruised skin there, so dropped my hands back down to the bed. 'Why're you just sitting there looking at me, you little creep?'

'You were shouting.'

'No I wasn't'

'Yes you were.' Colton was studying me closely, his eyes serious. 'What were you dreaming about?'

'I dunno.' I couldn't remember.

'You must know.'

'I don't.' I shrugged. 'What did I say?'

'I couldn't tell. You were shouting about something,

but you didn't make any sense. You sounded scared.'

'Didn't Gran hear?'

Colton raised both of his eyebrows as if to say *'what do you think?'* The Scottish lilt of Lorraine Kelly's voice was loud and it travelled from the telly downstairs straight up through the floorboards. She was saying something about skirts worn over the top of trousers being 'the height of style this summer'. It sounded, to me, like something Gran might try.

'How come you look so full of life anyway?' I said, groggily. 'Are you feeling better already?' I certainly wasn't.

Colton dipped his head and appeared almost sheepish. He gazed up at me through his lashes and grinned, looking far too impish. Lowering his voice to a whisper, he said, 'I was only pretending.'

'What?'

'I didn't want to go to school. And when I saw how poorly you are, I thought I could get away with saying that I wasn't very well.'

I cuffed him gently across the side of the head. 'Dad'll kill you, you idiot.'

'Only if he finds out.' Colton's mouth pulled tight and he gave me a warning glare. 'He doesn't have to know.'

Huffing heavily to let him know just how much I didn't condone what he'd done, I said, 'Okay, I won't grass you up. But you have to go to back to school tomorrow.'

He continued to frown and didn't respond.

'Colton!'

'Alright, alright.'

'For the whole day.'

'Maybe.'

'I mean it!'

'Alright.'

I closed my eyes and breathed in deeply. 'Now leave

me alone. I feel like the Ultimate Warrior power slammed me from the top of Gregory's Leap.'

Colton laughed. But I was being serious.

'I think I might be dying,' I told him.

Colton said something that I didn't quite catch, but it was too late to ask him to repeat himself because I was swept away into a restless sleep where black thoughts and dreams collided. I hovered just above the mouth of the cundy, as if I was the air itself, and watched a group of older teenagers congregate. They were dressed in black clothes, their t-shirts depicting screaming skulls and various scenarios of death. The three lads in the group had long, greasy hair and the one girl had a shaved head, Sinead O'Connor style. They all looked excessively aggressive. Not your typical group of introspective goths or brooding metal-heads at all, there was something decidedly dangerous about them. The blackness of their clothes seemed to extend to their auras. They were bad from the inside out. Filled with so much hatred and bad will.

One of them I recognised as Martyn Robson's brother, Tony. He didn't look like a Tony at all, more like a Sadist or Mad Bastard. He was only about seventeen, but looked more like twenty-five. He was built like a brick shithouse and had a goatee beard. A proper, bristly ginger beard which clashed terribly with his dyed black hair. Like Martyn Robson, Tony had a chronic case of acne. Silver rings decorated his ears, nose, right eyebrow and bottom lip. He sat down on the concrete footpath at the opening of the cundy and instructed the others to do the same. In his left hand was a red labelled bottle of vodka. The name of it was barely pronounceable. Something Russian-looking. In his right hand was a rat. A live rat. It squirmed beneath his fingers, thrashing its tail.

Holding the rat towards the darkness of the cundy,

Mad Bastard said something which sounded like, 'Lunhart Mohert.'

The others then joined hands with each other and echoed the words in an eerie chant. 'Lunhart Mohert. Lunhart Mohert. Lunhart Mohert.'

Mad Bastard closed his eyes and breathed in deeply, then brought the rat to his mouth and tore off its head with his teeth. Blood poured down onto his goatee beard and he spat the rat's head out into the flowing water of the beck. There were no voices in the water now. The only voices were those of Mad Bastard's mates chanting. Mad Bastard dragged his forearm across his lower face, mopping some of the blood from his chin with the sleeve of his shirt. He threw his head back and took a long swig of neat vodka. Then raised the bottle to the sky and cried, 'Lunhart Mohert!'

I woke up, sweaty and disoriented. Colton was at my bedside again, watching me with way too much interest. He told me I'd missed dinner. Gran had blasted a bowl of chicken soup on high in the microwave for two minutes. I told him I didn't care.

I still felt as though I was on the brink of death, rapidly switching between feverish and freezing. One minute I sweated with the delirium of a high temperature, the next I shook with a teeth-chattering coldness which matched that of the water in the cundy. My pyjamas and sheets felt damp and unpleasant. I imagined they retained some of the residue from my leaking illness, the moisture of which belonged with the voices. It made perfect sense that my pores should be secreting water from the cundy, because my body had absorbed so much of it the day before. I thought if I listened – if I really, really listened – I'd hear those watery voices from my dreams again. The ones from the cundy. Right here with me. Now.

Sully. Sully. Sullivan. Sully.
Lunhart Mohert.

I sent Colton downstairs to get me a glass of tap water. He must have come and gone without me knowing. When I woke up again, there was a glass of water on the bedside table but my room had dimmed along with the afternoon sun and I could hear Dad's voice downstairs. He sounded angry.

'Mrs Harper reckons you skived off school again yesterday,' he said. 'Do you want to tell me where the hell you went for all that time?'

Whatever Colton's response was, I didn't hear it.

'And what about Sully?' Dad yelled. 'I heard from his teacher that he was out of school all afternoon as well.'

Again Colton said something.

'I've just about had it with you two,' Dad said. 'I'm sick to death. Look at me when I'm talking to you. Do you understand what I'm saying?'

Colton made a noise. I imagined him nodding. His eyes wide. Angelic. But Dad was no fool.

'Don't think for a minute you're going to get out of staying with Aunt Julie over summer. You've had umpteen chances to prove yourself. In fact, as soon as school's out the pair of you can pack your bags and get out. And you know what? You can stay with Aunt Julie at weekends too, till you learn to do as you're told and how to bloody well behave yourselves.'

Another little part of my soul died. That was it then. A whole summer to be spent with Aunt Julie and my reprobate cousins. Six weeks of hell. I held my breath for as long as possible, to see what it might feel like to suffocate. To drown.

When I heard Dad's footsteps on the stairs, I rolled onto my side and curled up. Closing my eyes, I pretended to be asleep and hoped with all of my might that I'd still be ill the next day.

8

Exposed

The next morning, by the power of Sod's law, I was feeling fine. Weak from having not eaten anything the day before, but certainly well enough to go to school. The atmosphere at the breakfast table was tense. Colton kept making eyes at me and I could tell he was dying to talk to me about something. I suspected it was the Aunt Julie bomb that Dad had dropped with absolute conviction the previous evening.

Dad, himself, was sullen. He was sitting at the end of the table emanating invisible steam from a simmering rage that threatened to boil over at the least thing. He chewed on his toast way too slowly and at one point at least two minutes passed by where he didn't blink. Colton and I hardly dared to speak.

In a way I was pleased about Dad's silence. It meant he wasn't quizzing me about the dreadful afternoon at the cundy. I knew better than to think he'd just leave it alone, but I was all for delaying the inevitable. Aside from that, though, his mood made me nervous. He seemed on the brink of something. I didn't know what, but I knew it must be bad. I'd always been fairly good at gauging what his reaction to stuff would be and that morning, although not his usual self, instinctively I knew the littlest upset would send him crashing over the edge of all reason. And judging by his eyes, which were too wide and staring for my liking, I wasn't sure he'd ever return to a normal place.

In my head, I willed Colton to be quiet and for him to behave.

Dad picked up the sugar bowl and handed it to me. Gesturing to my bowl of cereal with a nod of his head, he made a grunting sound, giving me the go-ahead to cover my Rice Krispies in sugar. I'm guessing he thought I could do with the energy boost. I'm also guessing that he'd either sussed Colton for feigning illness the day before or was punishing him for playing truant on Wednesday, because the sugar bowl wasn't offered to him. Colton scowled, but didn't say anything.

Colton and I left the house at the same time with minimal goodbyes to Dad. Dad said he expected to see us home straight after school. He didn't bother warning Colton not to sneak out of school early; his countenance conveyed all the warning that any stern words would have had.

Colton walked as far as the bus stop with me, traipsing along and not saying a word. Whatever had been on his mind at the breakfast table didn't seem to be so important now. When he continued along the road towards Yohden Primary School, head bowed, shoulders hunched, I called after him, 'See you later, shit stain.'

He turned and gave me a half-hearted wave, but didn't reply. His face conveyed the sort of dejection I'd felt a lot myself lately. I wished I could call him back, so that we could run away together. Go someplace else. Anywhere. As long as it was somewhere where we didn't have to go to school or Aunt Julie's. I wished we could go to wherever Mam was, because it seemed like only she could make us happy again. My chest hurt with the empty ache of her not being anywhere I could find her. Inside, I cried and cried until the bus came.

At school, Miss Mawn, my form tutor, pulled me to one side. She was a thickset woman, probably in her late twenties, with dark, spiky hair and a penchant for turtle neck jumpers. We'd all presumed, without prejudice, that she was a lesbian. But a few weeks ago she'd announced that she was engaged to be married, to a man, and that next term her name would be Mrs Peacock.

'What happened to your face, Sullivan?' she said. Her voice was stern and her blue eyes were severe beneath the weight of her inspection of me. She had a white scar that ran down the full length of her top lip on the left side. I wondered what had happened to her. Whether she'd been severely beaten up at some point. I doubted it. Miss Mawn looked like she knew how to handle herself. I considered that maybe she'd been born with a cleft palate. She folded her arms over her chest, like she meant serious business. Her large breasts squashed together as she did. They looked soft and appealing, even though they belonged to her, beneath the thin knit of her navy jumper.

I looked to the floor. 'Fell off my bike, Miss.'

'Really?' She didn't sound in the least bit convinced.

'Uh-huh.' I nodded, keeping my focus trained on the toes of my shoes. My shoes which still felt slightly damp inside.

'Maybe I need to speak to your dad about it?' she said.

If she was to do that I suspected Dad would tell her about the bullying. Then I'd be forced to tell them both about Kevin England. Then I'd get beaten up even more for being a grass. I shrugged, hoping indifference would sate her curiosity. 'That's up to you, Miss.'

She narrowed her eyes and chewed on the inside of her mouth for an awkward and indiscernible amount of time, then dismissed me.

I made it all the way through to dinnertime before I saw Kevin England. He was standing outside the technology block with Watson and Hake. Robson was nowhere in sight. I prepared for a verbal attack, maybe even a physical one, but as I walked past, they all just fell quiet and glared at me. I didn't for one minute think that was a good sign.

After dinner break I had a double lesson of English literature followed by PE. By the time we'd dissected and evaluated large sections of Harper Lee's To Kill A Mockingbird, I was ready to let off some steam. I went to the changing rooms and changed into my running shorts, t-shirt and trainers then took off round the school grounds to try and beat my own cross country record. Straight away I knew I wouldn't; my muscles ached from all the running I'd done at the dene two days ago and I was still weak from fever. Still, the fresh air felt good and my timing wasn't too bad.

I could hear the other lads from my class shouting and cheering on the back field, as well as the occasional pip of Mr Hendrick's whistle. They were all playing football. I liked Mr Hendrick. He knew I didn't like football and once he realised how good I was at running, after the Kevin-England's-head-got-in-the-way-of-my-ball incident, he'd been happy to encourage my cross country goals. I expect that many other teachers would have made me play football regardless, even if just to find pleasure in making me miserable. Teachers are human, after all. And humans for the most part are sadists, I've found.

The sky was blue. All rained out. And apparently Mrs Carlton was doing okay after her run in with the electrics in the storage cupboard. She was due back at work the following week. At least she had a long weekend to recover and we had a weekend free from algebra. As I ran, I eyed the fence at the perimeter of the school grounds. I imagined jumping over it and continuing to run. To see how far my feet would take me before I keeled over. I reckoned I could run all the way home. To the beach even. Then the dene. And the cundy. To the darkness. To the water. To the voices.

No!

The lair of the creature, whose darkness lay beyond the alter of a headless rat, was not where I needed to be. Not ever again. No matter how beseechingly alluring those voices in the water became. I considered again how lucky me and Colton were not to have been mauled by the freakishly large dog. It could have been so much worse.

We could have been killed.

As home time drew close, I cantered back to the changing rooms. The air inside was thick with sour body odour, sweaty feet and a convergence of Lynx body spray. Most people were chattering loudly, gently ribbing each other. There was a general air of good spirits as everyone rushed to get undressed and redressed. It was Friday afternoon. An entire weekend stretched before us, enticingly close.

When I opened my locker door, my heart sank. It was empty. Someone had stolen my backpack, along with my clothes and shoes.

Shit!

Thomas Tremane, a podgy, ginger kid who kept himself to himself, pretty much like I did, and whose locker was next to mine, was hunkered on the floor, tying his shoe laces.

'Did you see who took my stuff, Thomas?' I said.

Thomas looked up and shook his head; a little too adamantly, I thought. Grabbing his holdall from the bench, he then scurried outside, appearing way too flustered. My insides wound tight. I had a bad feeling about this. I doubted I was the butt of some jovial wind-up, more likely the victim of some malicious prank. I started searching in other lockers, as well as on top of them and beneath the benches, but couldn't see any of my stuff. A few people laughed at my dilemma, but mostly I was ignored. Everyone was too eager to hurry home for the weekend. No one was willing to help find my stuff.

Soon, I was the only person left in the changing room and it was clear that my belongings weren't there. I imagined the school buses were already parked up at the gates, waiting to fill up and get going. The very thought of having to go home and let Dad know that someone had nicked my clothes and shoes wasn't a happy one. I really didn't know how he'd take the news. I decided I'd rather not go home.

But what the hell was I supposed to do?

Race over to reception and report my missing things to Miss Ward before she left for the day, that's what. She'd probably involve Mr Bainbridge, the head teacher. In fact, I knew with certainty that she would. An assembly might even be called on Monday morning, I imagined, for the entire school, because Mr Bainbridge took theft very seriously. Even so, I had serious doubts as to whether my stuff would ever be found.

As I trudged towards the door, downcast and empty handed, I jumped in alarm when it burst open. The handle slammed against the inner wall, making a dent in the plasterwork and a metallic blast which probably echoed throughout the adjoining gymnasium hall. Frozen to the spot, I then watched as England, Watson and Hake walked in.

'Lost something, Carter?' England said. He was grinning like a loon.

Fuck!

His blonde hair was darkened with grease and his squinty eyes were as sly and devious as ever. He looked like a member of some cutesy boy band gone wrong. His baggy grey t-shirt was blotched with sweat around the armpits. I wondered if this was from whatever exertion it had taken for him to steal and hide my gear. Next to him, Watson chewed gum too loudly and smirked. Looks were certainly deceiving. His face full of freckles and immaculately styled quiff made him look like a character from some wholesome Enid Blyton tale. Hake's face, in comparison, was a mask of unhinged seriousness. He'd shaved his hair since I'd last seen him on Wednesday. Two sections of it remained long-ish at the sides and had been gelled and spiked into what looked like a pair of broken bird's wings sprouting from his head. I'm guessing he thought he looked as cool and edgy as Keith Flint from The Prodigy, but in reality he looked like a total dickhead. I'm surprised Mr Bainbridge hadn't sent him home to shave the bits he'd missed.

I rolled my eyes to show them I was bored of their games, even though I was bricking it. 'Where've you put my stuff?'

'The same place I'm gonna put the rest of your stuff,' England said. 'You zombie-eyed freak.'

All three of them rushed at me and tackled me to the floor. Watson and Hake held me down while England began tearing at my clothes. His hands were rough, nipping and biting into my skin, and he was alarmingly strong. Although we were all in Year Nine together, England, Watson and Hake had almost a year on me. I was one of the youngest in our year group, with still a few weeks to go till I was fourteen, whereas England, Watson and Hake were fast approaching fifteen.

'How'd your dad like your new face?' England sneered. He ripped my t-shirt over my head with one quick tug, then started yanking at the waistband of my shorts.

I kicked and punched and wriggled furiously, but the

three of them easily overpowered me. I didn't stand a chance. When England got my shorts down past my knees, he tried to get them over my flailing feet. As he did, I managed to kick him in the mouth; a satisfying blow with the toe of my trainer. Blood erupted from his bottom lip and spattered down onto the floor. His eyes blazed wild with fury.

'Right, you fucking dweeb,' he said, swiping his tongue over his split lip. 'Let's see you get them *all* back, shall we?'

He yanked my trainers off, then slammed them against the back wall in rage. Foolishly, I thought that would be it, that he'd collect my stuff and just leave me alone, but he reached for the waistband of my boxer shorts and began to tug.

No!

Desperate to be freed, I turned my head and sank my teeth into Hake's wrist. His flesh broke under the pressure of my jaw, like a ripe tomato, and I could taste the metallic zing of his blood on my taste buds. He let out a yowl of pain, then punched me in the face. The already swollen skin around my right eye exploded with renewed agony and the scab from Wednesday afternoon's beating ruptured with fresh blood. Dazed, I lay still as a black and red bluster of unconsciousness swirled behind my eyes. All of the fight had, temporarily, been knocked out of me.

England tackled my boxer shorts and as I lay there naked on the changing room floor, he went and gathered all of my stuff together. Once his arms were full, he came and stood over me. Making a loud snorting noise at the back of his throat, he hacked up a mouthful of phlegm then spat at me. Watson and Hake laughed and let go of my arms. All three of them ran from the changing room block.

Groggy, I sat up and looked about, to assess my

situation. I'd been left with nothing but my socks.

Shit!

Black and red continued to pulse behind my eyes, but I eased up onto my feet. I had to do something. I had to find a way out of this scrape. Soon. Cupping my crotch with my left hand and blotting my bleeding eye with my right knuckle, I frantically glanced all about me. I needed to find something to cover up with else I'd have to streak across to the main building with no clothes on.

And what the hell would I do once I got there? Ask Miss Ward on reception if she would lend me her jacket to cover my naked body?

She'd probably have a heart attack.

Miss Ward was a timid woman of a nervous disposition who most likely cursed her choice to work in a secondary school on a daily basis. She seemed more cut out for organising cake and coffee mornings at the church hall or for pre-school story time at the local nursery. The idea of an adolescent boy's dick touching the inside of her jacket would probably be enough to send her over the edge of whatever meltdown she was on the brink of having. The mental image of Miss Ward's reaction to me rocking up to reception with no clothes on was so deplorable it was almost funny. Almost.

I searched the entire changing room for something, anything at all, that I might be able to cover myself with. The only thing I found was a girls' netball bib on top of the back wall lockers, which, ironically, had no business being in the boys' changing room. The blue garment was layered with goodness knew how many years' worth of dust. When I shook it a hideous cloud of foul smelling particles rose up and hit me in the face, keen to irritate my sinuses. In bold, white sans serif letters, **GS** was emblazoned across the front of the bib.

Goal Shoot.

I don't even know how I knew that, but I did.

With little choice, I undid the Velcro straps at each side and fashioned a modesty piece. It was extremely short, but hid all the essentials. The neck line was a gaping hole at my left hip, which meant most of that leg was completely exposed. I felt incredibly vulnerable as I pulled open the door to the changing room block and peered outside. I couldn't see England, Watson or Hake anywhere, but suspected they'd be watching from somewhere close by. They'd be enjoying this way too much to risk missing the most entertaining part of their efforts.

Their humiliation tactics had gone to a whole new level.

I'd only just started down the path towards the main building, creeping like a cat in my sports socks, when I heard the shrill voice of Mrs Simons, the fit, Italian-looking history teacher, call out, 'Sullivan Carter! What on earth are you doing?'

That's when I saw England, Watson and Hake rush from behind the gym and head towards the buses which were still by the gates. All three of them laughed raucously and England shouted, 'Loser!'

By the time Mrs Simons reached me I thought I might cry – with rage.

'What are you doing?' she said, looking me up and down as though I'd just pissed up her leg. Her long black hair was tied in a ponytail, but wispy bits had come lose about her face. Her makeup looked stale, like it had put in an extra hard day, but still, she looked good – for someone her age.

'Someone stole my clothes, Miss,' I said. I was clinging to the flimsy fabric of the netball bib so tightly my fingers ached. It was by no means cold outside, but the air was fresh enough to make gooseflesh prickle all over me. My nipples were shrivelled and small. I imagined my knob was too. I'd never felt so self-conscious in my entire life.

'Who would do such a thing?' Mrs Simons wanted to know. Her chocolate brown eyes were unyielding and I suspected she thought I was telling fibs.

Scrunching my eyes shut in frustration, I fought the urge to tell her, *Actually, no one, Miss. You totally busted me. I'm just a loony exhibitionist who thought it'd be a great idea to parade around the school grounds in a random piece of girls' sportswear, because, hey, that's just how I roll. Obviously, I don't get picked on nearly enough. And I just love taking beatings.* When I opened my eyes, to reply properly, I noticed with dread that someone else was coming towards us.

Ginny!

The pretty strawberry blonde from the school bus.

Right about then I wanted to die. It was bad enough that Mrs Simons had to see me like this. But Ginny as well?

Nooo!

Ginny approached cautiously. So much so, her long legs and graceful countenance made her look like an inquisitive deer.

'Excuse me, Miss,' she said. 'I saw what happened. It was Kevin England, Ian Watson and Keith Hake.'

Mrs Simons turned to face Ginny, her expression becoming less suspicious already. 'Oh. Okay. Did you see what they did with Sullivan's clothes?'

'Yeah.' Ginny looked at me and winced, then pointed her finger at the top of the gym block. 'They threw them up there, Miss. On the roof.'

Mrs Simons thanked Ginny, then escorted me to the sick bay. I had to stay there till Mr Barry the caretaker had got some ladders to retrieve my stuff from the roof of the gym. By this time, I'd long since missed the bus home. When Mrs Simons said she'd call my dad to let him know what was going on, that's when I started to cry. And I cried like I hadn't cried before. Not even when Mam had died.

'There, there, you poor thing,' Mrs Simons said, bundling me into an awkward hug. Guiding my head onto her shoulder, she patted me on the back. 'Has this bullying been going on for long? And was it Kevin England, Ian Watson and Keith Hake who did that to your face?'

Becoming lost to the grown-up smell of her perfume, the silkiness of her blouse against my cheek and the taboo softness of her breasts pressed against my chest, I couldn't find it within myself to answer. Yes, England's crusade to destroy me had been going on for way too long, but how could I explain that it wasn't just the bullying that was making me cry. It was everything. Every-single-fucking-thing.

After a ten second hug which felt more like ten minutes, Mrs Simons walked me outside to her black Vauxhall Tigra, then insisted she'd drive me home. On any other day, I might have been thrilled. As it was, I couldn't have been any more horrified. The atmosphere was tense the entire way to Horden. I was all cried out and felt utterly foolish. Like a great big snivelling cry baby. Gripping the leather upholstery beneath my legs for the duration of the journey, I wished I could teleport myself to anywhere else. Even the cundy. Because I'd rather deal with the ginormous dog and the remains of Mad Bastard's weird sacrifice than Mrs Simons as she persisted in her efforts to coax more information from me about England, Watson and Hake. I remained quiet, unspeaking, while the memory of her breasts pushed against me was much too fresh. Too tantalising. Too awkward. And that I was thinking about her breasts when she was right next to me was even more awkward.

How I hated my life.

After directing Mrs Simons to Murray Street, she

pulled up outside my house. I looked to the sitting room window, to see if Dad was there, watching. He wasn't. Before I scrambled from the car, Mrs Simons placed her hand on my shoulder and squeezed, then promised she'd deal with England, Watson and Hake – as if that should make me happy. It didn't.

Inside the house, Dad was waiting for me. I was almost an hour late and I could tell by the thunderous expression on his face that he was about to launch into an incessant rant, something along the lines of, 'Where the bloody hell have you been?' But within seconds of him seeing me, his black rage fizzled to a smouldering greyness of confusion tinged with concern.

'Sully, what happened?'

He could probably see that I'd been crying.

'Doesn't matter.' I dropped my bag by the front door and started up the stairs.

'Hey, I'm talking to you, sunshine,' he called after me. 'Where've you been?'

'School.'

'Why are you late?'

'Some stuff happened.'

'What stuff?'

'Doesn't matter.'

'How did you get home?'

'Mrs Simons' car.'

'Is everything okay?'

I didn't have the energy to lie and pretend that it was. I simply shrugged. My eyes stung with the threat of new tears.

Suddenly, Dad was floundering. I could tell. He didn't know what to do with all the pent up energy he'd imagined unleashing as soon as I walked through the door. More to the point, he didn't know what to do with me. Stroking his beard, he said, 'Your tea's in the microwave. Do you want me to heat it up?'

'No, thanks,' I said. 'I'm not hungry.'

I went straight to my room and lay face down on the bed. Less than two minutes later, Dad came in.

'Tell me what happened,' he said. His hair was bedraggled, as though he'd been running his fingers through it too much, and his eyes were rimmed with dark unhappiness. I'm guessing he'd had a bad day too. He stayed by the door, looking at me as though I was some sort of exotic wild animal that he didn't know how to handle. Would I bite? Or take flight? Or would I retreat into my shell and never come out again?

'Nothing.' I sat up and faced him. Didn't mind him seeing how utterly miserable I was.

'Sully.' Dad's tone was a stern warning that regardless of whether I was upset or not he'd lose his temper if I didn't start talking.

'It's okay,' I said. 'It's getting sorted.'

'Alright.' He nodded and eyed me for a few moments, as if testing my resolve, to make sure I wasn't lying. He looked unsure.

'Mrs Simons is sorting it on Monday,' I said, trying to get him off my case already.

Exhaling loudly, Dad moved away from the doorway and sat on the edge of the bed. He put his hands together and laced his fingers. Making a steeple with his forefingers, he touched his bottom lip with the tip of it while he thought.

'If they do anything to you again,' he said, eventually, 'anything at all, I bloody well mean it, son, you'll give me their names.' He had that mad look back in his eyes.

Dad was naturally stocky and in his younger days he'd been a weightlifter and dabbled in martial arts. He had a fiery temper, much like Colton, which is why I'd purposefully kept the bullies' names from him. If he paid a visit to Kevin England's house to speak with his dad, but got no joy in resolving the issue of his son kicking my arse every time he saw me, things would, undoubtedly, turn nasty. Then I'd be left to deal with whatever consequences such a scuffle would yield: Dad in trouble with the law for GBH, most likely, and me permanently at the top of Kevin England's hit list.

I didn't want Dad fighting my fights. And I certainly didn't want to have to give him England's name. I nodded, nevertheless.

'Listen, I was thinking about going out tomorrow,' Dad said. 'I mean, I don't have to if you don't want me to. I know I've got the day off and was supposed to be spending some time with you and Colton. It's just, I've got a few things that I need to sort out. And it'd just be for a couple of hours or so. Is that okay?'

'Uh-huh.'

'Are you sure?'

'Yeah.' I shrugged. I could do with some quiet time.

'Would you be able to watch Colton?'

Instantly, my thoughts sparked with an idea. Could this be our *final* chance to prove ourselves? Could we make Dad reconsider and break the promise he'd made to send us to Aunt Julie's over summer?

'Okay,' I said, managing a smile.

Dad tried to reciprocate, but it looked more like a grimace. Like he was partway through pulling off an Elastoplast somewhere hairy about his person. 'You're a good kid, Sully.'

'I know.'

'You can invite a friend round if you like,' Dad said. 'To watch some films and play some games.'

We both knew that I didn't have any friends, but I guess it didn't stop him from hoping that one day I might.

'Thanks,' I said. 'But I'm okay on my own.'

9

AWOL

The stray dog from the cundy ran amongst the trees of Castle Eden Dene and for a while it was me. That is, I could see through its eyes. Everything was highly defined, depicted with shocking clarity. Running on all fours, my hands and feet were paws. Fast and nimble, they carried me over ivy and other entwined foliage which covered the floor of the dene like spiky carpet. The smell of wild garlic was strong and tantalising; an aroma that evoked in me a sense of freedom and nature. All of my senses were finely tuned to the dene's wooded essence. As the dog, I felt at home. Alive. But the boy within me was anxious. Carried along by this great, carnivorous beast, whether he wanted to be or not. Like a shiver of cold air on my skin, I could feel his reluctance. His fear.

My fear.

All around me the light was dim. Night hadn't yet fallen or morning hadn't yet risen, I didn't know which, but it was some in-between time, of dusk or dawn, when the dene's wildlife comes out to graze or hunt or do whatever it does when no one's watching.

I saw a flash of white up ahead.

A rabbit's tail.

I was chasing a rabbit.

I snorted with exhilarated exertion. The sound was loud above everything else. The underside of the rabbit's tail showed bright like a beacon as the small animal zipped around trees and through the same undergrowth that my paws were trampling. It was fast, its speed a frantic energy fuelled by its need to escape me, the awareness of which stoked my excitement. I *had* to catch the rabbit. It was my primary objective. The small, agouti-furred blur enticed me with a trail of musky wonderfulness which, bizarrely, was as familiar to me as it was exotic. The promise of its meat was just as tantalising as the succulence of lamb. My mouth had filled with saliva as I anticipated tearing apart tender flesh with my teeth, nuzzling my nose in spoiled pelt and tissue, and tasting rich blood in my mouth. I needed to quench my thirst. To sate my appetite. Because I could feel the hunger pangs of an empty stomach like never before. Raw, sharp stabbing pains. I was more ravenous than I think I ever had been.

It was only now that I became aware of a new, maddening noise which was loud above the gentle susurration of leaves above me. It was the lure of water rushing through the cundy. Somewhere behind or in front, it was impossible to tell. The undercurrents spoke in loud whispered voices, none of them gender specific.

'*Sully. Sully. Sullivan. Sully.*'

The voices were almost urgent in appeal, needy in nature. But on I ran, ignoring their pleas. I was the dog now, after all, not Sullivan Carter. And so I ran and ran and ran and ran, disregarding the haunting charm of the boy's name, *my* name, being uttered on the tireless breath of whatever it was that churned and flowed within the dark tunnel. Because if I listened and obeyed, if I went to the source of those voices as they wished, I worried what might transpire.

I feared what might happen to me inside the cundy.

The cundy…

No! Don't go.

I had to stay focussed on…

The rabbit.

Don't listen to the voices.

Sully!

The rabbit.

Don't listen.

Lunhart Mohert.

The rabbit.

Sully.

Don't listen.

'Sully!'

I awoke with a start to find sunshine filling my room like an acid attack and Colton sitting on the end of my bed like some deathbed angel. He must have opened the curtains and appeared to be emitting a radiant glow. Even his hair shone golden like the corona of a Christmas card cherub.

'Sully, get up,' he said, grabbing my foot and shaking my leg.

'Uh.' I groaned. 'What are you doing?' Rolling over, I buried my face in my pillow. The bruising and swelling on my cheekbones hurt, but the sunlight was worse than the pain, so I stayed there. The voices were still too strong in my head and the dog's hunger was very real in my belly.

'Can we go out?'

'No. I'm not up yet.'

'So get up.'

'It's bloody Saturday, man.'

'Exactly, we don't have to go to school. Get up, lazy bones.'

I looked up at him in exasperation. 'Did you shit the

bed or something?'

'Stop wasting time, Sully.' Colton shook my leg again. 'Get. Up.'

'Why?' I tried to remember if I'd been such an enthusiastic (irritating) little shit on weekend mornings at his age. I didn't think so. But maybe I had. It was forever ago, back in the days when Mam used to tell me stories about solar eclipses and a boy called Sully who lived on the moon. 'Where do you want to go?'

'For a walk.'

'Where to?'

Colton reached over and picked my Sony Walkman off the bedside table. Clicking it open, he pulled out the tape inside and feigned interest in the blue biro handwritten label which read: Metallica – Ride The Lightning. I could see some sort of nervous energy playing in his eyes. Perhaps even slyness. He was being evasive. Like he had a plan but wasn't forthcoming with the details. Like he was still plotting but hadn't yet decided how to get me on board. Which made me think that whatever it was would be likely to land us both in trouble.

'Can I borrow this?' he said, waving the tape in my face.

Making stern eyes at him, I said, 'Why are you avoiding the question?'

'I'm not.' He slid the tape back into the Walkman, then returned it to the bedside table. 'I just wanna listen to some of your music.'

'Fine, I'll make you a copy.' I wafted a hand in the air. 'Now tell me where you want to go. Why's it so important that we go for a walk right this minute?'

'It's not.' Colton started fidgeting with his hands in his lap. His head was bowed and he avoided looking at me, cementing my suspicion that he was plotting something ill-behaved. 'We can go out on our bikes if you'd prefer.'

'That's not the point.' I huffed, to let him know he was trying my patience. 'Whether we walk or go out on our bikes, you have somewhere in mind that you'd like to go, don't you?'

He shrugged. 'Maybe.'

'Where?'

Sighing, he relented. 'The beach road. The beach. The dene. The cundy.'

'What?' I couldn't believe what he was saying. 'Why the hell do you want to go back there? I got my head kicked in and we got attacked by a bloody big dog. Remember?'

'It wasn't a dog.' Colton looked up at me. The sunlight, which made the white walls of my room emanate stark brilliance, was lighting up his face with a healthy glow, but his eyes remained darkest blue. Insusceptible to brightness. 'I'm not scared of it anymore.'

'Well, that's good.' I was pleased to hear it. I certainly wouldn't bother telling him that it still scared the shit out of me.

'I keep dreaming about it, Sully. I think it wants us to go back.'

My skin pricked with gooseflesh and my mouth became dry.

What?

I wondered if he too had dreamt about being the dog. I wondered if he'd chased the rabbit. I wondered if the voices in the cundy had called his name. But I couldn't ask. Couldn't encourage this silly notion, whatever it was, that stirred in my gut. I just couldn't.

'That's stupid,' I said, sounding more churlish than I'd intended. 'Why would it want us to go back?'

'I dunno,' he said. 'But I think it does. And besides, I need to go back anyway.'

'Why?'

'I lost something.'

'What?'

'I can't tell you.'

'Why not?'

'It's a secret. I just can't.' Colton looked agitated. Not quite on the verge of an episode, but his eyes harboured some kind of wilfulness which promised to be unpliant to any amount of reasoning or goading. I got the impression we were scraping the surface of whatever it was that had been playing on his mind for the past few days. He still wasn't ready to talk about it fully, but he was reaching out to me nonetheless. Asking for help.

'How can I help you look for something if I don't know what it is you're looking for?' I said, trying to coax just a little more from him. Not feeling at all hopeful.

'You would if you saw it.'

'No.' I sat up and swung my feet out of bed. If he wasn't willing to be straight with me, then I wasn't going to cooperate. Not this time. The idea of retracing our steps along the beach road, through the dene and to the cundy made my guts churn. The chance of bumping into England and his gang was probably slim to none, but a possibility nevertheless. One I wasn't yet ready to deal with. I thought about the day before, of standing in the schoolyard in front of Mrs Simons and Ginny wearing nothing but a pair of sports socks and a girl's netball bib. The memory made my face burn with shame. The methods England was willing to deploy in order to humiliate me had got out of hand. He'd moved the bar and I had no idea what he'd be capable of next. I dreaded to think.

'But Sully...' Colton sprang to his feet, ready to follow me.

'No,' I said, more firmly. 'It's not happening. Not if you can't tell me what it is you lost.'

'But, I can't. And I can't go on my own. Dad really would kill me.'

'Too bloody right he would. And if he didn't, I would.' I stormed from my room, more annoyed about my own inability to stand up to England than Colton's persistent badgering. I didn't want to become a prisoner, trapped indoors because I didn't dare leave the house in case I got attacked.

'I *need* to go,' Colton whined. 'Sully, pleeease.'

'Unless you tell me what's so important,' I said, glancing over my shoulder. 'Tough shit.'

Colton wouldn't speak to me after that. He followed me downstairs but refused to so much as look at me. As we poured Rice Krispies into bowls at the table, I could feel that his 'huff barrier' was firmly in place. Great, I thought. Colton's huffs could last for days.

If Dad noticed there was an atmosphere between us, he didn't say. He was standing at the counter with his back to us, making himself a cup of coffee.

'I shouldn't be gone too long,' he said, chinking a teaspoon against the side of the mug as he stirred in milk. 'But whatever happens, I'll definitely be back no later than teatime.' He turned round and leant against the counter. His hands were wrapped around the steaming mug, as though he had no pain receptors. Or as though his skin was made from asbestos. 'So, what are you gonna be getting up to today?' he said to me.

Funnily, I wanted to ask him the exact same thing. Not only was he dressed in a pair of smart trousers and a crisply ironed shirt, which was hardly casual attire for a day off work, he'd also had a shave. His face was smooth and bare. More youthful. Fresher. He looked almost like 'old Dad' again. It didn't escape my attention that he was wearing aftershave too. He smelt like Friday nights of years gone by, when he'd done the Horden pub circuit with Mam while Ella Bear (yes, that really was her name), a teenager from Glanton Terrace, used to come and babysit me and Colton. I wondered if Dad was meeting another woman. Like, if he was going on a date.

This thought made me entirely too anxious. Maybe even a little bit angry. Because didn't that mean he'd be cheating on Mam? It hadn't even been a year yet. Some of her clothes were still hanging in the wardrobe. They still smelt of her.

'I dunno,' I said, trying to keep the sulk out of my voice. 'Might just play on the Amiga for a bit.'

'And what about you?' Dad looked at Colton.

Colton shrugged. Without looking up, he chased Rice Krispies round his bowl with his spoon. 'Dunno.'

Dad's face fell into a reproachful frown. 'You must have some idea.'

As if sensing the danger of sparking an argument if he didn't give a valid answer, Colton looked up from his cereal and said, 'I might see if Danny wants to go down the bee-em-ex-ee or something.'

The 'bee-em-ex-ee' was a BMX track behind where Nimmo's on Third Street used to be. Locals affixed an 'ee' sound to the end of BMX for ease of identifying the recreational area. Evidently 'BMX track' was much too formal terminology for the folk of Horden.

'Er, I don't think so, matey.' Dad's frown deepened. He put his mug down on the counter and crossed his arms over his chest. 'You're bloody well grounded, remember?'

'What?' Colton's eyes blazed with outrage.

But Dad's did even more so. 'After bunking off school and playing silly buggers in the rain the other day, I already told you, you're not allowed out for a week.'

'No way! That's not fair. It's Saturday.'

'It'll be a month of sodding Saturdays if I get anymore backchat from you.' Dad's voice was a coarse, warning growl.

Colton resisted the urge to answer back. Dad tended to be rigidly unmoving about the groundings he dished out and if he threatened extra time, you most definitely got extra time.

'But what am I supposed to do all day?' Colton said, in a whiny-as-he-dare voice. He put his elbows on the table and cradled his head in his hands.

'Play on the Amiga with Sully.'

I looked at Colton, poker faced. He gave me stink eye in return.

I was increasingly curious about what he'd lost, what was making him so sulky. But racking my brain, I just couldn't think what it might be. The blueish white piece of the moon and the green piece of Uranus that he'd found? I seriously doubted it. There were plenty more chunks of sea glass scattered about the beach. It wasn't like those two were particularly special. Or maybe he'd been carrying his Spider-Man action figure in his pocket and it had fallen out. But then, why the secrecy? The more I thought about it, the more it unsettled me. It seemed like more Colton mischief to me.

Dad finished his coffee then brushed his teeth. By the time he was tying his newly polished dress shoes at the front door he seemed overly nervous, which concreted my suspicion that he was going on a date. I decided not to voice my concern to Colton, not because he was in the huff and wasn't speaking to me, but because if he was too young to have picked up on this himself, then it was probably best that he didn't have to dwell on such things. Goodness knew how he'd react anyway.

After Dad had left, Colton slinked away from the dining table and stomped up the stairs.

'What are you up to?' I called after him.

'I'm going to my room, is that *okaaay?*' he shouted. Seconds later his door slammed shut.

In hindsight, I should have known that he'd still be

plotting and planning. That he was too stubborn and obsessive to leave the 'lost thing' alone. But I went to my own room, settled on the floor in front of the television and switched on my Amiga. I played Lemmings till I ached from craning my neck to look at the screen. There was something so addictive, almost therapeutic, about guiding those green-haired pink lemmings towards their end goal without having too many of them fall off a ledge and splat on the ground. So much so, I reckon a good hour and a half must have passed by till I decided to check on Colton. Because now I thought about it, he was being way too quiet. And no bloody wonder. He wasn't in his room!

Standing on the landing, outside his room, I called out, 'Oi, shit stain. Where are you?'

There was no answer. Just the quiet hum of a dormant house.

Dashing to the top of the stairs, I gripped the bannister and called down the stairwell, 'Colton? Are you down there?'

Still no answer.

Shit!

I raced down to the hallway, my socked feet seeming merely to skim each stair, then checked every downstairs room in turn. He wasn't in any of them. When I got to the kitchen, I found that the back door was unlocked.

Oh man. Not good. Not good at all.

Dashing outside into the yard, I saw my bike propped against the wall. But the space next to it, where Colton's bike should have been, was empty.

Shiiit!

I slumped against the wall and ran my hands through my hair. How could Colton go against Dad's warning? He knew how tightly wound he was, yet he kept doing stuff to aggravate him. Again and again. And I was like some stupid mediator, getting caught up in the crossfire.

No matter what.

No matter what.

That's right. I said I'd have his back no matter what.

Fuck, Colton. Fuck!

I went back inside and shoved my trainers on. I had no choice but to go out looking for him. There was a slim chance he might be at the bee-em-ex-ee with his friend, Danny, but I didn't hold much hope. Common sense told me otherwise. My heart was filled with dread at the prospect of where else he might be. But I couldn't think about that. Not yet.

Back outside, I steered my bike away from the wall and wheeled it out into the back lane. I looked up and down. There was no one about. Seconds later, I was bombing down Murray Street, my thoughts dominated by the many ways in which I'd like to kill Colton when I found him. I came to a screeching halt at the crossroads on Cotsford Lane. There were no cars coming in any direction, so I hurtled straight over onto Third Street. Mounting the pavement to avoid the cars which were parked on both sides of the road all the way down, I blasted along with the wind in my face. About halfway down, a middle-aged biker stepped out of Eddie's Tattoo Studio just as I was approaching. I pulled on my brakes and did a silent scream. I was on a direct collision course with the man's denim-clad bulk, which wouldn't bode well for me, the man or my bike. The man jumped backwards, however, flattening himself against the door of the tattoo studio, when he heard the shriek of my tyres. I managed to curve round him with expert dexterity, or maybe just fluke, although the tip of my right handlebar just grazed his rounded gut. All of the air left my lungs in a rush of relief.

'Watch what you're doing, you little shit!' the man bellowed after me.

I held up my hand in apology. I doubted it made a

difference.

As I passed Cotsford Junior School, I heard some people talking in one of the yards round the back of Third Street. My guts clenched. For a moment I thought one of the voices belonged to Kevin England. It didn't. But even when I decided that it most definitely didn't, I still felt extremely vulnerable. Because what if he was round the next corner? Or the one after that? I realised I couldn't go on living this way. Living in fear. Burying my head in the sand wasn't working, so I needed to reassess all of my options.

Cutting across the rubble patch of what used to be Nimmo's, a pub where Aunt Julie used to work, I headed down Southeast View towards the bee-em-ex-ee. As I neared the track, my heart sank. I could see that Colton wasn't there. No one was. Not even any Saturday morning dog walkers. If Colton wasn't at the bee-em-ex-ee, then I knew exactly where he would be.

Shit, shit, shit!

I pedalled my bike then like I'd never pedalled it before, up through the dirt track of the allotments to Acacia Avenue, then down the beach road. When I got to the tank blocks at the top of the beach, my mind hardly registered what had happened there a few days ago. The beating I'd taken. Because now all I could think about was the dog. The portentous black dog inside the cundy with its snarling mouth and sharp teeth.

I had to get to Colton as quickly as possible.

If it wasn't too late already.

10

Rabbit

As I neared the cundy, I got off my bike and steered it along the dirt path. I could see the red frame of Colton's bike gleaming in the sun. He'd left it lying on the grass verge in plain view of anyone who might happen to pass by. An act of recklessness or indifference? With Colton, who knew?

A crow called out from a tree at the other side of the dried up beck. I squinted and saw its stooped, black shape amongst healthy, green foliage. Its button-shiny eyes blinked inquisitively as it watched me and the memory of its voice haunted the surrounding dene with lasting eeriness. I got the impression that whatever it had just said, its corvid cry had been directed at me. But what did it mean?

Stay away? Go home?

If the crow was foretelling danger, I was already well aware of the possible perils of the cundy. If it simply wanted me to go away, to get off its patch, I was working on that just as fast as I could. I shrugged my shoulders. *No worries, Mr Crow. Believe me, I don't want to be here.*

When I got closer to the cundy's entrance, I dropped

my own bike on the floor and stood gaping into the tunnel's darkness.

'Colton?'

I felt apprehensive, but also vexed. Vexed that Colton had forced me to revisit the scene of my recent trauma. The swellings on my face had gone down a little since Wednesday, but hurt with nauseating persistence. So much so, Dad had allowed me to take an ibuprofen before bed each night. My skin was displaying all different shades from the bruise spectrum, from yellow to purple. And even if I hadn't had any physical afflictions, my dreams wouldn't let me forget this place.

I was not ready to be here yet.

My bladder twinged even though the cundy had dried up and there was no sound of water rushing through it to encourage an unreasonable urgency to pee. There were no voices either. Not that there had been last time, of course. The voices were nothing but an extension of that nightmarish afternoon, added to the mix by my own subconscious, inspired by Colton's dreams. In fact, now that I thought about it, Colton had put the voices in my head to begin with.

Squeezing my fists tight, I took a deep breath and stepped closer to the brooding darkness.

'Colton?'

I heard his unhurried footsteps before I saw him emerge from the black mouth of the tunnel; a stoop-shouldered, red-shirted waif. I could see he'd been crying. At first I wasn't sure whether to placate him with a shoulder squeeze or chastise him. But at the sight of him standing there, framed by the cundy's terribleness, my anger, which I'd imagined would spew forth like a hot, unstoppable thing, began to dissipate. Colton's expression of sheer wretchedness yanked something deep inside me. He looked so small. So forlorn. And I could tell that something was terribly wrong.

'What're you doing here? Looking for the thing you lost?'

'I can't find it,' he said. His hair was wheaten blonde in the sun and he looked like a miniature, smooth-skinned version of Dad. Especially because of the sullenness of his navy blue eyes. His eyes, like Dad's, always balanced on the edge of some tumultuous temper. *Meteorite storms raging.* He began to tug at the front section of his hair. 'I looked but I can't find it, Sully.'

I felt annoyance flutter like black moth wings in my head. That I might have come all the way to the cundy to find some pieces of sea glass or a plastic Spider-Man figure made my swollen, scabbed lip throb with vexed energy. 'You need to tell me what you lost.'

'I can't,' he insisted. 'You'll kill me.'

'I bloody will if you won't tell me.'

The crow cawed again. This time it sounded like dark laughter.

Turning his back to me, Colton looked into the black murk of the cundy. 'I think Mam's in there,' I thought I heard him say.

'What?' Every inch of me prickled. 'What did you say?'

'And look at that.' He pointed to a grassy area not too far from the tunnel's entranceway. There was a cluster of unblown dandelion heads and a pile of crushed, empty lager cans. I was about to object, to demand that he rewind and go right back to what he'd said before, about Mam, but then I saw it. Just beyond the dandelions and cans there was a dead rabbit, lying on its side. And, as with the rat, it had no head.

Lunhart Mohert.

A swarm of flies was busying itself around the small carcass, making the collective maddening buzz that flies tend to make around dead things, rubbish and shit. Now

I was aware of it, I was surprised I hadn't noticed it before. Once it gets in your head, that sound, it can't be ignored. Repugnantly distracting, perhaps because of its strong association with dirt and decay.

Sully. Sully. Sullivan. Sully.

The voices inside my head – obtained from nightmares and preserved in consciousness – called to me. The agouti colour of the strewn rabbit, at least what was left of it, and the whiteness of the underside of its tail taunted my rational thought. Could it be the rabbit from my dream?

Surely not.

My innards flipped.

'Who'd you think did it?' Colton said. His tone was too casual by far, like he didn't much care about what the answer would be but mild curiosity had prompted him to ask the question anyway. He may as well have asked me who I thought would win in a fight between Jake 'The Snake' Roberts and Shawn Michaels, neither of whom was a particular favourite wrestler of his. I could be wrong, but he seemed indifferent to whatever horror had befallen the rabbit. Not at all fazed, as he had been when we'd found the headless rat earlier in the week. I wondered if he'd been desensitised to the horror of such dismemberment or if he was too preoccupied by whatever it was that he'd lost. Either way, his lack of empathy disturbed me.

'I dunno,' I said. I could hazard a guess, but my judgement was clouded by bad dreams. I couldn't know for certain that Martyn Robson's big brother, Mad Bastard, and his mates had done anything to the rabbit. Neither could I condemn them for taking the rat's head. Definitely not while chanting obscure words. Words which meant absolutely nothing to me and probably nothing to anyone else. My imagination's creative licence had maxed out; of that I was certain. Mad

Bastard hadn't bitten the head off that rat, it had been sliced off cleanly, so why was I giving my dreams such credence? Why was I so sure that he had anything at all to do with the beheading of small animals?

'It's bloody sick.' I turned away. Appalled. I wanted to get away from there. My nerves were rattled and I was overcome by such an omnipotent sense of threat that for a moment I was convinced that the dene itself was a terrible, insidious place that had sprouted and grown from the dark depths of the cundy, the core of which was even blacker and more depraved than the devil's own heart. Or Mad Bastard's hair dye.

The dene was aeons older than the manmade cundy, however, so I knew that couldn't be the case. I considered that something else, something unseen, had seeped from the cundy and soaked into every porous surface, thus tainting the entire wooded area with badness. A badness so profound I could feel its chill on my skin, beneath my clothes. Filling the areas between fibre and flesh. Even aside from the watchful crow, which was still on its perch, I felt as though we were being observed. From all around by one source. Perhaps even stalked. Lured. Primed for something much bigger than I thought I would ever be able to comprehend.

'What did you say before?' I said to Colton, looking past his shoulder into the gaping blackness of the cundy.

'When?'

'Before you showed me the rabbit, you said something about Mam.'

He shrugged and edged backwards. As he did, daylight seemed to leave him a little and the darkness from inside the tunnel clutched at his small frame with greedy, malicious intent. I wanted to grab his shoulders, to pull him fully out into the open again. Because as much as I was repelled by the dark space that ran beneath the coast road, Colton seemed to be drawn to it. Dangerously so.

This scared me more than anything.

How could he not feel the evil that was leaching from the very core of the manmade structure? How could he not sense that we were in grave danger? Because what if the dog was in there? What if it came bounding towards the sound of our voices and snatched Colton away? What if Mad Bastard and his mates turned up with their vodka and knives to do some weird shit?

Dipping his hands into the pockets of his jeans, Colton bowed his head and said, 'I lost her bracelet, Sully.'

I stared at him wide-eyed, unable to speak. The words were so weighty, they took a while to settle into place. 'Mam's bracelet?'

'Uh-huh.'

'But...why did you even have it?'

'I like to carry it around with me. So she can be with me. It was in my pocket. It must have fell out.'

I scrunched my eyes shut and screamed in my head; a scream so profound, I imagined blood vessels might rupture inside my brain. I couldn't believe his admission.

This was bad. *Really* bad.

He'd lost Mam's bracelet which he'd had no business taking from Dad's room in the first place. Yet the reason he'd taken it was because he was struggling to cope.

Who could be angry about that?

Dad?

Probably.

My eyes stung blurry with the intensity of sentimental loss.

'Ah Colton,' I groaned.

One of Mam's favourite possessions was now gone. Possibly forever. I tipped my head back and looked to the sky. The dirty white expanse hid everything that Mam said I should be able to see through. All I could make out was what looked, to me, like misery, etched on the underbelly of stagnant clouds. It touched everything else with hard edges of sombre joylessness too, making everything dull. And if by chance this misery *was* the thing beyond all everything, I thought, then I didn't want to exist at all.

Colton whimpered.

The crow opened its jet black wings and glided down to the grassy area in front of the tree, then it just stood there openly watching us. *Now, now children, let's not bicker,* I imagined it saying. Like the spirit animal parody of an intervening adult.

I looked at Colton. His eyes were glazed and his bottom lip trembled. I knew his sadness only too well. I felt it myself. Inside my own chest. Raw. Like a wound that had never healed. I would have hugged him, but that was a step too far, one that would have triggered other anxieties in him. So I put my hands on his shoulders and squeezed.

'It'll be okay, shit stain,' I told him, trying to make myself believe the words. But I couldn't, not for one second. 'We'll figure something out. It'll be okay. Okay? It's okay.'

Okay.

But I doubted things ever would be. Everything just seemed to go from bad to worse lately, as though we were cursed. The thought that the cundy might retain some part of Mam – some part of us all – made me feel sick. The bracelet that Colton had lost was a sterling silver chain with charms attached to it. The charms were novelty stuff for the most part: a sun, a moon, a star, an owl, a wolf, a tree, a butterfly and a rabbit.

A rabbit.

I looked over my shoulder to the headless, furry carcass. Bile rose up my throat.

Where was the rabbit's head?

Adorned with Mam's bracelet in the dried up gullet of the cundy?

Maybe.

It was a world in which such awful things were allowed to happen.

As well as the novelty charms, there were four silver discs affixed to the bracelet, each of them individually engraved with our names. One for Catherine, one for Hugh, one for Sullivan and one for Colton. On the backs were our birth dates and star sign symbols. Mam was really into astrology. She believed in all that stuff.

The pendant bearing my name had a small '69' on the back, symbolising Cancer. Colton's had two arches standing back to back with a horizontal line running through the middle. This symbol represented Pisces. Mam had pointed out more than once that we were water signs and that we both rolled with the same tides as the oceans and lived by the same rule of the moon's push and pull. She once told me that in time I'd find I had more abilities than Colton. Being the crab meant I could dwell on both land and sea and would, therefore, have the skill to move between the kingdom of the deep and the vast realms of the Earth. She said that was no bad thing though, because my Cancerian traits, which lent me great intuition and emotional sensitivity, would see to it that I always made sure Colton was okay. Looking back, it's as if, subconsciously, she knew she wasn't going to be with us for the long haul.

I felt a sudden spark of anger that so much had been laid at my feet. Anger which wasn't necessarily directed at Mam, but at whoever or whatever was in control of our fate. That I had to be the carer, the emotional rock. How was that in the least bit fair?

Me and Colton, we were supposed aquatic brothers in arms, but I was the older and by default, under the law of some time-old obligation, this meant more duty befell me. I understood this, I accepted it. He was only ten. Too young for this shit. Much too young. But who was I supposed to turn to when I felt weak?

My inner rage surged with such frightening force, I felt like it might channel out of me and split the atmosphere all around us with great lightning bolts, powered from within but generated by the entire cosmos without. Behind my eyes a bluster of blackness made me lightheaded. I gripped Colton's shoulders tighter and imagined the cundy behind him might crack open and a hellish vortex of black lava would spill out.

'But what if we can't find it?' Colton said.

And just like that it was lost, all of the rage within me crushed. I dropped my arms and stepped back, away from him. Unable to keep the frown from my face, I shook my head. I didn't know.

'Did you bring a torch with you?' I thought to ask.

'No.' Colton looked embarrassed that he hadn't thought of this himself.

I felt queasy. Sick with nervous dread. Checking my watch, I said, 'Shit, we really need to go home.'

'We can't.'

A blast of cool sea breeze ruffled my hair and massaged the nape of my neck. The trees all around us shivered. The crow ruffled its feathers and began to pace.

'If Dad gets back before us we're in big trouble.'

'But, can't we have a quick look for the bracelet first?' Colton said. 'Together.'

'What'd be the point? It's pitch black in there. We need a torch.'

'So what should we do?'

'Go home and come back later with a torch.'

'But I'm grounded,' Colton reminded me. 'This was the only time I could come out without Dad knowing.'

'Then I'll have to come back and look for it by myself, won't I?' The idea didn't fill me with any sense of joy whatsoever. But what else could I do?

Colton's mouth tightened into a scowl. 'It's not fair.'

'No, you're right, it's bloody not,' I snapped. Again, I was having to sort out the mess that Colton had made. 'But whose fault is it that you're grounded in the first place? Bunking off school isn't fair,' I said. 'You'll get Dad into trouble if you keep doing it, you know.'

'But I don't want to go to school.'

'And you think I do?' I glared at him, my beaten up face surely proof enough that my school days were no more fun than his.

Colton began to respond, but I shook my head and said, 'Come on. We're going home.'

The trees whispered above us, as if deciding amongst themselves whether or not they would let us go. I had an overwhelming notion that if we didn't leave then, right at that very moment, something bad would happen. There was a building of tension all around us, so thick with wrongness I could feel it on me like static. Either the black dog would skulk from the darkness and savage us or we'd come face to face with whoever had decapitated the rabbit and rat: the torturer of animals.

Lunhart Mohert.

And maybe we'd find out first hand if they were fledgling serial killers. Maybe they'd cut us with their knives and make our heads disappear.

Desperate to get going, to climb back on my bike and race towards home and not stop till I got there, I pulled on Colton's arm and said, 'Come on. We have to go.'

'But...just one more look.' His eyes were desperate. He clutched my forearm. 'Please, Sully.'

'No. *Come on.* It's too dark in there. What if the dog's still around?'

Colton shook his head. 'It's not.'

'How do you know?'

'I've already been in.'

'That doesn't mean it's not there, doofus.'

'But it's not. I can tell.'

'How the hell can you tell?'

'I dunno. I just can.'

'No.' I kept hold of his arm and continued to pull him away from the cundy's entrance. 'It's not happening. Not without a torch.'

'But I need to find it,' he whined.

'I know. But it'll have to wait till tomorrow. I'll think of a way to get Dad to let you come out with me and we'll come back tomorrow. With a torch.'

Colton was reluctant to move at first, but then he huffed and stomped over to where his bike was. 'Promise?'

'Promise.'

Pulling his bike off the ground, he looked longingly over his shoulder, towards the cundy. 'What if we can't find it though?'

'I dunno. We'll just have to try, that's all we can do.'

Straddling my bike, I looked to the other side of the dried up beck and watched as the crow took off and disappeared into the trees. It went silently.

As did we.

11

Ginny

We got back with about ten minutes to spare. Dad was in such a good mood when he came home, if we looked at all flustered he didn't notice. He changed into a pair of blue jeans and a plain white t-shirt then pottered about the place and whistled a lot. We had Chinese takeaway later that evening, which was something of a rarity, and Dad drank a few cans of John Smith's, which was even rarer. While he was so upbeat, and merrier still off the booze, I decided to broach the subject of me and Colton going out the following day. It was now or never.

'I forgot to mention,' I said, fiddling with my tumbler of cola, feeding the glass round and round with my fingers. 'I have to go down the beach tomorrow.' I knew I'd have to make my reason for wanting to go sound sensible if I was to stand any chance of convincing Dad to let me take Colton along too. Even better if I could put some sort of educational spin on it. 'I need to look for some fossils for this piece of geography homework I have.' I hated lying, but the idea that Mam's bracelet might be inside the cundy, waiting to be reclaimed, goaded me on. I crossed my fingers behind my back as I spoke.

'Okay.' Dad nodded. He looked happy enough about that.

So far so good.

'So, I was wondering…' I began picking at the edge of the cork placemat in front of me, hoping I didn't look too guilt-ridden or shifty, but feeling pretty certain that I did. 'If, er, Colton might be able to come along as well.'

Dad's jaw tightened and he gripped his almost-empty beer can, which created two large dimples at either side. I could tell he was about to say 'no.'

'It's just, it'd be helping me out,' I hurriedly explained. 'And I could teach him some of the stuff he'll be learning when he leaves junior school and goes to the Comp.'

Colton, who was sitting directly opposite, looked at me with wide eyes, like he couldn't believe that I'd actually asked. Or perhaps he was surprised that I'd lied so easily. I willed him to keep his mouth shut. He did.

After a few moments of quiet deliberation, during which I was convinced the answer would be 'no', Dad huffed and retracted Colton's punishment of being grounded the next day. He said that Colton could go with me with the proviso that we were both back by four. He then had a quick talk to Colton about the importance of not playing truant ever again. Colton nodded in agreement, his eyes full of remorse, and said that he wouldn't. If I hadn't known any better, I'd have believed him.

I suspected Dad's date, or whatever mysterious business he'd been on, must have gone extremely well. There was an element of 'old Dad' back. Not wholly, but he certainly resembled the man we loved best from the days when Mam was around. We chatted and joked all evening around the dining table. Even got Cluedo out. My Colonel Mustard kicked Dad's Professor Plum and Colton's Miss Scarlet to the kerb with his detecting skills (well, my die-rolling luck mostly). We didn't bother having a second round though. Colton got a bit stroppy about losing, so we packed up the pieces and put the board away. Neither me nor Dad, it seemed, wanted to lose the jovial connection we'd rediscovered amongst ourselves. On the whole, it was a good night. The sort of quality time spent together that we'd all been craving.

When I went to bed I had dreams, most of which weren't memorable. They were like a subconscious sorting of jumbled thoughts which provoked no sense of emotion one way or another; an amalgamation of no-coloured indifference. But when I woke up needing the loo, thanks to all the pop I'd drunk earlier, this must have given me a mental shake. After visiting the bathroom, I climbed back into bed and fell asleep, landing myself in an almost familiar dream.

I was the dog from the cundy again. Running through the dene, same as before. My breathing was laboured; rough, grating lungfuls of extended exertion which were loud in my head. Thorny undergrowth pricked the pads of my galloping paws, but I was driven on by a need too strong to allow me to care about much else: the ferocious, primal need to eat.

I could taste the hunger within me; an intense tang that clawed its way up from my empty stomach and coated my mouth with sourness. I could feel the same excitement and adrenalin coursing through me as before.

Dodging trees and leaping over nettles, I waited for the white flash of a rabbit's tail up ahead, because I knew I must be chasing something. The smell of wild garlic clung to the air, masking everything else that might have a scent. Birds chirruped, busying themselves in the treetops. Finches, wrens and blackbirds. A pheasant cawked from some indeterminable spot within the dene; the raucous sound of it resounded through the expansive gulley. I thundered past a tree whose sprawling branches extended from a thick trunk which looked like a mass of plaited wood. Its leafy boughs were jewelled with red berries. It looked way older and grander than any of the other trees round about. Like a gnarled sentinel that was bearing rubies.

Veering to the right, I headed in the direction of the cundy. This time I could feel its pull. Its blackness drew me to it like iron to a magnet. Like human nature to sin. Obedient to its call, I felt as insignificant as a surge of water hoping to rise all the way to the moon. Or the ghost of a death's head hawkmoth aiming for a charred, blackened sun. This time I knew exactly where I was. There was no uncertainty or sense of disorientation amongst the trees. I was stronger now. Faster.

Straight ahead dry branches snapped and crunched. The sound of my prey running away. I was closing in.

So close.

Above the aroma of wild garlic, I could now smell a tantalising trace of blind fear, tender meat and the beginnings of surrender. Then I saw that it wasn't a rabbit, but a boy that I chased. A dark-haired boy who was heading straight for the cundy. When he turned his head to look, to check on my advance, I saw the panic on his face and the white-blue of his pale eyes. His eyes! The moon's light was caught right there in them in broad daylight.

And that's when I realised that he was me.

Sullivan Carter.

So close.

So close.

My speed increased and my mouth salivated.

I was about to devour myself whole.

But then, I heard other voices coming from the cundy. Four figures bowled out from the darkness into the light. It was England, Robson, Watson and Hake.

'Yo, Carter,' England said. 'We're all dead in there.'

He pointed to the gaping mouth of the tunnel. 'We've been waiting for you to come and join us. You'll fit in really well, you zombie-eyed freak.'

Watson and Hake laughed, but Robson's face contorted into a mask of fury.

'Lunhart Mohert, motherfucker,' he yelled. 'You're gonna get ripped to pieces.'

I woke up in a cold-sweated state of terror, tangled in my sheets as though I'd been grappling with them all night long. The early daylight that seeped around the blinds made my white bedroom walls light grey, but the memory of the dream held me in a red fugue. I panted at the memory of the chase. The dream had felt so real, I half expected the massive black dog to come bounding out of my cupboard, sending the louvre doors crashing and splintering against the wall.

It didn't. But Colton chose that moment of all moments to come barging into my room.

'Come on,' he said, pulling the sheets away from me. 'Why aren't you up?' He was fully dressed and bursting with urgency. 'Get up! Get up! We have to go.'

I squeezed my eyes shut and rubbed my temples. I couldn't get the dog from the cundy out of my head. I lay there, unmoving. Intuitively sensing that the threat of the dog was much worse than the trauma of a bad experience which, subsequently, had morphed into a nightmare. I sensed that whatever it was was more like a real thing which had transmitted itself through the realms of dreamscape to touch my actual psyche. To let me know that it very much existed. And that, actually, Colton had been right after all, that the hulking black beast was much more than just a dog.

'Sully!' Colton said, gripping my wrist and tugging my arm. *'Get up!'*

He was relentless.

'Alright, alright.'

Downstairs, we ate a hasty breakfast and I managed to pilfer Dad's spotlight torch from the back of the cupboard without him seeing. I stuffed it into my backpack. Dad was still in a favourable mood. As me and Colton put our trainers on at the back door, he called out, 'Have fun, lads. Be back no later than four, mind!'

'Right-oh,' I called, pushing Colton outside.

Colton looked at me and grinned.

We'd done it.

I'd done it.

I'd lied and got Colton his freedom. Only, now we had to go back to the cundy. Really, there was nothing to grin about.

The dog skulked at the edges of my mind. Restless. Powerful. Hungry. Even though the sun was shining there was a sharp nip to the air. I contemplated going back inside for a hoodie, to pull over the top of my t-shirt, but decided not to. The less I saw of Dad till this whole business was over, the happier I'd be. I felt bad for having lied to him about wanting to search for fossils. My lie overstepped the boundary of trust I'd established with him, and this wasn't something I took lightly. My priorities were in a tangle. As were my loyalties. So much so, I hadn't been able to look Dad in the eye as I'd eaten my cornflakes.

At the bottom of Murray Street, Colton and I turned right onto Cotsford Lane, then headed towards the beach road. We intended to retrace our steps from the previous Wednesday afternoon. Mam's bracelet wasn't necessarily inside the cundy, after all. Colton didn't know at what point it had fallen from the pocket of his raincoat. It could be on the beach. It could be in the dene. Or maybe it had been swept away by the water inside the cundy, taken straight to the sea.

I held very little hope of us ever finding it. Even so, I kept this negativity to myself.

As we passed the red-bricked building of Yohden Primary School, Colton's mood dipped. His chatter about whether or not he thought Bret 'The Hitman' Hart would return to the ring after losing the WWF Championship to Shawn Michaels in Wrestlemania 12 diminished to a quiet funk. It was as though the building itself had some dark hold over him. I wanted to ask him why he hated school so much, but didn't dare broach the subject. Didn't want to tempt further thoughts of truancy, not after he'd promised Dad never to do it again.

I kicked a stone at his foot, in an attempt to cajole him into a game of pass. But he wasn't interested. He didn't even scowl at me or punch me on the arm.

'Maybe the Hitman'll come back for Summer Slam,' I said. 'Because, you know...' I squared my shoulders and deepened my voice. 'He's the best there is, the best there was and the best there ever will be.'

'Hmmm.' He was still having none of it.

It wasn't till we approached Kingy's coal yard and the school was safely behind us that I felt Colton's bristliness lift. But my own mood soared into a frenzied panic when I heard a jingle of bells across the road and saw the pretty strawberry blonde girl from school coming out of the corner shop.

Ginny.

My heart hammered inside my chest. On Friday afternoon she'd seen me wearing nothing but a netball bib. I realised I was still very much traumatised by this, therefore I prayed to goodness that she wouldn't look over and see me now. She was with a boy around Colton's age, maybe younger. I guessed he must be her brother. He had a thick, unruly shock of hair the same colour as hers, which clashed spectacularly with the orange t-shirt he had on.

Ginny was wearing an oversized white t-shirt over the

top of black cycling shorts. Her legs were long and skinny, not quite as white as her t-shirt, but not far off. White slouch socks were bagged around her ankles and her white trainers had seen better days. The tongues of her trainers were massive though, so they were pretty cool all the same. I felt myself blushing, still praying she wouldn't see me.

But she did.

'Hey!' Ginny's face brightened with a smile and she gave me a wave. 'Where are you off to?'

Shit!

She began to cross the road, coming straight towards us. Her little brother trailed behind her.

'Er…' Awkwardness stole my ability to respond and I just stood there entranced. Embarrassed.

Colton answered instead. 'What's it got to do with you?'

'Colton!' I was mortified. 'Stop being cheeky.'

'But it's none of her business,' he complained.

Ginny laughed and shook her head, obviously not offended or deterred by Colton's bluntness. Up close, when her eyes fixed on mine, I could feel my face burning even redder at the embarrassment of having turned red in the first place.

'We're, er, going to the…er, beach,' I said, annoyed with myself. Why couldn't I talk to a girl without turning into a gibbering wreck? 'And maybe the, er, dene.'

'Sully!' Colton hit me on the arm. 'Stop telling her everything.'

'Can we go with you?' Ginny's little brother said, tearing at the end of a Cadbury's Fudge wrapper with his teeth. 'We're staying at our gran's today and it's proper boring there. All she does is watch Murder, She Wrote and Colombo repeats on telly *all day.*'

Ginny laughed. 'They might not want us to go with

them though, Rory.' She rolled her eyes in some assumed grown-up manner of apologetic courtesy.

'Aye, you're not wrong there,' Colton said. His brow had furrowed, marking a deepening sulk, and the meteorites in his eyes raged.

'Why not?' Rory wanted to know. Half of his chocolate bar was gone already. 'Why don't you want us to go with you?'

Huffing, Colton stormed off ahead without another word. He was just as socially inept as me.

Torn, I began to follow him, but walked backwards so I wasn't outright dismissing Ginny. After all she'd done on Friday, speaking up about England, Watson and Hake and helping me to get my stuff back, I felt bad for running off. It was like some sort of gross ingratitude towards her, I thought.

Pulling my mouth to one side, I shrugged as if to say *'sorry, it would have been okay with me'*.

Evidently, this was enough to give them the go ahead to tag along. Ginny and Rory both jogged to catch us up.

Colton glanced over his shoulder and glowered. 'Stop following us,' he said.

'Chill out,' I told him. 'Maybe they can help us.'

'No. They can't!'

'Help with what?' Ginny asked. She was holding a long, blue ice pop, which she must have bought in the shop. She tore the top of the plastic wrapper off with her teeth, then spat it out to the wind. My thirteen-year-old self thought this was oddly sexy.

'Never you mind, nosy,' Colton told her.

'Well, we can be your lookouts at least,' she said.

'Lookouts for what?' I buried my hands into the pockets of my jeans, trying extra hard to look cool.

'Kevin England and his mates.'

I stiffened. Hearing England's name spoken aloud put a massive dampener on my mood. And suddenly I felt very paranoid about Ginny's motive for wanting to hang around with us.

Why would she want to?

I didn't know her and she didn't know me. She must think I was a total wimp. She'd seen me at my most vulnerable only two days ago. At my most cringeworthily uncool. Not that I was ever deemed anything close to cool by other kids, but still, at that age I was self-conscious enough around girls to berate myself for not *trying* to be cooler.

'Why do you want to come with us?' I said.

Ginny's long hair whipped about in a freak gust of wind. It looked like wildfire all about her head. She shrugged. 'Dunno. Just do.' Already her tongue was stained blue off the ice pop but her teeth gleamed white. Her breath smelt of blueberries. I knew I was way too young to fall in love, but at that moment my heart did something that was both pleasant and unpleasant. It sort of lurched.

'Sully, *come on!*' Colton was practically speed walking now.

'Hey, I know you from school,' Rory said, jogging to catch up with him.

'Well I don't know you.'

'You're in the year above me.' Rory fell into step beside him, not at all deterred by Colton's bad mood, just eager to make friends.

Ginny walked alongside me. Her nearness made me nervous. When she made eye contact at such close range, I found the experience intense. Unsettling.

'Kevin England did that to your face, didn't he?' she said.

I nodded and looked away. Why did everything have to boil down to Kevin England?

'Does it hurt?' Ginny wanted to know.

I shrugged as if to suggest not really, but told her

truthfully, 'Yeah.'

'That's really shit. He'll get what's coming to him one of these days.'

'Hmmm.' I wasn't so sure.

As if sensing my reluctance to discuss Kevin England, Ginny motioned to Colton with a tip of her head and said, 'You two don't really look like brothers.'

'Well, we are.'

'I know, it's just, you have really dark hair and he's fair. And your eyes are, like, *really* light blue.' Her cheeks coloured then and she looked away.

'Colton looks like Dad,' I thought to tell her.

'Do you look like your mam?'

I kicked a stone with the side of my foot. It bounced off the kerb and landed in the gutter. 'Yeah, I suppose.'

'Me and Rory, we look pretty similar.' She made a face as if to suggest that this was a hardship she really wasn't happy to bear, then laughed. 'We take after Dad. Our older sister, Donna, though, she has dark brown hair like Mam. She's *way* prettier than me.'

Sensing that Ginny was perhaps baiting for some sort of complimentary response, for me to disagree with what she'd just said, I felt my tongue become rigid and throat tighten. How could I tell her that she was wrong when I had no idea who her sister was. All I could think was that Skunk from Year Eleven reckoned he'd seen Ginny's sister's tits and that he thought they were better than Ginny's. This fleeting thought made me feel even more awkward and I couldn't slacken my tongue enough to say anything. All I could do was raise my eyebrows. I didn't even know what I meant to convey with this particular facial tic, but my eyebrows were the only part of me that seemed capable of communication.

Ginny looked indifferent, however, and I realised then that I'd read her wrong. She hadn't been baiting for a compliment at all. I could see that now. She was simply stating what she thought to be true. I wondered then if she realised just how pretty she was.

I doubted it.

This made me like her even more.

Wanting to raise the awkward topic of me wandering about the school grounds with no clothes on, so that I might overcome the embarrassment and move on, because to pretend that it hadn't happened at all seemed somehow worse, my tongue finally unfurled and I said, 'Anyway, I've been meaning to say thanks for Friday, Ginny.'

Instead of smiling and accepting my offer of gratitude, as I thought she'd do, her shoulders became stiff and she looked at me coldly.

I gulped hard.

Was highlighting the fact I was a wimp a bad move?

The coldness of her stare seemed to pass quickly, however, and she shook her head. 'Er, yeah. Anytime. No problem. Kevin England and his friends are total dicks.'

'Yeah.' I smiled. 'They totally are.'

Narrowing her eyes, she smiled and regarded me carefully. 'You do realise that my name's not Ginny, right?'

12

Mythology

'What?' I felt the blood drain from my face. 'But I thought…I dunno, I thought…'

'That my real name is Ginny?' She studied me closely, her baby-doll eyes not so much cute as unnerving in that moment. They had the ability to transform her from playful, shy kid to frosty Ice Queen in a heartbeat.

'Well, yeah.'

'No. It's just a nickname,' she said. 'Some bullies gave it to me in junior school. It kind of stuck, then followed me to the Comp.'

'But, why Ginny?' I thought it was a perfectly nice name.

She frowned, as though reluctant to tell me. Then pointing down, she said, 'Because of my legs.'

I didn't get it.

'They're long and skinny,' she explained. 'Like a ginny longlegs' legs.'

'What's a ginny longlegs?' Colton said.

I hadn't realised he was listening to our conversation.

'Same thing as a daddy longlegs,' I said. 'A crane fly. They're all the same thing.'

'Your legs aren't *that* skinny,' Colton thought to tell

Ginny. 'They are really long though.'

Yes, I thought, finding myself staring at them. *They are.*

'So...' I said, feeling the blood rise back to my cheeks. 'What's your real name?'

Feeding the dregs of blue juice up the clear plastic ice pop wrapper with her fingers, she sucked all of the bubble gum syrup out of it then told me, 'Katrina. Katrina Delaney.'

Katrina.

It was just as nice as Ginny, I thought. But more of a feline-bold name which flashed burnt orange and yellow in my head. Like orange and lemon boiled sweets. Citrusy fresh.

'It's okay though,' she said. 'You can still call me Ginny, if you like.'

Narrowing my eyes, I gave her a quizzical look. 'But why?'

'I dunno. I guess I don't mind when you call me it.'

I shrugged, like, *whatever.*

We passed under the red brick bridge at the top of the beach road and Colton shouted, 'Hello!' at the top of his lungs. He revelled in the subsequent echo, evidently having forgotten about the bad mood he'd been in before.

Rory whooped then cried out, 'Fart-head!'

He and Colton fell into fits of giggles, while me and Ginny shared a look of sufferance, like we were thirteen going on thirty. The forced sensibleness sparked some amusement between us though and we both began to laugh along.

For a while, as the four of us walked down the beach road together, chatting and laughing, enraptured by birdsong and the smell of early summer, I forgot about a lot of the bad stuff that was going on in my life. And for that short snap of time, I'll never forget, I actually felt content. As though I was part of a unit. Me and three other kids who had the capacity to 'play nice'.

It felt good.

Ginny stooped to pick a dandelion head from the grassy verge at the side of the road. Her arms and fingers were long and slender, just like her legs. She was as tall as me, even though she was younger. Technically, though, since I was one of the youngest in my year group, I figured I might not be all that much older than her. Could be by a couple of months, maybe even weeks. She pursed her lips and blew the dandelion's fluffy white head to the wind. The seeds scattered far and wide. One of them landed on my t-shirt. I left it there.

'Did you know there used to be a medieval Saxon village called Yohden in Horden?' Ginny said. As she spoke, I couldn't help but notice that her tongue was still blue.

'Yohden's the name of my school,' Colton said, without looking up from the road. He was no doubt watching and hoping for a glint of silver. A glimpse of Mam's bracelet.

As was I.

'Yeah. And it's no coincidence.' Ginny nodded. 'The name's pretty significant in the area. Some say the name Horden was probably derived from the original settlement of Yohden.'

'Whereabouts was it?' I asked. I'd never heard of any such settlement. Not even from Miss Resnor, the raven-haired, witchy junior school teacher who liked to tell stories of urban legends to Year Fives on gloomy afternoons.

'Near Sunderland Road,' Ginny said. 'Further along from the pony field.'

'What happened to it?'

'It got deserted. No one knows why.' She stopped walking and hunkered down to tighten her shoelaces. I watched as she did and my heart did that thing again.

Ginny Longlegs.

'The northeast of England was taken over by the Norse king, Reignwald, in the 900s.' Ginny spoke in a well-recited manner, as though she was some history buff who gave regular talks on the subject. 'He gave East Durham to Scula, one of his Viking warlords. I reckon the people of Yohden would have been pretty shit scared of him, so that's probably why they upped and left.'

'How do you know all this?' I said. Not only was Ginny pretty, it seemed that she knew loads of cool stuff too. I was well impressed.

Ginny shrugged. 'Our Donna's history teacher at college is pretty cool. He tells her all that sort of stuff during lessons, then she tells me. It's a shame Mr Wiggins at school doesn't. All I get to hear about is the bloody Industrial Revolution.' She feigned a yawn. 'I mean, *bor-riiing*. I'd rather learn about our area and its history. And Norse mythology too. I'd love it if we could do Norse mythology in RE. How cool would that be?'

'What's Norse mythology?' Colton asked, still scouring the road ahead for mislaid jewellery.

'An old, polytheistic Germanic religion,' Ginny said.

She had no way of knowing it, but the more she spoke, the sexier she became. Her talking of ancient legends in this adult manner gave me a strong desire to kiss her bubble gum lips. I was definitely developing a crush.

'What's polly-thee-stick?' Colton said, scrunching his face in bewilderment.

'Polytheistic,' Ginny corrected. 'It's a religion where there's more than one god.'

'A bit like Clash of the Titans,' I told him. 'Only Norse, not Greek.'

'Exactly,' Ginny said, looking at me and beaming, as though she'd just discovered someone else who liked pineapple on their pizza. For the record, I don't. But you get what I mean. It's just, it was the sort of quietly elated look which suggested she'd discovered a rare kindred spirit. Someone else who liked a fantasy film from the early eighties that probably not that many other kids our age had heard of let alone seen.

'So the gods in Norse mythology are different to the ones in Clash of the Titans?' Colton said, lifting his gaze momentarily, his interest piqued.

'Yeah, but they're just as well known. You've probably heard of Thor before?' Ginny said. 'I'd say he's probably the most famous of the Norse gods.'

'He's the god of thunder,' I said.

'And his dad, Odin, is the big daddy of them all,' Ginny said. 'He has two pet ravens as well as two wolves and he sacrificed one of his eyes for wisdom.'

'He sounds bonkers,' Colton said.

Ginny laughed. 'His wife, Freya, or Frig, as she's sometimes known, is the highest ranking goddess. She totally stands on her own merit.'

'Frig?' Colton sniggered, then so did Rory.

'She's, like, totally kick arse,' Ginny said, ignoring them both. 'She was the one who brought magic to the gods and humans. She even has some bird of prey feathers which allow her to shapeshift. How cool's *that?*'

'Pretty.' I nodded in agreement.

'Oh shut up, Kat,' Rory said. 'You're being all feminist again.'

'And you just copy whatever Dad says.' Ginny flashed her little brother a scathing look.

'No I don't.'

'Yes you do. And you're talking out of your bumhole anyway. You don't even know what a feminist is, do you?'

Everyone looked at Rory. He blushed furiously.

'So stop trying to poke fun at me over something you know nothing about,' Ginny said, still scowling.

'You don't believe in God,' Rory said, churlishly, as if this was a valid answer that would get him off the proverbial hook he'd got himself onto.

Ginny groaned and rolled her eyes. 'What's that got to do with the price of cheese?'

'Dad says you don't believe in God because He's a he.'

'That's not true. I don't believe in God because I don't believe in monotheistic religion. How can there be a He without a She? Nature doesn't work like that. At the very least, if there *had* to be only one God, then It would have to be a hermaphrodite.'

'What's one of them?' Colton asked.

'When there's no defining gender. As in, male and female parts. A bit like an earthworm.'

'*What?* Do you mean, like, earthworms don't have dicks?' Colton sounded unduly mortified about this. So much so, I laughed out loud.

'No. I mean, I think they do. They have male *and* female parts.' Ginny shrugged, uncaring. 'But it's not like I was suggesting that God's an earthworm with no dick anyway. It was just an example.' The wind buffeted us head on and Ginny's oversized t-shirt moulded to the shape of her body. For a fleeting moment I could see the swell of her small breasts. 'You get hermaphrodite people as well.'

'You sound just like our Donna,' Rory complained.

'She's the only person in our house who talks sense.' Ginny huffed. I felt the earlier pleasantness of the conversation rapidly waning. 'Monotheism is man-made religion made by men for men to control the masses. To instil fear in people. Give me Freya, Thor and Odin any day. At least they didn't try to make people feel guilty just for being alive.'

'You're *so* going to Hell,' Rory told her, wagging his finger right in her face.

'That's not very Christian of you to say,' Ginny said. 'And anyway, why should you care? Whatever happens to me when I'm dead is not your problem, so don't concern yourself.' She looked at me then. 'What about you, Sully? What do you believe in?'

I shrugged, like *leave me out of this*.

As it was I didn't have any set beliefs. I was open-minded; wary enough not to fall into religion and all of its rules and hyperbole, but cautious enough not to dismiss it outright. It was too complicated a subject and required much faith; a certain faith that not everyone has within them.

Dad used to proclaim to be a believer, but I got the impression that he believed out of fear. That he worried if he said he didn't believe in God then something bad would happen and he'd end up being struck down. Maybe not by a lightning bolt from the sky or anything as dramatic as that, but certainly punished in terms of God's preordained fate. Or that he'd be put on some naughty list that would get him a ticket straight to Hell once he died. He was never a church goer and he did nothing else that would categorise him as being religious, he just maintained the right to call himself a believer without the practising part. After Mam died, however, I don't think Dad believed in much. Or if he did, I suppose he didn't give a monkey's arsehole about upsetting God anymore. He'd already taken the figurative lightning bolt right on the chin, so what did he have to lose? And I dare say he was so angry about Mam's untimely passing, he'd have challenged God to a physical fight if he was able to.

Mam, on the other hand, was more, I dunno...spiritual? She believed there was something out there in the cosmos, something far greater than us, she just didn't know what. I decided Ginny would probably have liked her.

'I believe in Heaven,' Colton said. He was scraping his feet along the tarmac and tipped his head back to gaze at the sky. 'Heaven's a nice place, right up there with the stars.'

Ginny looked up and said, 'I think so too.'

I wondered if she already knew that Mam was no longer with us, because whatever her thoughts were on Heaven, she was willing to let Colton have that. For which I was grateful. My chest swelled with something like happiness; it felt just as pleasant, but was too ephemeral. The pleasant feeling was quickly swallowed by a gaping pit of fear in my stomach when I saw the cundy in my mind's eye. The utter blackness of it consumed my thoughts. I heard the imagined, whispered voices churning in the gushing current of remembered water.

Sully. Sully. Sullivan. Sully.

'Do you think the dene's haunted?' I asked Ginny, before I could stop myself.

She averted her gaze from the sky to look at me. 'You mean by regular ghosts? Or by Norse land spirits?'

'Well, I dunno. Just...whatever.' Her question had taken me aback. It wasn't at all what I'd expected. 'I guess I just meant by all the people who've killed themselves there. But, I dunno. What's a land spirit?'

'Oh. Right. Well maybe it is haunted by all those people, yeah.' She considered what I'd said and nodded. 'Land spirits tend to dwell in certain areas. Natural places. I mean, the dene is a good example. They impact on the wellbeing of the land itself and can curse a place as well as anyone who travels through it.'

'Uh, there you go again,' Rory complained.

'Shut it, dicksplat.' Ginny stooped and picked up a stick then bounced it off her brother's head.

'What do land spirits look like?' I wanted to know.

'I'm not sure.' Ginny held her arms out and deflected Rory as he tried to barge into her in retaliation. 'I suppose they could take the form of anything really. A deer. A rabbit. A fox. Probably even a tree.'

'What about a black wolf?' Colton asked.

A rash of goosebumps made my flesh zing. I knew exactly what he was thinking.

The dog in the cundy.

'I'd imagine so, yeah.' Ginny nodded. 'The spirit is just the essence of a place, so I suppose it could take the physical shape of anything it wanted to. You know how sometimes a place might give off certain vibes, whether that's good or bad? Well, I think those are the places that are inhabited by land spirits.'

'Like the cundy?' I blurted out.

'Yes.' Ginny grinned. '*Exactly* like the cundy. That place is definitely haunted.'

'What makes you say that?' My response was so quick, I sounded almost defensive.

'Well, why would you doubt it?' She gave me a look to suggest I was being weird. 'I mean, you've been inside, right?'

'Course I have.'

'So then, you must know.' Her large, mesmeric eyes were unreadable and I wondered if she was indeed a normal girl and not some land spirit herself. Or a Norse deity reformed. She seemed too knowledgeable. Her choice of words almost too mature. Intuitive. She'd rocked up, pushing her way into my life, the very same day as the dog (wolf?) from the cundy. Was it all part of some greater plan?

'Why don't we go there now?' she suggested.

Rory gasped. 'We aren't allowed to go to the cundy,' he said. 'You know that.'

'So? Who'd find out?'

'Dad.'

'No he won't. Not unless you tell him.'

'Dad finds out everything.'

Ginny rolled her eyes, then looked at me. 'I'll show you Yggdrasil on the way.'

'What's that?'

Rory groaned.

'I'm only kidding,' she said. 'Or maybe I'm not. I dunno. There's this tree, see, in Castle Eden Dene, which is quite close to the cundy. It's a yew tree and it's the only one of its kind in the entire dene.'

'So why's it called Yggdrasil?' I asked.

'That's the great tree of life and death in Norse mythology. It grows up from the Urd well and its roots and branches hold the nine worldly planes. Legend has it that Yggdrasil was an ash tree, but many believe it was actually a yew tree. I'm open to the suggestion that it was the latter, if only for the fact I can say that Yggdrasil is rooted in Horden.' She grinned and did a pirouette. Her red hair fanned out behind her and she looked particularly pretty in that moment. Still, my skin flashed cold because I couldn't help but think about the tree in my dream. The one with the entwined bark which looked like thick braided strands. The one with berries like red gemstones.

'What does a yew tree look like?' I said.

Ginny seemed to contemplate this, then eyed me mischievously. 'I dunno, sort of tree-ish.'

I groaned.

'Ha! Don't worry,' she said, nudging my arm with her elbow. 'I'll show you.'

But I couldn't wait. 'Does it have red berries?'

'Yeah, that's the one. You've seen it before then?'

Yes. But how could I tell her that I'd seen it in a dream?

Lost for words, I shook my head. I had a feeling that if

I was able to show my dream to her, she'd decipher it. That she'd know the dog – or wolf – and the rabbit it had chased, perhaps even by name, from Norse legend. Mam had often talked about fate and I wondered now if that's what had brought me and Ginny together like this.

I still do wonder.

We arrived at the end of the beach road, where the tarmac dips down to the shaded car parking area. Immediately I knew something was wrong. I'd say we all did, in fact. We couldn't see beyond the leafiness of the trees to the car park below, but all four of us fell silent and shared a few moments of uncertain apprehension.

It was as though the sea air was carrying a trace of badness with it. A wrongness so subtle, but distinct nonetheless, which seemed to warn us to turn round. To go back. But we didn't. We continued on till we reached the car park. And that's where we found a police car, parked like an abandoned vehicle.

'What do you think it's here for?' Rory said.

We all stopped to stare at it.

'Dunno but look.' Ginny pointed towards the beach.

Striding up past the tank blocks, two policemen in short-sleeved black uniforms were making their way towards us. One of them was stocky, about the same age as Dad. He had a bit of a strange gait, as though his shoes were too tight, and he'd lost most of his hair to middle-age. The other policeman was quite a bit older. By comparison, his thick mop of hair had faded to a nondescript shade of grey which, bizarrely, was almost the same colour as his face. As they reached us, they brought with them an air of bad news.

'Where're you off to, kids?' The stocky one held out his arms to block our advance, even though none of us was moving. His voice was every bit as authoritative as I'd expected it would be, but something about his countenance was off. He seemed rattled.

Something terribly bad had happened.

'Down the dene,' Colton told him.

'Nah.' The stocky policeman shook his head. 'No you're not. Not today, son.'

'Why not?'

'Because I said so.' Using his bulky presence, he ushered us away from the car, then tried to herd us back the way we'd come.

'But, what's going on?' Ginny said, daring to challenge the policeman for a better answer. 'Has something happened?'

'Look, I suggest you find somewhere else to play today, flower,' the older policeman said, stepping in. He put his paw-ish hand on Ginny's arm and spun her round.

'But *why?*'

'I'm afraid there's been a nasty accident.'

13

Bruised Knuckles

On Monday morning the school bus was filled with a sizzling buzz of excitement. The same sort of nervous energy that had spellbound everyone after Mrs Carlton had been electrified in the storage cupboard. As soon as I stepped on board I could tell that something had happened. Something big. Probably bad. I wondered if it had anything to do with the alleged nasty accident at the beach or dene yesterday, which the policemen hadn't given us any further details about. Gut instinct told me the answer was yes.

Ginny was sitting by the window, four rows back. When she saw me, she raised a hand and waved. My stomach flipped. She dragged her backpack onto her lap when I reached Row D and urged me to sit down next to her. The fact she'd saved a seat for me made me think we must be friends at least. I sat down, more than a little bit happy with this knowledge.

Ginny's hair was loose and especially voluminous that morning, I noticed. Her eyes were eager, sparkling with whatever sensational news she had to tell me – the same news, I expected, that everyone else on the bus was already buzzing about.

'Have you heard what happened?' She leaned in close. Her voice was an urgent whisper, right in my ear, as though she was telling me a secret which no one else knew. Her breath had a faint minty edge to it, of lingering toothpaste perhaps, and I could smell her hair too. Soapy and fresh, like almond and air. She clutched my arm, her slender fingers, warm and soft, surprisingly tight around my wrist.

'Er, no,' I said, going into some sort of sensory overload. Could anything be more important right now than Ginny sitting next to me, gripping my arm and radiating nice smells? I could hardly think. My hormones fizzed.

'Martyn Robson jumped off the viaduct. Yesterday. That's why we couldn't go onto the beach or through the dene. That's why the police were there.'

I jolted away from her, my hormones crashing as quickly as they'd soared. 'Seriously?'

'Uh-huh.' Ginny's eyes were wide, simmering with the taboo excitement of having shared news of someone else's tragedy. News which has not yet sunk in properly and, therefore, feels too much like fiction; meaning there's a possibility that the words can be taken back at any time, made not true.

'But...' I found it hard to absorb the information. Even harder to process just how I felt about it. 'Why?'

'I dunno. I only just heard about it myself.'

'Is it definitely true?'

'Yeah. Someone back there,' Ginny thumbed over her shoulder, to the back of the bus, 'says he lives in the same street as the Robsons. He said he saw police coming and going from their house all day.'

Still, that didn't make it true.

I thought about the last time I'd seen Martyn Robson. Near the cundy. Not too far from Gregory's Leap. I'd punched him in the face. Twice. Might even have broken his nose. I looked at the knuckles of my right hand; they were still bruised. An ugly brownish purple edged with yellow. I found it more than slightly disturbing that my knuckles bore the marks of having smashed into the face of someone whom, if hearsay was correct, was no longer alive.

A cold chill ran through me.

Could it be true? Was Martyn Robson *really* dead?

If so, who or what had made him go to the top of Gregory's Leap and look down, all that way, and decide to jump?

The voices from the cundy rushed through black rivers in my head, haunting me with their whispered babble. I felt chilled from the inside out, as though the marrow in my bones was packed with ice crystals.

'Who found him?' I wanted to know.

Ginny sat back in her seat. As she did, her fingers left my arm. Immediately, I wished I hadn't asked.

'Dunno,' she said. 'But I'm sure we'll find out more as the day goes on.'

Hmmm. I wasn't sure I wanted to.

While everyone around us gloated or commiserated about Martyn Robson's death, or simply talked about the weekend, I was troubled by much deeper thoughts. It was as though my intuition was barbed with supernatural hooks which tore through the gossamer layer of whatever awareness was presented to me. The whole situation was too grisly, touching several nerves and making me feel as though, that day down the dene, something had been set in motion. Something dark and dangerous. Something beyond my control. The dog, it still chased me. And the voices in the water continued to haunt me.

The knuckles on my right hand throbbed. I squeezed my fist tight.

The dream I'd had on Saturday night sprang to mind,

sudden and unwelcome. England barrelling out from the cundy. His words: *Yo, Carter. We're all dead in there.* Then Robson's acned face contorted in anger. *Lunhart Mohert, motherfucker*, he'd shouted. *You're gonna get ripped to pieces.*

Did any of it mean anything? Was my dream a premonition?

Had the wolf got Robson?

Was it coming for us all?

No, that was silly.

Wasn't it?

I thought about the rabbit from my earlier dream. Could it be that there was a connection? Were my dreams perceptive of some weird hocus pocus? Mad Bastard's hocus pocus. And what about the creature from the cundy? Could it be that it was some aggravated land spirit? Ginny had said they could curse the land in which they dwelt as well as anyone passing through it. Therefore, I had to wonder, had we all been cursed on the day of the storm? Me, Colton, England, Robson, Watson and Hake.

My consciousness fought hard to piece together the puzzle, of which I believed my subconscious was withholding bits. That I'd dreamt of a rabbit the night before having discovered the headless body of a rabbit near the cundy was odd. But the fact that I'd gone on to dream about Martyn Robson the night before he'd died was…what?

Mere coincidence.

In fact, it wasn't even unusual enough to be classed as a coincidence. I was being paranoid, that was all. Massively paranoid. None of it meant anything beyond the boundaries of me being stressed to fuck. Not even the dream about Mad Bastard.

'Do you know what Lunhart Mohert means?' I asked Ginny, almost sure that she would.

But her eyebrows scrunched downwards and she looked only vague. 'Er, no. Should I?'

I shook my head. 'No. Doesn't matter.'

My knuckles continued to throb. I squeezed my fist again.

When we passed the graveyard on Thorpe Road, I watched as rows upon rows of gravestones rushed by in a blur of grey. They inspired new thoughts about Martyn Robson and the fact he might be 'gone'. I can't say I felt all that sorry about it. In fact, if I'm completely honest, I felt some small relief that he might be one less person for me to worry about. Granted, it would have been better if he'd just moved away or stopped being a dick. But it was what it was. There was certainly no love loss between me and him. For weeks he'd aided and abetted England in the pursuit of torturing me. Whatever demons had chased him to the top of Gregory's Leap, that was his business. I was just a kid and I had my own demons to deal with. Robson had earned no sympathy from me.

Maybe he'd have grown into a decent human being eventually. Who knows? I guess we never will. All I did know for certain was that up until that point, as far as I was concerned, he'd always been a deplorable arsehole. So for that reason I wouldn't be rushing to the front of the queue to mourn his death.

I didn't even want to think about him.

Covering the bruises on my knuckles with my left hand, because they cemented some sort of guilt in me which I couldn't quite figure out, I said to Ginny, 'Your hair looks nice today.'

I don't know where this fleeting boldness came from and if Ginny was shocked, I was even more so.

'Oh, er, thanks.' She touched it self-consciously.

'I mean, I'm not saying it doesn't usually look nice or anything,' I said, recognising the potential hole I was digging myself into. 'It's just that today it's, er…big.'

Thankfully she laughed at my weird observation and the fervour that had been in her eyes since I'd got on the bus didn't go away. I wasn't an expert at reading girls, far from it, but I would have sworn she liked me. I hoped she did, anyway.

'So, what did you get up to yesterday afternoon?' I asked, by way of diversion. What I really wanted to ask was if she'd like to come round mine one day to play Lemmings or Lotus Turbo Challenge 2 on my Amiga. Or go down the bee-em-ex-ee. I imagined she'd be the kind of girl who could pull wheelies and do bunny hops. I also wanted to ask if she'd like to go and find the medieval village of Yohden sometime, to see if the field where it used to sit was as mystical and haunted as it sounded to my mind. Most of all, however, I wanted to ask if she'd mind if I kissed her at some point, because I really, really wanted to. But I kept all of those questions and ideas to myself and listened as she told me about her dog, Buster, who had broken out of their yard and ransacked the neighbour's dustbin last night. All the while my heart did that thing – that weird, contradictory, pleasant but unpleasant thing – about half a dozen times.

By the time we pulled up outside school, my tongue was still incapable of relaying any of the ideas my brain had thought up. I didn't have the nerve to ask Ginny for anything more than what she was willing to instigate herself. We got off the bus and said goodbye to each other at the corner of the tennis yard, then I trudged my way to registration.

Miss Mawn, my form tutor, arrived five minutes after everyone else. It wasn't like her not to be punctual. She looked flustered as she bustled in with the register clutched to her chest. We already knew what tidings she brought. Fussing with her short hair for a moment, she coughed into her hand then confirmed that Martyn

Robson had indeed passed away.

Which made it official. Non-retractable.

It was really, really true.

Miss Mawn didn't give any other details, but just in case anyone didn't already know, Seth Granger, the class clown, decided to announce that Martyn Robson had jumped off the viaduct. Miss Mawn lost her shit a bit then and started booting off. Shouting and gesticulating with her arms, she ordered Granger out of the class and demanded that we all show 'a bit of damn respect'.

I kind of zoned out at that point. All the daylight in the room snapped off, as though a light switch had been thrown. Blackness fully absorbed me and I found myself inside the cundy.

Sully, Sully, Sullivan, Sully.

The wolf-dog snarled. It was waiting for me in the dark. I anticipated the feel of its fur on my skin. The force of its powerful body ramming into mine. Then I saw its eyes. On fire. Burning into my soul.

I must have passed out because the next thing I knew I was lying on the floor and light was filtering back to my eyes and Miss Mawn was slapping my face with moderate force. The knuckles on my right hand ached.

'It's a shock to the system, Sullivan, I know,' Miss Mawn said. She was so close, I cowered away. Her morning breath was like a blast of cottage cheese in my face. 'Would you like to go outside for some fresh air? Or to go and sit in the sick bay for half an hour?'

I shook my head and climbed to my feet, my legs unsteady. 'I'm okay, Miss.' *So long as you stop breathing on me.*

Sitting down in my seat, I felt self-conscious. Someone giggled. I looked around. There was a lot of concern shown on the faces of the girls in the class, but some of the lads had wry smirks. They probably thought I'd fainted at the idea of Robson jumping to his death.

'Would you like some water?' Miss Mawn said. She was too close again and the scratchy material of her skirt rubbed against my bare arm. Like coarse fur. I pulled away, clutching my elbows to my sides. The wolf-dog's flaming eyes had seared my brain, causing a headache.

'No, Miss.'

'Go and get Sullivan a glass of water, Kelly,' Miss Mawn said to Kelly McGee, a bottle-blonde with dark roots, who was sitting closest to the door. 'Hurry.'

'No,' I snapped, hating the fuss.

Miss Mawn regarded me suspiciously. The scar on her lip puckered and I knew I was in danger of losing her concern to irritation.

'Really, I'm alright, Miss,' I said. 'I'm tired, that's all.'

Pulling her knitted grey waistcoat over the rounded swell of her breasts, Miss Mawn exhaled heavily through her nose. 'Then in future,' she said, 'I suggest you make sure you get to bed at a more reasonable time.'

'Yes, Miss. I will.' *Now leave me the hell alone.*

I struggled through morning lessons, lost to thoughts of the cundy, the wolf-dog, Robson and his final moments, as well as Ginny. All of it was a blur of confusion. At noon I went to the dinner hall. I wasn't really hungry, but it was drizzling outside and I had nowhere better to go. England, Watson and Hake were sitting at a table by themselves towards the back of the hall, near the doors. All three of them were stoop-shouldered, none of them speaking. They prodded at their food with their forks, but didn't seem to be eating much of anything. No one occupied the tables closest to them. It was as though their association with Martyn Robson made them ill-omened pariahs. When I walked past, they didn't react at all.

Since around mid-morning an overall air of moroseness had spread through the entire school like a numbing vapour. The shocking manner in which Robson had died had had time to sink in. He was gone for good. It was no hoax. There was no coming back for him. That initial buzz of excitement had waned to nothing. No, not nothing. It had swung completely the other way. Melancholy tainted everything with drab greyness. That a fourteen-year-old could actually die was on every pupil's mind. Life was not a video game and it couldn't be reset. Sometimes shit got real. Too real.

Now my classmates were pondering their own mortality; I could see it in their eyes as they walked through corridors, sat in classrooms and queued for food in the dinner hall. I'd done plenty of the same sort of pondering myself over the past six months. It never got any less confusing. Or any less frightening.

At the front of the queue, I slid my tray along the counter and asked a burly dinner lady, who had coloured tattoos on her forearms and a silver ring in her eyebrow, for cottage pie. She slopped a portion of mashed potato and gravied mince fusion onto a plate and handed it over. The bruising on my knuckles looked more prominent under the fluorescent light of the counter, I saw. I recalled the way Martyn Robson's nose had crunched beneath my fist.

Sully. Sully. Sullivan. Sully.

I snatched up my tray and scurried away. Ginny stood up from a nearby table. She was slim and graceful like a deer. I raised a hand and waved. She waved back and beckoned for me to join her.

'Hey, how's it going?' I said, taking a seat next to her. She was sharing the table with some geeky Year Nines. I knew their faces, but not their names. They were an okay bunch – I'd sat with them before.

Reaching out, Ginny touched my arm. Her fingers were gentle this time. 'Have you heard the rumours about Martyn Robson?'

Martyn Robson. Ugh.

153

Sighing inwardly, I said, 'No. What rumours?'

'Well...' She shifted on her seat, so she was facing me more. 'There's this lad in my class, right? Scotty. He hangs about with Keith Hake sometimes. Out of school, when Kevin England's not about. Their mams are good friends or something. They might even be related. Hell, who cares?' She wafted a hand in the air. *Certainly not me.* 'Anyway, Scotty says that Hake says that Robson started acting all strange after the pair of them went down the dene with England and Watson last week. Last Wednesday. The day of the storm.'

My skin prickled and my knuckles ached. 'Acting all strange in what way?'

'Hake said he just wasn't himself. Robson told him that he'd been having some weird dreams about the dene.'

Now I felt nauseous. Sick with dread. Pushing my plate of cottage pie away, I said, 'What sort of dreams?'

Ginny shook her head. 'I dunno. But it gets weirder.'

'Really?' I wasn't sure I wanted to know, in that case.

But Ginny was going to tell me anyway. 'Hake told Scotty that Robson's older brother is always down the dene. Him and his mates hang about at the cundy. Hake reckons they practice devil worship there.'

I thought about the headless rat. The headless rabbit. The news didn't exactly surprise me. I'd already heard that the cundy was the favourite haunt of Mad Bastard and his mates and my subconscious had already made its own hare-brained assumptions as to what it was they did there.

Lunhart Mohert.

'I don't get it though,' I said, absent-mindedly running a finger over my bruised knuckles. 'What's that got to do with Martyn Robson jumping off the viaduct?'

'I'm not sure.' Ginny's hand fastened around my wrist and she leaned in closer, her voice becoming a whisper.

'Maybe Robson's older brother and his mates have invoked some sort of evil presence at the cundy and then, by association, the thing went after Martyn Robson. I mean, Hake told Scotty that they all saw something inside the cundy last week.'

I swear I felt the blood drain from my face. 'Did Hake say what it was they saw?'

'No. He said he didn't know what it was.' Her fingers tightened on my wrist. 'But what if it's a demon?'

That jet black pelt. Those fiery eyes. It could well be.

'Or what if it's a land spirit,' I said.

Ginny thought about this then shook her head. 'Nah. They're not satanic.'

'But who can say for sure that Mad Bastard, I mean, Martyn Robson's older brother, is definitely into satanic rituals?' I argued. 'And what if they don't know what they're doing? I mean, even if they do perform black arts and shit, that's not to say they'd succeed in summoning the devil or one of his minions. What if they've pissed off some land spirit instead? You said yourself that land spirits are the essence of the land itself.' It sounded ridiculous, yet still I shivered. I thought of the wolf-dog.

Ginny clamped her bottom lip between her teeth as she considered this.

'Anyway,' I said, shrugging. 'If you really believe there might be a demon in the cundy, that sort of skews your view on Christianity, doesn't it?' I mustered a grin to show I was only teasing.

'Don't be a smart arse, Sullivan Carter.' Ginny loosened her grip on my wrist then pulled the hair on the back of my arm. Even though she was scowling, her eyes glinted with good humour. 'No one likes a smart arse.'

'Ha!'

'Whatever it is,' she said, 'apparently Hake, England and Watson are bricking it.' Ginny cast a look over her shoulder to where they sat, about seven tables away.

'Why?'

'In case they're next. They really do think that the devil's after them.'

14

The Promise

I sat next to Ginny on the bus home. She'd secured a window seat and saved the one next to it for me. Her hair had calmed down – as in, it wasn't as big as it had been that morning – but it still retained a certain wildness. A natural appeal. She smelled of almonds and fresh air still. I relished breathing her in. We talked non-stop all the way to Horden, mostly about the upcoming holidays. There were only four days to go till school broke up for half term. It felt good to talk about normal stuff with someone my own age. In fact, it felt good to talk to anyone besides Dad or Colton, full stop.

I made a conscious effort to steer the conversation away from Martyn Robson, the cundy and demons. They'd already occupied my thoughts way too much that day. Ginny, consciously or not, seemed happy to oblige. She nattered about the launch of the free webmail service Hotmail for a while, saying she thought computer stuff would 'totally take off' and become the way of the future. When she spoke, her grey eyes glinted with enthusiasm and every now and then she would touch my arm. She had a zeal about her that was totally addictive. I imagined she'd be able to make a conversation about the benefits of double glazed windows seem interesting.

While we talked, it came as a pleasant surprise that I didn't feel nearly as awkward around her anymore. Not to the extent that I'd have dared to ask her out on a date – I mean, let's not be too rash – but to the point where I didn't blush at anything and everything she or I said. We sort of fell into a much easier mode of banter, as though we'd known each other for ages. Which was a pretty big deal for me.

Typically, I'd always been an outsider. Not because I wanted to be, but because I found it hard to mix with others. I never knew what to say. Never knew what others expected of me. I lacked communication skills and looked too deeply into situations, analysing the shit out of every minute detail of any social encounter, always self-berating. It's not that I never looked at the popular kids and wished I was more like them. I was just too shy to be one of them. Too self-conscious. Lacking in confidence. Painfully introverted. I always felt different to everyone else.

Ginny was like a breath of fresh air. A kindred spirit, in that she seemed to float about like a loner, much like me. Only, she seemed more confident within herself. She'd made the first move, extending that initial hand of friendship. And that was that, a bond had been made between us. A bond that I hoped could never be broken.

By the time the bus was trundling along Sunderland Road, I'd told Ginny about how Dad was probably going to send me and Colton to live with Aunt Julie and our three cousins in Wingate. I explained that it was Colton's errant behaviour of late which, ultimately, was likely to sway Dad's decision. Ginny condemned the unfairness of it all and agreed that it was totally shit. When she asked if I'd be coming back to Horden at all during the summer, her eyes were wide and her fingertips touched the back of my hand. I said I didn't know and she looked disappointed. We both fell quiet. Took some time to dwell on what this meant.

Our silence stretched on for the time it took to travel from the traffic lights outside Memorial Park to David Sykes' bike shop at the top of Cotsford Lane. Then Ginny said she was going to her gran's house for tea. Somewhere along Alder Road. So when I got off the bus outside Ellwood's gym, she stayed on till the next stop. I raised my hand as the bus pulled away and was pleased to see that she returned my wave. I walked home feeling like a new person. Within the space of a week my life had changed for the better. It still wasn't great by any stretch, but it had gone from being utterly shit to a little more bearable. I'd gained a friend and lost the bullies, the irony of which didn't escape me: England, Watson and Hake were leaving me alone because they were too preoccupied by the devil that they imagined was on their backs.

Well, good, I thought. *Let them feel terrorised for a while.*

My own involvement in what had happened down the dene, inside the cundy, didn't slip my mind, however. I'm not sure I could ever forget. If they had the devil on their backs then so did I. I saw the wolf-dog each day and night in my thoughts and dreams. I'd even tasted its hunger. But unless it came looking for me in the flesh, I told myself that I couldn't allow myself to get too worked up about it. Not like how England, Watson and Hake supposedly were. I had to have that edge on them at least. I had to grasp this opportunity to be free of them with both hands and not be cowed by something else in their place. I needed room to breathe. Besides, I had Mam's dreamcatcher; the dreamcatcher which had put an end to Edith's visits. Surely it was capable of stopping the wolf-dog from breaking beyond the realm of dreams too.

I had to believe that it could.

And I also had to stay the hell away from the cundy.

No matter what.

Dad was waiting for me when I got home. He'd been standing by the front door, ready to nab me on the off chance I tried to flee. I didn't. I just stood there, absorbing the blackness of whatever fury he was about to unleash. The air in the house was so tense, I swear it felt colder than usual.

What now?

Dropping my backpack on the floor, I kicked my shoes off. Colton, I saw, was sitting at the dining table already. His white-faced look of dread made me even more nervous than I'd been initially.

'Sit down,' Dad told me. He pointed to where Colton was. 'Right this minute.' He was so angry he didn't even shout. The clipped tone of his voice marked him as incensed. He trembled with unspent rage. He hardly blinked and his lips were pulled tight, curled inwards to reveal his teeth.

Holy fuck, what now indeed?

I made wide eyes at Colton as I walked towards him.

Had he been playing truant again? And if so, why was that my fault?

But then I saw it.

Oh man, I saw it. Right there on the table. Glinting in the weak daylight which was casting its spidery way through the net curtains of the front room window.

Mam's bracelet.

Slow, long seconds passed while tension mounted and the golden pendulum of the mahogany wall clock behind Colton did nothing but add to this growing pressure. I couldn't move. Felt like I was playing a game of musical statues and if I did anything but breathe I'd be caught out. Colton shook his head and shrugged; a miniscule gesture but enough to let me know that he hadn't been the one to have found the bracelet.

But if he hadn't, then who had?

I didn't like this one bit.

Dad broke the awful silence. He came storming up behind me and slammed his hand down on the table, making me, Colton and Mam's bracelet jump. 'So, are you going to tell me what happened?'

Freed from the imagined game of musical statues, I slumped down onto one of the dining chairs. Feeling small and overpowered, I wanted to slide right off it and hide beneath the table. Had Colton already been interrogated, I wondered. And if so, would our stories correlate?

'Sorry,' was all I could manage to say, even though I had nothing to be sorry about. I bowed my head, allowing my hair to fall forward and cover my eyes.

Dad bent over, resting his arms on the table, so that his face was right next to mine. So I couldn't get away from him. So I couldn't escape his oncoming interrogation. 'Why was your mam's bracelet found down the dene, Sullivan?'

Fuck shit fuck.

I looked across the table at Colton, his head was bowed. He wouldn't meet my gaze.

'It was the day it rained. Last week,' I said, fiddling with my fingers. 'We were down the dene. I know we shouldn't have been, but…we were.'

'I see,' Dad said, breathing heavily through his nose. 'And who took the bracelet?' He looked at Colton. Then back at me.

Neither of us spoke.

'Someone better own up to it,' he said, spittle flying from his lips. 'If it was you.' He pointed a finger at Colton. 'You can damn well stay at your Aunt Julie's for the rest of the year. In fact, till you're bloody well sixteen for all I care.' Veins bulged at the side of his head and his eyes blazed. 'I've absolutely had it with you.'

Swiping my hair upwards, I glanced across the table at Colton again. His face had drained of all colour. He'd really done it this time. I don't think I'd ever seen Dad so riled.

I wondered if Dad would understand why Colton had taken the bracelet if I was to explain.

At that moment, I seriously doubted it. Given his volatile demeanour I wouldn't have expected any sort of empathic reaction at all. But was he bluffing about sending Colton away indefinitely?

I didn't think so. Colton had pushed him too far this time. Hell, I expected Dad might even pack Colton up and drop him off at Aunt Julie's that very evening.

As Dad's weighty words settled about us with all the after-sting of a punch in the face, there was an urgency for someone to say something. To do something. But no one did.

Colton's eyes were peeled, his gaze affixed to the table top so rigidly it was as though he had vertigo and didn't dare move. He looked traumatised. So small. And suddenly I remembered his words, like a stake through the heart: *I like to carry it around with me. So she can be with me.*

My chest heaved.

Hadn't I promised to always have his back?

No matter what.

Breathing in deeply, I felt my heart lurch.

'It was me,' I said. 'I took it.'

It's difficult to describe it any other way, but I felt Dad's disappointment like an actual blast of frostiness. As if the front door had opened and a winter squall had rushed inside to wait out the next five months with us. It clung to me like a cellophane layer of disapproval, gripping me tighter and tighter till I thought I might cry. Truth be told, I'd have preferred a crack across the arse with Dad's belt, because his disappointment hurt worse than any physical punishment he'd ever dished out. With my false admission I'd managed to undo so much that I'd worked to build up between us over the years. Mostly his trust in me.

You really fucked up for me this time, Colton.

'Do you want to know where your mam's bracelet was found?' Dad's tone returned to that same brutal-calm ferocity as before. He flexed his fingers then pulsed his fists. I imagined he might be entertaining thoughts of taking my head clean off my shoulders right there and then with one swift blow.

'Where?' I managed to say.

Dad began pacing the length of the dining room, running his fingers through his hair. His movement made me edgy. 'Right next to the body of that Robson lad.'

Oh man.

What were the chances?

'I take it you've heard about that?' he went on, talking to me as though Colton wasn't even in the room.

I wasn't sure if he expected me to answer the question or if he was simply stating what he knew would be true; gossip amongst kids spreads like wildfire after all, of course he knew that I'd heard about Martyn Robson. Still, I nodded out of courtesy.

'Any idea how that happened?' he said.

How Martyn Robson had killed himself? Or how Mam's bracelet had wound up next to Robson's body? I didn't know which part he was querying. He wasn't making himself clear. But to ask him to clarify would only incite his rage further, so I shook my head.

'Was Robson one of the lads who bullied you at school?' Dad's eyes narrowed, became suspicious even.

'Did he lend a hand in doing that to your face by any chance?'

I burned red under his scrutiny. What was he suggesting? That *I* might have had something to do with Martyn Robson's death?

Jesus.

Covering my right hand with my left, I shrugged and said, 'Yeah. As well as three others. But it's just coincidence. About the bracelet, I mean. It must have fallen out of my pocket at the same place that Martyn Robson, er...fell.'

'Well that's a bit of a big bloody coincidence, isn't it?' Dad shook his head disparagingly.

'Well, yeah. Totally,' I agreed, not liking at all where this line of conversation was headed.

My knuckles throbbed and Dad continued to stare at me. If my eyes were as iridescent as the moon's visible face, as Mam had always said, then Dad's kept its dark side.

Eventually he nodded. 'You'd better be telling the truth, Sullivan. Because if I find out that you...' He pointed at me, his index finger like a loaded weapon, and left the threat hanging.

Wow, I thought, completely stunned. *What kind of psychopath do you think I am, Dad?*

'Maybe Robson found it after I'd dropped it,' I said, 'and still had it on him when he...you know.'

'Lucky for you,' Dad growled, either having not heard or totally disregarding what I'd said, 'when the police brought the bracelet back, they asked me a few questions and don't seem to think it's necessary to speak to either of you. At least, not for now.' He turned to Colton and jabbed a finger in his direction. 'And don't think you're home and dry, sunshine. There's more to this than meets the bloody eye and I'm betting you had something to do with it.'

Colton didn't say anything. He caught my eye and I could tell he was sorry for the way things had turned out. But still, I was mad at him. Mad as hell.

Dad ordered us both to our rooms 'without tea or supper' and said he didn't want to see or hear a peep from us again. In the heat of the moment I think he actually meant it in a perpetual sense.

As I walked upstairs in front of Colton, I fought the urge to stamp my feet. Life was so unfair. No matter what I did, I always seemed to get bitten on the arse. I cast a glance back downstairs, through the wooden spindles of the bannister. Dad was still standing by the table. He looked like an angry, wounded woodland creature. I don't know why that particular comparison sprung to mind. I guess his dishevelled hair and the bobbly brown jumper he'd changed into since getting home from work lent him the look of an animal. The jumper had holes around the neckline and would have been more suited to line the bottom of a dog's basket. I can only guess that it held certain memories which he wasn't yet ready to part with. The way he held himself, stooped over like he'd been winded, made him look physically hurt. Like he was riding painful waves of some new injury. He picked Mam's bracelet up off the table then gripped it in his hand. I wanted to shout down, to tell him that it hadn't been me after all. That Colton had taken it. But I didn't.

I couldn't.

At my bedroom door, Colton lurched forward and gripped my arm. He started to say something, but I shrugged him off and stormed into my room, slamming the door behind me. I was much too angry for his apologies or words of gratitude for me having put my head on a platter. I contemplated playing on my Amiga, but reasoned that Dad would come thumping up the stairs and take it away; and the mood he was in, he'd probably throw it straight in the bin. So I decided to read instead. I lay on my bed with a paperback and somehow knew it was going to be a long night.

I just knew it.

15

Stalked

I dreamt about the dene again, only this time I wasn't the wolf-dog. I wasn't me either. I knew this because of the vague yet resolute self-awareness that's often permitted in dreams. I was some other boy. A dead boy roaming. Lost.

I was Martyn Robson.

Even in sleep, this prospect disturbed me. I could see, hear, feel and smell everything that he could with intense clarity. An altogether too frightening perception. My fingers were insipid grey, like raw shelled prawns. The tips of them were numb with cold. My limbs were stiff, lending me an awkward gait and as I shuffled through undergrowth my left leg dragged behind me. From the knee down something felt horribly incorrect, like my foot was on the wrong way round. I didn't dare look down to check – or to inspect what other damage there might be, for that matter. I'd rather not see what injuries my – Martyn Robson's – body had suffered at the merciless call of Gregory's Leap. My entire body hurt with the constant nerve-zinging sting of what I could only presume was ripped flesh and torn muscle. Whatever mangled skin there was beneath my clothes would never bind together again. I was a flesh-wounded dead boy walking. A zombie or a ghost. It didn't matter which. Either was horrific.

Daylight had burnt out, causing a caustic grey sky to simmer above the darkening canopy of the treetops. Each tree shushed and cackled as the baying wind sang some melancholy lullaby through them, and a restlessness of birds and squirrels shifted about on leafy boughs. Now that the sun had surrendered to night, making way for a greyscale dusk, I knew the dene would soon be teeming with nocturnal wildlife. Of which I had no doubt some would be headless. The pitter-pattering of many nimble feet would be all around me, while the black shape of the viaduct, which stood like a many legged monster no matter what time of day or night, continued to guard the mouth of the dene. Whichever way I turned it was always there, right behind me.

A full moon blinked between the black outline of trees, directly above. A cyclops' eye. It glowed silver blue, highlighting my surroundings and tracking my non-progress. As I hobbled aimlessly, lonely and scared – my dead fingers probing rough bark – a feeling of indomitable dread gripped me so suddenly it felt like a cold, rigid hand on the back of my neck. Squeezing so hard, its coldness transferred through my flesh and travelled down my vertebrae. Shivers coursed up and down my painful skin. I wanted to curl into a ball and lie on the dirt beneath me and hide from the moon's spotlight. I felt hunted.

Something deep within the dene, perhaps the dene itself, threatened – no, promised – to consume me if I didn't get out. But somehow I knew there was no way out. No matter how far I walked or how much I searched, the trees would go on and on, ad infinitum, foiling my attempts. And Gregory's Leap would forever loom right behind me. Never any larger, never any smaller, always just there. Making escape impossible.

After all, how could I retract what had already been done?

Even though I couldn't see them, I was aware of others there too. Others who'd gone before me. Others who were also trapped. The dene had retained their souls, as it had mine, claiming all of them for itself. For every haunting crow's caw that resounded through the tenebrous gulley, a handful of lost souls wept. We were a legion of spirits, divided by our own misery. Perhaps we had cursed the land with the emotive burden of our untimely deaths, or maybe we'd been cursed by the land. A spiteful land which had been damned in the days of Scula the Danish Viking warlord's rule, or maybe many more millennia before that, when glaciers were still modelling the terrain of this North Sea inlet. Who knew what land spirits existed and what caused them to react, be that positively or negatively, to any living thing that trod on its soil?

As if in arrogant response to my fearful pondering, the black wolf-dog – no, definitely wolf – came into view. It slinked into a clearing before a cluster of silver birches, just ahead, with its head held low.

I froze.

It was enormous. A great hulking predator whose coat was as black and pure as the dark matter which occupies the space between stars. It regarded me with sly interest. Telepathically or perhaps just instinctively, I knew that it had been watching me all along. Stealthily stalking. Its eyes were amber; fiery pieces of fossilised tree resin which had likely trapped and collected many dead things over time. Baring its teeth, it crouched low to the ground, readying itself to pounce. I could feel death radiating from it in great waves of warning.

Or maybe I was exuding my own state of death. I mean, could the wolf kill me anymore than I was already dead?

I didn't know. And I didn't want to find out.

Turning to run away, my broken leg buckled beneath me. The wolf snarled. The sound was loud in my head. Too loud. My hands scrabbled at the thick trunk of a sycamore tree. Somehow I managed to prop myself against it and stay upright. I didn't dare look back, didn't want to see those hellfire eyes. Using the tree as leverage, I hoisted myself forward and was appalled to see that the viaduct was no longer looming behind me, as it had been all along. Now it towered ahead; an immense mocking beast which had welcomed irrational urges and irreversible choices since it had been built.

Caught between the wolf and the viaduct, I whimpered and froze.

What now?

I shuffled backwards. Didn't dare turn my head. With my back against the tree, I slid down its rough bark and crumpled to the floor. The moon winked at me. I closed my eyes, but not before the wolf sprang towards me with an almighty roar.

'Sully!' Colton shook me awake.

Lurching into a sitting position, I looked about, expecting to see the wolf's massive form; teeth bared, already salivating at the thought of having my flesh and blood in its mouth. It wasn't there though. Just Colton. I wanted to ask him *What the hell are you doing?* but couldn't speak. My mouth was dry and my tongue felt rigid. Paralysed. As though it was a slab of old meat. My skin felt too hot but at the same time it was damp with a film of cold sweat. Goosebumps stood to attention all over my arms and torso. I shivered. My pulse was racing too fast. The memory of the wolf's amber eyes, with their burning intensity, had seared deeply into my fears. It had almost touched me. The wolf had been mere inches away from latching onto my flesh with its hungry white teeth. If Colton hadn't come to my room when he had, if he hadn't woken me, I wondered if the dream catcher would have been strong enough to catch the wolf as it slipped right out of the dream – which I was almost certain it would have done.

For once I had doubts. As much as the dreamcatcher was enough to keep Edith tangled in its threads, the wolf was more powerful by far. Omnipotent, if you like. And even though it hadn't ruptured from my nightmares yet, or indeed the black space in the cundy, I had a crushing feeling that it was coming for me now. The chase was on. It was actively hunting me.

Clamping a hand over my mouth, I thought I might be sick. I could still smell the musky stink of its fur. The malodour of its presence.

And what about Martyn Robson?

Holy shit.

The fact I'd dreamt that I was Martyn Robson trapped in the dene was horrifying because it opened the question: what if he really was? What if on some other plane he was there right now? Wandering aimlessly. Lonely and afraid. Broken and hurting. He might have been a massive knobhead in life, but he didn't deserve that unending fate.

'Sully.' Colton gripped my arm, demanding my full attention. He looked like a ghostly form in the darkness. 'I dreamt I was in the cundy,' he said.

Reaching over, I snapped on the bedside lamp so I could see him better.

'What happened?' The words rushed out as one, like *whatappened.*

Colton scrabbled onto the bed and settled beside me. He seemed excited. Buzzing with some newfound elation. 'I think Mam's there.'

I was taken aback. Confused. 'In the cundy?'

'Uh-huh.'

I remembered the day we'd found the headless rabbit. Colton had uttered something about Mam while looking into the cundy. I hadn't caught what he'd said. 'What do you mean? What the hell are you talking about?'

'I think Mam's in the cundy,' he repeated, as though I hadn't heard him the first time. 'Or at least, I think there's a passageway to get to her.'

'No.' I shook my head. Couldn't believe that. Wouldn't. 'Definitely not.' I felt upset at the thought of Mam being in there. That Colton would suggest something so terrible made me angry. I was annoyed with him all over again for having made me lie so badly to Dad. For not 'fessing up when he'd had the chance. For not taking the opportunity at least to share the rap for everything. Yes, he was only ten, but would I always make excuses for him just because he was younger than me?

But then, that wasn't fair. It had been my own fault, hadn't it? I'd played myself as a sacrifice, landing myself in this god-awful situation. Colton hadn't asked me to do it. So how could I blame him?

To what length was I willing to go to have his back? Would it reach a point where he'd never learn right from wrong because I'd always be the one to pick up the punishment for him? He'd been the one bunking off school and he'd been the one who stole Mam's bracelet from Dad's room, not me. But I was suffering as a result.

That wasn't all that troubled me either. The look on Colton's face when he'd thrown the rock that hit Kevin England on the back of the head had been one of such feral rage it still gnawed at my sensibilities. In some deep, guarded place within my heart, it bothered me more than I dared to admit. He definitely had an underlying dark streak. An unpredictable nature which, I was loath to admit, I didn't always like. As much as I was repelled by and scared of the cundy, Colton seemed to be enamoured by and drawn to it. His difference in character worried me.

'You know it yourself,' Colton said. 'I can tell.'

Sully. Sully. Sullivan. Sully.

I closed my eyes and squeezed at my temples with my fingers; fingers which I was thankful weren't grey or dead. What Colton was suggesting was alarming because I also felt that there was some sort of portal within the cundy. Only, I didn't believe that it led to Mam. No way. I was more inclined to think that it had something to do with Mad Bastard's dark rituals. Whenever I went to the cundy – in real life or dreams – I found it an ill-omened place that might snap a person right out of existence. Certainly, I thought, it was no place where Mam would be lingering.

'No,' I said. 'Just leave it be. It's dangerous there. Stop talking about it.'

'But why don't you care?' Colton's shoulders sagged and he looked at me deploringly. His eyes were like Dad's. The dark side of the moon.

'I do care,' I said, through gritted teeth; a warning for him not to push the boundaries of my tried patience any more than he already had.

But he did. He went there. He stomped all over that last scrap of patience and may as well have clouted me in the face for good measure.

'No you don't,' he said. 'You don't care at all.'

I couldn't believe it. Couldn't believe his audacity.

'How can you even say that, you ungrateful little shit? After all I've done for you.' Resisting the urge to knock him off the bed with a side swipe of my leg, I thrust my arm out and pointed to the door. 'Get out. Now!'

There was a moment of irate staring between the pair of us, then Colton slid from the mattress and walked towards the door. When he got there he turned his head and said in an eerily monotone voice, 'I'll go and find

Mam, with or without you.'

'Don't you dare go back there,' I spat, almost ready to launch myself off the bed to give him a good hiding.

He gave me a scathing look, as much as to say that he'd do as he damn well pleased, then left.

Shit!

I lay back in bed, my thoughts a tumultuous whir of confusion, fear and hopelessness.

Mam, if you can hear me, I thought, *tell me what to do.*

There was a long moment of ear-buzzing silence. Nothing more.

I was hardly surprised. How many other times had I spoken to Mam and got no response?

Countless times, that's how many.

Next door's dog barked, breaking the quiet spell. Then further up the street someone's wheelie bin lid clattered shut and a woman shouted, 'Shut that bloody door, Frank!'

I was still clammy with sweat and the room was stifling. There was barely any air to breathe. It seemed Colton had taken it with him. Dragging myself out of bed, I opened the window. The back street was glowing orange from the two streetlamps which were stationed at either end. I stuck my head outside and gasped in fresh air.

Only…it wasn't fresh.

There was an unpleasant stink of stagnant water. Maybe blocked drains. I considered closing the window against the smell, but the outside sounds were a good distraction from the silence of my room and noise of my thoughts. I stayed where I was, listening; the window thrown wide. Cars passed along Cotsford Lane every now and then; an infrequent hum of engines that came and went. The sound of a horn blaring was so distant it could have been anywhere in Horden.

I looked up at the sky, imagining the stars and moon

above the blanket of dark grey, and wondered what it would be like if I could glimpse the millions of galaxies beyond our own, just as Mam had suggested I could. But I couldn't. I could see only the murky underside of rainclouds. No farther.

The sound of a dog's *tick-ticking* claws on cement brought my attention back down to street level. Craning my neck, I looked in next door's yard, expecting to see Denver the Rottweiler there, having a late night toilet break. But the big old dog was nowhere to be seen.

I waited. Watching. Listening.

Something black flashed past the wrought iron gate of our yard. I heard claws again. *Tick-tick-tick.* There was definitely a dog out there in the street. Perhaps it was Denver. Maybe he'd escaped from the yard.

Somehow I knew that wasn't the case, however.

I waited and waited, becoming altogether too tense. Even though it wasn't cold my arms bristled with gooseflesh. I shivered. The untroubled ambience of the street below was replaced with a growing sense of menace. Because something was down there. Hiding behind the wall. And I could tell that it knew that I knew.

I waited and waited, not daring to blink. Not daring to move. Clouds shifted. The moon peeked through a narrow gap. Like an eye peeping through a keyhole. Checking up on things.

Hey, Sully. You okay down there?

No, not really.

An enormous black dog jumped on top of the yard wall, directly opposite my window. Only, it wasn't a dog at all. No way could it ever have been a dog. Even in the dark – or maybe *because* of the dark – the immense size of it chilled me. It was the black wolf. The wolf from the cundy. Right there outside my house. Looking right at me.

Yo, Moon Boy. I've found you.

I gawped at it with bone-chilled awe. It was really, truly there. *Right there.* Watching me. Communicating some silent threat via eyes which shone orange in the streetlit night. It was the kind of encounter that I just knew, should I survive, would stay with me for years afterwards. To be catalogued in my brain, to haunt me at every given opportunity. Because how could it not? The black wolf belonged in some horror fantasy film. It was bigger, I imagined, than your average wolf and its eyes – oh God, its eyes – were every bit as fiery as they had been in my dreams. Every bit as mesmeric as it had shown me they were within those nightly voyages to wherever the subconscious mind drifts.

Also, the unpleasant smell which tainted the night air, I realised, was emanating from the wolf itself. It filled Murray Street, perhaps even all of Horden for all I knew, with a fetid bouquet of ripe stink; a strong musty odour of turned earth, bad water and mildewed spaces. It clung to the back of my nose as invasively as a sinus infection.

It seemed like whole minutes passed by while we stared at each other, but it must have only been seconds. Hell, I wasn't brave enough to spend minutes looking at those amber eyes, I'm sure. Clapping the window shut, I smothered the glass pane with the flimsy material of my curtains, then stood for a while, listening. Hearing nothing but my own heart in my ears. I expected the wolf to crash through the window. When it didn't, I jumped into bed and hid under my duvet where I lay, not sleeping, for the rest of the night.

16

Truant

The next morning at breakfast, my attention kept wandering to the kitchen window which overlooked the backyard. I could almost picture the wolf standing on top of the wall out there, as it had done the previous night, glaring at me with its scarily incandescent eyes. I was overly tired and anxious. Several times I glanced across the table at Colton, wondering if he'd seen the wolf from his room. I guessed not though, his attention didn't once slip to the kitchen window.

He wouldn't look at me at all, which meant he was still in a huff after our spat last night. But that was okay because I was still angry at him. Dad banged stuff about to let us know that he was mad too. He didn't bother speaking at all. In fact, no one did. We went through the motions of having breakfast and getting ready for school and work without any of us uttering a single word. I suspected Dad had hidden Mam's bracelet somewhere that Colton and I wouldn't be able to find it. I couldn't really blame him. I was just pleased it had found its way home.

Colton left the house first, without waiting for me. If Dad noticed, he didn't ask why. I left shortly afterwards, closing the door without so much as a goodbye. This upset me. My stomach churned.

Despite the fresh sea breeze whipping in from the east, I walked to the bus stop imagining I could still smell the wolf at the back of my nose. I considered again that it might be a land spirit. The idea still seemed somewhat absurd, but I wholeheartedly believed that it was some sort of personification of the dene. It felt right in my gut that the wolf *had* to be a land spirit.

I wondered if it might have the ability to emanate a more pleasant smell, something like wild berries and bluebells, when it wasn't so pissed off about the likes of Mad Bastard and his mates desecrating its soil and disrespecting its resident creatures. But then, maybe the agedness of the land was so fully embedded into the very heart of the thing, its skin and fur would be forever imbued, even after each season's moult, with the smell of rot. Perhaps it loathed all of mankind because of the forceful intrusions we'd inflicted on it – the coast road, the viaduct and the cundy. We take what we want, after all. Arrogant and aggressive. Changing things for our own advantage and gain. I could see, then, why the wolf would choose to haunt the cundy. To scare off the very ones who'd built it.

Ginny wasn't on the bus that morning and I ended up sitting next to Raymond Foster. He smelt almost as bad as the wolf. His sour, ferrety BO was so ripe, my gag reflex kicked in at least half a dozen times. Someone somewhere on the bus was steeped in dewberry perfume, or maybe it was just the sickly, sweet combined effort of several girls who all shopped at The Body Shop. Dewberry seemed to be the fragrance of choice for adolescent girls and seemed to be as much of a statement of social hierarchy to them as their Harmony Hairsprayed quiffs. Either way, whoever was responsible, the dewberry scent was persistent and acted in some way like an air freshener against Raymond Foster's pong. By the time we reached Thorpe Road, the amalgamation of the two contrasting smells had made me feel nauseous however. My cornflakes felt like poison inside my belly.

As well as negotiating with my breakfast to stay put, I spent the journey to school wondering where Ginny was and when Dad would speak to me again. I also thought about the cundy and of what Colton had said, about Mam being there. I suppose that was the thing that was eating me up most. Not that I believed what Colton said held any truth, but it worried me that he thought that Mam was in the cundy. Did he hear voices in his dreams calling his name too? Was their appeal more alluring to him? Or was his grief taking some new, unexpected twist?

How much more could I take? How much more could we take as a family?

The bruise on my knuckle had faded a little, but still it throbbed. I rubbed the copper-coloured flourish of skin and wondered if the sensation was all in my head. Some psychosomatic guilt presenting itself as a physical symptom. But then, what the hell did I have to feel guilty about? Punching Robson in the face had been an act of self-defence. I was in no way responsible for his death. Whatever had made him take his own life, it was nothing to do with me.

Yet, why did I feel uncertain about this?

Something was bugging me, itching the far edges of my conscious thought with ghostly imprecision. I couldn't figure out what it was.

I wondered when Robson's funeral might be and if Dad would be involved. Almost everyone in the village used McGregor's Funeral Home and I couldn't see why the Robsons would be any different, so I expected he would be. Dad never talked about work though. Besides,

Robson was no friend of mine, so why would he tell me? He wouldn't expect that I'd want to go.

Part of me wanted to though, to make sure Robson's foot wasn't back to front. To see if he looked at peace. I thought about him wandering around Castle Eden Dene, his spirit body dysfunctional, while his mind was fully cognisant. As much as I'd disliked Robson, I disliked that thought even more.

The school day went by slowly. Too many hours of science. A distinct feeling of isolation. And finding that I didn't care a damn if lessons never came to an end because going home was no more appealing than the sound of Mr Davidson's dull monotone prattling on about photosynthesis.

Before my last lesson, I saw Kevin England. He was on his own. I was walking to the geography class when I passed him in the corridor. He put his head down and didn't so much as glance at me, let alone hurl any insults. I wondered if the wolf haunted him, as it did me. I hoped so. He deserved it. It might teach him some humility.

When the final bell rang, I traipsed to the bus stop entertaining thoughts of running away. Of not getting on the bus back to Horden, but instead walking in the opposite direction to wherever my feet might take me. But I didn't. I got on the bus. Like I knew I would.

That evening Dad made gruff announcements to let us know when tea would be ready and when me and Colton should do our homework, to which we replied with monosyllabic words. It was a worse atmosphere, I thought, than when nobody was speaking at all. By eight o'clock I went to my room and didn't bother wishing anyone good night. I drew the curtains against the lingering day, knowing that I wouldn't dare look out of the window again till the next morning. I thought I would lie awake for ages, my mind too busy to make way for sleep, but I dozed off pretty quickly.

I dreamt about the dene. Which was no surprise. I wasn't the wolf and I wasn't Martyn Robson. This time I was me. I was standing at one end of the cundy and could see a figure standing in the circle of grey daylight at the other end. So much blackness stood between us, I squinted to try and make out who it was. In my heart I already knew.

It was Mam.

Hey Moon Boy, how yer doin'?

I heard her voice inside my head. It echoed all around the cundy.

'Mam?' Taking a step forward, the toe of my shoe was swallowed by the darkness. I hesitated.

She opened her arms.

Come here, sweetheart.

'Sully!' Someone was behind me, gripping my shoulder and pulling me back.

I turned my head and saw Ginny.

'What are you doing?' I asked, surprised to find her there.

'Don't go in.' Her eyes were wide, dulled by the darkness. They were the same unreachable colour as the swatch of daylight at the other end of the cundy.

'But my mam's there. Look.' I pointed, to show her. But there was only darkness.

'She was,' I insisted. 'She was right there.'

'You'll get lost in all that black.' Ginny's hand loosened on my shoulder.

'Not if I walk in a straight line...'

'It's not that simple. It never is.'

'But I'm not scared anymore.'

'You should be.'

'Why?' I turned to look at her again, but she wasn't there. 'Ginny?'

She was some twenty yards behind, beneath Yggdrasil,

the yew tree, which shouldn't be there. The wolf was standing between us. Surveying me with cool interest.

Sully. Sully. Sullivan. Sully.

I heard my name being called inside the cundy.

'Mam?'

'Don't go in, Sully,' Ginny implored.

The wolf stalked towards me, its head held low, forcing me backwards, into the dark.

That's right, Sully, Mam said. *Come here. I've been waiting for you.*

I don't remember what happened after that, I'm guessing the blackness of the cundy extended itself to deep sleep and I stopped dreaming. When I awoke the next morning I felt like my sanity was as precarious as a thin, suspended pane of glass upon which many heavy things were piled. It was bound to crack beneath the weight, I thought, and shatter spectacularly.

Ginny wasn't on the school bus again that morning, which raised alarm bells in my head.

The first hairline crack?

I'd dreamt of the wolf chasing the rabbit the night before me and Colton had found the headless rabbit at the cundy, and I'd dreamt of Martyn Robson the night before he'd jumped off the viaduct. I hoped my dream about Ginny wasn't a prophesy that something bad had happened to her. I nursed a sickly feeling of dread the whole way to school and worried in case some announcement might be made by Miss Mawn at morning registration about a second pupil having lost their life to Castle Eden Dene. By lunch time I was so concerned about Ginny's absence that when I saw a dark-haired girl who I'd seen Ginny walking between lessons with a couple of times, I ran over and asked if she knew where Ginny was.

The girl looked at me as if I was an alien and shook her head. 'Dunno.'

She was short and squat with a square-ish face, possibly made squarer because of her fringe, which was sitting on top of her eyebrows with all the straightness and thickness of a brand new masonry paintbrush. She looked a bit like Velma off Scooby Doo, only without glasses and all the orange and red. Not one of the popular kids, there was no Harmony Hairspray quiff or dewberry perfume here. She made to step past me, making it clear she had no intention of giving me any more of her time. But I couldn't let her go. Needed to know more.

'Do you know where she lives, by any chance?' I said, sidestepping to block her escape. Dangerous thoughts were already coasting through my mind: thoughts of bunking off school to go and find Ginny.

Velma shrugged her shot-putter shoulders, which I imagined would be able to tackle me into the middle of next week if I wasn't careful. 'Not sure.'

'Not even a rough idea?' I pleaded, feeling reckless enough to challenge her. 'It's *really* important.'

Velma rolled her eyes and huffed. She looked like she might thump me, but didn't. Instead, she said, 'I think she lives next door to the vets, alright?'

'Which vets?'

'The one near the park. Now, if you don't mind.' She bouldered past, clipping me with her left shoulder.

'Memorial Park?' I called after her.

But Velma was done talking to me.

'Cheers,' I shouted anyway, before dashing off towards the fence at the bottom of the playing field. If I hurried, I reckoned I could be at Ginny's house by the time afternoon classes started and Mr Dunn realised I was missing from his physics class. It was the first time I'd ever bunked off school, but I was in the dog house anyway so what did it matter? I may as well commit an act of delinquency and give Dad a real reason to be angry with me.

Throwing my bag over the fence first, I climbed up the metal slats, swung my legs over and jumped down onto the pavement at the other side. A silver Vauxhall Corsa drove past at the same time. I hoped it wasn't a teacher. Without waiting to find out, I scooped my bag off the floor and sprinted to Little Thorpe roundabout. Once there, I slowed to a jog and headed along Thorpe Road. By the time I'd passed the crisp factory and the graveyard, I was only a little out of breath.

The sea was a blue band in the distance and yellow rape fields picked Horden Hall out as a haunted house in Oz. Veering right, I ran along Sunderland Road, hoping Dad wouldn't happen by and see me. I never knew what jobs he had on any given day. It wasn't kids' business was all he'd say if I ever asked him about work. And I guess that was true, unless you happened to be Martyn Robson.

By the time I rounded the bend on Sunderland Road, opposite the bingo hall, I'd developed a stitch. Memories of running away from England, Robson, Watson and Hake barrelled into my thoughts. It was hard to believe that it had been just a week ago. So much had changed since that day.

I stopped to wait for traffic to pass before crossing Blackhills Road. Feeling insurmountably guilty, dreading that someone might see me. My legs felt like jelly. As I ran past the gates of Memorial Park, I checked my watch and was impressed to see that only half an hour had gone by since I'd decided to skip afternoon classes. If I really wanted to, I could turn around and go back without anyone knowing that I'd been gone. But I couldn't. I was almost at Ginny's house now. I needed to see her.

In Hardwick Street, I slowed to a steady walk and looked down the row of terraced houses. I didn't know which house either side of the veterinary practice, at the bottom of the street, Ginny lived. Nor what I would say to whoever answered the door. I couldn't dwell on those finer details, however, else I'd chicken out. I had to be spontaneous and just take it as it came.

There was a blue Seat Ibiza parked outside the vets. Inside it, a woman and a worried looking collie watched me approach. I stopped at the house immediately to the left of the veterinary practice and raised my hand to knock on the white uPVC door. But something didn't feel right. Gut instinct told me it wasn't the correct house. So I moved to the one on the right of the veterinary practice. I still wasn't sure, but it didn't feel as wrong. The woman in the Seat Ibiza watched me through her wing mirror. When we made eye contact, she didn't look away. This made me feel thuggish, like she expected I was up to no good. I could hardly blame her. Lifting my hand, I knocked on the door. Then waited.

Minutes passed. My stomach wound tighter and tighter into knots. The fresh breeze was cool against my face, but I was still flushed from the exertion of the run. When a man answered the door, I knew straight away that I'd got the right house. Ginny's dad, Mr Delaney, had the same colour hair as Ginny, only his was greying at the sides. He was older than my dad, I'd say by maybe about ten years. His eyes were the same grey as Ginny's, but aloof.

'Who are you?' Mr Delaney barked. 'And what do you want?'

'Is Ginny in?'

Mr Delaney crossed his sinewy arms over his chest and shifted his weight from one foot to the other. His eyes narrowed. 'Who?'

Blushing profusely, I said, 'I mean, Katrina. Is Katrina in?'

'Depends who's asking.'

'Sullivan Carter. Her friend.'

'Kat doesn't hang around with boys,' he said. 'She isn't allowed to have boyfriends.'

'Er, I'm not her boyfriend.' My cheeks burnt with unnecessary guilt; I wasn't her boyfriend, but my god did I want to be. 'I'm just a friend. And I wanted to know if she's okay, that's all.'

'No, she's not,' Mr Delaney told me. 'Else she'd bloody well be at school, wouldn't she?'

'So, is she poorly then?' I dared to ask. Pushing my luck, but needing to know that Ginny's absence from school was nothing to do with the dene.

'Aye, she is.' Mr Delaney rocked back on his heels. 'Not that it's any of your business, like, but she's had a touch of the squits.'

'Oh.'

Ginny's dad beamed, as if pleased with himself for having embarrassed his daughter in front of a potential suitor.

'Is there any chance I could have a quick word with her?' I said, already knowing what the answer would be.

'Not likely.' Mr Delaney leaned forward and thumbed up the street. 'Now piss off. And don't let me catch you sniffing round here again.'

Not that I'd have known how to respond anyway, but Mr Delaney closed the door on me so I didn't have to. I glanced across at the blue Seat Ibiza and saw that Collie Woman was still watching me. Nosy cow. As pleased as I was that Ginny had nothing more than an upset stomach, I was crestfallen that I hadn't got to see her. It would seem that my afternoon of truancy had been in vain.

I carried on walking to the very end of the street. When I got there I thought I might try walking up the back lane, to see if I could see anything of Ginny there.

Counting the houses from the bottom up, I worked out which was Ginny's. I must have loitered long enough because her face appeared at a window that was framed with red curtains. The window opened with a dull thunk and Ginny leant out.

'Sully!' she whisper-shouted down to me. 'What are you doing here?'

'I came to see you,' I told her. 'But your dad wouldn't let me.'

She cast a look over her shoulder, then said, 'Gimme five minutes. I'll come down. Meet me at the end.' She pointed to where I'd just come from.

It was more like fifteen minutes by the time she showed up.

'Did you bunk off school?' she said, sidling up to me and leaning her back against the end house.

'Yeah. I needed to know if you're okay,' I said, feeling awkward. 'I had a dream last night. About us. In the dene. And the wolf.'

'What wolf?'

Shit.

I hadn't told Ginny what had been going on. Not even to mark my own involvement when she'd told me about what Scotty, the boy in her class, had said about the thing that Hake, England, Robson and Watson had seen in the cundy. She was the only real friend I had and so I decided there and then that I would tell her everything. Get it all off my chest. A problem shared and all that jazz. I told her about how things were at home and about the day Kevin England, Martyn Robson, Ian Watson and Keith Hake had chased me and Colton. I told her about Mam's bracelet and about how I'd punched Martyn Robson in the face. I even showed her the bruises on my knuckles as proof. I told her how Colton thought Mam was in the cundy and how I'd dreamt that she was. And lastly, I told her about the beast inside the cundy. The wolf that England, Robson, Watson and Hake had seen. The very same wolf that had paid me a visit the night before last.

'I really do think it's a land spirit that's proper pissed off,' I said. 'So I just had to make sure that you were okay.'

Ginny's eyes sparkled with excitement, as though I'd just told the most amazing story in the world.

'Quick,' she said, linking her arm through mine and pulling me down the alley towards Third Street. 'Before my dad sees.'

'Why?' I laughed in bemusement, allowing myself to be dragged. 'Where are we going?'

'The cundy,' she said. 'I wanna see the wolf.'

17

Once Bitten

'No, we can't,' I said. 'It's too dangerous. Didn't you listen to what I just told you?'

'But what if Colton's right?' Ginny clutched onto my arm tighter and forced me to turn right along Sixth Street. 'What if there's a passageway inside the cundy?'

I couldn't believe she was siding with Colton.

'If there is,' I said, 'then it's guarded by a great big massive fuck-off wolf.'

'Which I just *have* to see.' Dark humour, or something like it, glinted in Ginny's eyes. 'Besides, it's never actually hurt you, has it?'

I looked at her, incredulous. 'It *attacked* us.' I could remember all too well the force of the wolf's body as it had slammed into me inside the cundy. The feel of its coarse fur against my skin. The feel of its hot breath in my face.

'Ah come on, I really want to see it.' Ginny was full of bravado and I knew there'd be no talking her out of it. 'We'll be really careful,' she said. 'And we'll tell it we mean no harm.'

'Tell it *we* mean no harm? And wait, you want to *talk to it?*' This was crazy.

'Yeah, why not?'

'What if it won't listen?' Which I suspected it wouldn't.

'It will. We'll tell it we respect its land.'

'What if it's not a land spirit?'

'What else could it be? The way you described it...' She left the response open, was putting the onus on me.

My heart lurched. I wanted to spend time with Ginny. But going to the dene with her? The cundy! It wasn't at all what I'd had in mind. And it didn't escape my attention that if Dad found out then I was likely to spend the rest of my days till I turned eighteen at Aunt Julie's.

Did I care enough not to go though?

In that moment, no.

Ginny was about the only person who 'got' me. If I threw a hissy fit and refused to go with her, she might not want to hang around with me anymore. Besides, going to the cundy would create the perfect opportunity to show her that I wasn't a total wet blanket. So, even though I knew it was absolute madness, I decided it was worth risking an encounter with the wolf.

Rather than go the long way to the dene via the beach road, we cut up the back of Murray Street, chancing being seen by my neighbours – as it was, I don't think anyone saw us. Soon we were on the coast road, headed down the bank towards the iron kissing gate which offered direct access to the dene. The coast road was busy enough with traffic coming from and going in the direction of Blackhall and I cringed the entire time we walked alongside it in case someone I knew spotted me and pulled over to ask why I wasn't at school. At the same time, my heart swelled with the excitement of wild abandon; that I was sharing this moment of rebellion with Ginny was the best feeling I'd had in a long while.

Once we slipped through the kissing gate at last – Ginny first, then me – and dipped into the cooler air beneath the dene's leafy canopy, I felt a little more at ease. Even though we'd pitched ourselves in the wolf's domain. I had this false sense of boldness, I guess, simply because I was acting so recklessly. I wondered if this was how Colton felt every time he bunked off school. I could see the appeal.

'Will your dad go mental when you go home?' I said, glancing sideways at Ginny. She looked especially pale that day, her porcelain skin lending her eyes more of a doll-like appearance than usual.

'Nah, he didn't see me leave. He'll think I'm in bed.' She tilted her head back to look at two squabbling finches above us. They chased each other, flitting and weaving amongst green branches. 'He's too busy trying to fix the kitchen tap before Mam gets in from work. If he sees me trying to sneak in when I go back, I'll just tell him I popped to the shop or something. I don't really care to be honest. He does my head in.' She looked at me then. 'What about your dad? Will you get wrong?'

'Without a doubt. I'm already in the bad books.'

Ginny frowned. 'You should really tell him the truth, you know. Stop taking the blame for everything Colton does. I certainly wouldn't do the same for Rory. The way I see it is that if he does the crime, then he can bloody well do the time.'

'It's different with Colton though,' I said, quick to defend him without really knowing why.

'How come?'

'I dunno.' I jammed my hands into my trouser pockets and shrugged. 'He's a bit messed up. After Mam. And, I dunno...he's just different to other kids in general.'

'Different in what way?' Ginny stooped to pick a long, thin branch off the floor. She trailed it behind her as she walked. 'He seems normal enough to me. No different to Rory really. A typical little shit.'

'Maybe.' I shrugged again; my favourite mode of body

language it would seem. 'I'm not sure.' Was I ever sure about anything these days?

Ginny cast a mischievous look at me and smirked. 'You're not exactly normal yourself, you know.'

I was taken aback by her frank observation. Couldn't find the words with which to ask her to elaborate.

This seemed to amuse her. She laughed.

'Which, I suppose,' she said, 'is why I like you so much.'

Likes me so much? Dumbstruck, I was unable to unravel my tongue enough to say any more than, 'You do?'

'Would I have risked coming down the dene with you now if I didn't?' She drew her arm back and swung the branch she was carrying into the undergrowth to her right.

I continued to stare at her, unsure what to say. Unsure if she was winding me up. Feeling awkward. Probably looking stupid. 'Er, yes, because you want to see the wolf.'

'Well, okay, that's true enough.' She rolled her eyes like she thought I was being pedantic.

Maybe I was.

We walked in silence for a while. I couldn't hazard a guess as to what her thoughts might have been, but mine were gleefully elated that she'd admitted she liked me. For an awkward thirteen-(soon-to-be-fourteen)-year-old it was a pretty big deal.

A pheasant bawked. Its deep cry pierced the afternoon calm and served to remind me that other things existed beyond me and Ginny. Its wings, as it took flight somewhere close by, made a heavy flapping sound, ruffling leaves and foliage. I willed it to be quiet, in case it stirred other things.

'You have the strangest looking eyes, you know that, right?' Ginny said. It seemed like a totally random thing to say, but I wondered how long she'd been wanting to acknowledge the fact.

Keeping my gaze trained on the ground, trying not to show my embarrassment, I said, 'Er, yeah. That's why my nickname's Zombie.'

As she was Ginny Longlegs to schoolyard bullies, I was Zombie or Zombie-Eyed Freak. My eyes were the sort of white-blue more befitting a Hollywood undead corpse than the regular kid I was supposed to be. I didn't have to look at them all that often though, only in the mirror when brushing my hair or washing my face, so most of the time I forgot how unusual they were to everyone else.

'Oh, I didn't know that.' Wafting a hand in the air, possibly sensing my discomfort, Ginny said, 'I mean, I was just saying, that's all. No offense or anything.'

'None taken.' But I felt crushed. Crushed to learn she thought I looked strange.

She must have picked up on this. Her expression turned all serious and she said, 'Hey, I'm sorry. Really. I didn't mean it in a bad way. Honest.'

'It's okay,' I insisted.

Reaching out, she grabbed my hand and yanked my arm to make me stop and look at her. It took all of my will to maintain eye contact.

'Really, it's okay,' I said. 'Just forget it. I have freaky eyes. I know.' I tried to pull my hand away, but she wouldn't let go.

'Bloody hell, man, Sully.' She huffed. 'I meant it in a good way. I like your eyes. In fact, they're probably what I like most about you.'

It felt like a backhanded compliment. 'Er, thanks.'

'That didn't sound right, did it?' She shook her head and rubbed her forehead, as if trying to massage her thoughts, to straighten out the tangle of awkwardness she was creating. 'Your eyes were the first thing I noticed about you, that's all. They're like… I dunno, a bit like…'

'The moon?'

Her face lit up and she laughed. 'See, that's exactly why I like you and your eyes, you nutter. You're so bloody weird.' She leaned forward and kissed me on the lips then. It was just a quick peck which was over too soon. But she kissed me nonetheless. She didn't taste of bubble gum ice pops, as I'd imagined, or much at all for that matter, but her mouth was warm and soft and I wanted more of it. She squeezed my hand and hooked her fingers more tightly between mine and said, 'Come on, we'd better hurry up. Time's getting on. We need to find the wolf.'

Right then I didn't give two flying fucks about what time it was or where the land spirit was. The dene could have split down the middle, swallowed us whole and shat us out next Christmas for all I cared. Ginny Longlegs was holding my hand and she'd kissed me and told me she liked me. That was all I could think about.

As we wandered deeper into the dene, Ginny chattered away and I barely got the gist of anything she said. My thoughts were moving too fast. This was a day of firsts. Truant and kissing. I was high on emotion. Eventually Ginny came to a stop and let go of my hand.

'There's Yggdrasil,' she said, pointing to a tree.

That got my attention.

It was the yew tree from my dreams, bedecked with arils that looked like rubies. A chill surged through me and I was rendered suddenly fearful; reminded of the grave danger this place threatened us with. I scanned the area around us, looking for the wolf. I couldn't see it, but that didn't mean it wasn't there. The viaduct was off to our left, watching. Ready to grind our bones beneath one of its many feet if we strayed too close. Everything had taken on an unfriendly edge. Even the gentle breeze had a spiteful air about it as it teased and goaded my hair and shirt.

There was movement in the trees to the right of where Ginny and I were standing. I looked and saw a crow perched on a bough some ten feet up. It cawed and I felt somewhat relieved. My nerves were rattled.

Just a crow.

It's only a crow.

But I heard broken twigs crackle underfoot and caught sight of something at ground level. Someone was lurking amongst the trees. Squinting, I could just about make out a boy's misshapen figure propped against the trunk of a birch tree, watching us. My breath caught. I couldn't breathe.

It was Martyn Robson.

There was no denying it. His face was familiar, yet broken all the same. He was staring at me so intensely I could feel hatred oozing from him in great waves of what I can only describe as festering regret. Regret for what, though, I didn't know. Maybe that he hadn't hurt me more when he'd had the chance, when Kevin England had held me down. Or maybe that I was still alive and he wasn't. Whatever the reason, his hate-filled bitterness was almost as tangible as the crunch of his nose beneath my fist. His lips were pulled back in a terrifying sneer and his skin was the colour of rancid chicken. One of his legs was on back to front, just like my dream. Only, this time I wasn't dreaming.

Lunhart Mohert, motherfucker, I heard him say, in my head. *The wolf did this to me. Now it's coming for you.*

Everything around me tilted by about twenty degrees and I thought I might pass out and fall to the floor. The knuckles on my right hand ached sharply with bone-deep pain. I scrunched my hand into a fist and winced.

Ginny gripped my arm. 'Sully, what's the matter? Are you alright?'

'Can you see him?'

'Who?' There was alarm in her voice and she followed my gaze. 'The wolf? Is it here?'

'No. I…Can't you see Robson?' When she didn't respond I looked at her and pointed to the birch. 'Right there.'

'Martyn Robson?' Ginny's brow crumpled. She shook her head. 'I can't see anyone.'

And neither could I. When I looked back to the birch, Robson had gone.

'Sully, seriously, are you feeling okay?'

'Not really.' My hands were shaking and I felt unsteady on my feet. 'Let's just get to the cundy,' I said, staggering away from the yew tree. 'We should head home soon, it's getting late.'

And it was. I needed to get back by the usual time at the very least. Or not at all. Which, lately, was becoming too much of a recurrent thought for me to ignore.

If I didn't go home though, where would I go?

The cundy?

Maybe.

As we drew close to the mouth of the tunnel, both of us, consciously or not, were unspeaking. Walking close together. Our arms almost touching. It seemed less of a game now to have come poking around. Not so much reckless fun as idiotic foolishness. Ginny was walking with less swagger. I guess my Martyn Robson episode had rattled her too, but not as much as it had me. If she'd thought I was weird before, I dreaded to think what she must think of me now. We both stopped walking and regarded the blackness of the cundy's innards from what we deemed to be a safe enough distance.

'Reckon it'll be in there?' Ginny whispered.

'I dunno.' I had no intuitive inkling either way. I rubbed my neck. I'd been bitten by a midge and could feel a small swelling forming. 'Do you know anything else about land spirits, by any chance? Like, what they want?'

'I doubt if anyone does,' she said.

A new collection of crushed lager cans had been scattered about at the entrance to the cundy. It seemed strange to me that Mad Bastard might have been back with his mates, doing whatever weird shit they did, given that his younger brother had killed himself just days ago not far from this very spot.

'Horrible bastards,' Ginny said, pointing to a nearby tree.

I couldn't have said it better myself. There was a dead cat nailed there. The kind of image that can never be unseen. My stomach roiled, hot and heavy. I hoped that the cat might have been road kill and brought here to be used as sick decoration. Because the alternative, that it had been brought here and murdered, was too much to bear. I felt sickened to my core that someone could commit such an atrocity to an animal, dead or alive. My head swelled with the glittering blackness of space. A place I imagined was safe and without people. A place where, suddenly, I wanted to be.

'Let's just go home,' I said.

'No, we're here now.' Ginny crept forward. 'People making sacrifices and offerings to gods and land spirits they don't understand is just plain stupid. They should be shot with shit and nailed to trees themselves. But they're not here, are they? And I wanna see the wolf.'

The term 'curiosity killed the cat' sprang to mind. I glanced over my shoulder at the cat on the tree. Someone's pet. Someone's heartache. Ginny disappeared into the darkness of the cundy. I slipped in behind her.

The black dankness accommodated us too well. Squinting into the distance, I found the grey swatch of daylight that marked the other end of the tunnel and was disappointed to see that no one waited for me there. In my head I heard Colton's voice: *I think Mam's in the cundy. Or at least, I think there's a passageway to get to her.*

My knuckles pounded in time to my racing heartbeat. Even though the darkness had fully absorbed us, I could sense Ginny's whiteness right there in front of me. It was like a bright light within. Not enough to instil a sense of ease, but there all the same. I was consumed by an idea that we were walking through some swirling dark threshold of death and that we were cursed, both of us, for having entered it. Just like Colton and England and Watson and Hake. Even Robson. All of us had been cursed by the land or whatever it was that didn't want us mooching in its dark spaces. This portal.

'I don't think it's here,' Ginny whispered.

Oh it's here alright, I wanted to tell her, but someone shoved me from behind and cold, dead fingers gripped my elbow, zinging the nerves and sending pain waves right down to my fingertips.

Yo, Zombie Carter, are you ready to join me now?

Martyn Robson.

Jolting forward, to escape those cold hands, I smacked into Ginny. Her hair was like a mass of cobwebs in my face.

'Whoa, what's wrong?' she said, spinning round. Her warm hands clutched at my bare arms, replacing Robson's deathly cold ones.

I was about to lie, to tell her that nothing was wrong, but then the cundy all around us echoed with a deep, resonant growl. The sound pitched me further into the void of nightmares. I could smell the old fusty stink of decomposed vegetation and stagnant water crawl all over me, as well as the musky scent of an animal.

Oh shit. Oh God. Oh fuck. It's here.

Dread rushed through me and I found myself rooted to

the spot, gripped in a state of total paralysis. Why was I even here? I'd promised myself that I'd stay away.

Ginny's hands tightened on my arms. 'Is that it?' she said. 'The wolf?' Her voice was shrill with panic and I remembered that she was the reason I was here.

There was another snarl. Closer this time. Louder. Released from my temporary immobility, my feet became unstuck and I began to edge backwards, pulling Ginny with me. A large, hulking shape augmented the blackness directly ahead of us.

It was coming.

The wolf was coming for us.

'Ah shit,' Ginny groaned, apparently not willing to try reasoning with the thing after all.

I pushed her behind me, to shield her with my body, and shuffled backwards, urging her to start moving more quickly. To go back the way we'd come, even if we were to bump into Robson on the way. Her fists bunched the fabric of my shirt tight about my waist and I could feel the rigidness of her fear extending from both hands. The blackness of the wolf loomed no more than ten feet away. It mirrored our movement, was even quicker maybe. I fancied I could make out its amber eyes, like the embers of a fire. I wondered if this time I'd lucked out. If this time I'd die. When it growled again, with a much deeper, throatier warning, I spun round and shoved Ginny.

'Run!' I cried. 'Go, go, go!'

I felt her slight body twirl beneath my hands and she bolted. Lightning fast. I ran after her, my legs pumping. I was right behind, running in her slipstream. When she splashed out into the daylight, her hair was a vivid trail of luscious colour. And I followed straight after. Was right on her heels. But then I felt something sharp tear through the flesh of my right arm – teeth or claws, I couldn't tell which.

Stumbling free from the cundy, I lost my footing and fell to the ground. I put my hands out and skidded to a stop. The sting of gravel rash ripped right up my arms to my shoulders, but I didn't much care. I rolled over onto my back and held my arms above my head in anticipation of the wolf landing on top of me. Teeth bared. Hackles raised. To end it all here. But it didn't. Instead, above the clamour of my own pulse and gasping breaths, I heard the sound of its claws retreat back into the depths of the cundy.

Ginny stooped to help me up, her hands clutching at my arms. Pulling.

'I saw it,' she said, panting. 'I saw it. Shit. I *saw* it.'

And I was totally sorry that she had.

Once I was on my feet, Ginny looked at her fingers and gasped. 'Bloody hell, Sully, you're bleeding loads.'

Lifting my arm, I inspected the wound. She was right. I touched the ragged, torn skin with cautious fingers.

Ginny's eyes met mine and she sucked in air. 'Shit, what do we do now?' she said. 'You've been bitten by the wolf.'

18

More Lies

I walked to the corner of Seventh Street with Ginny. An ice cream van hurtled along the main road just as we got there. Its *Pop Goes the Weasel* jingle was a grinding noise, more sinister than alluring. Like some ancient music box, the mechanism of which, no matter how much you wound it up, never kept the right speed and was therefore unsettling. Three girls of about six were walking down Cotsford Lane bank towards us, perhaps following the ice cream van. As they passed us, all of them fell into a hushed silence and stared at my bloodied arm.

'Will you be alright?' Ginny said to me.

'Yeah.' My arm had stopped bleeding and the blood was beginning to congeal. I thought it probably looked worse than it actually was. I just needed to clean it up.

Ginny gave my hand a quick squeeze. There was a fervour in her eyes which made me think she might kiss me again. But she didn't. She scurried off and I watched her lithe figure slip away from me. Light blue jeans emphasising her crazy-long legs and a white t-shirt which made her hair look redder than it was. She stopped at the alleyway that led to Hardwick Street and turned back.

'Good luck!' she said. 'Hope you don't get into too much trouble.'

'Same,' I said, with a wave. I turned and started to walk away, falling into step behind the three small girls who kept glancing over their shoulders to look at me. Maybe the blood on my hands, shirt and arm made them think I was a real zombie. I wondered if they'd run away screaming if I shouted *Brains!* It might have been an amusing idea had I not felt such dread about going home.

I stopped walking, hit by another thought. If I was destined to be miserable about almost everything else in life, then what the hell, I may as well be happy about something at least. Backtracking a few steps, I shouted, 'Hey, Ginny! Wait.'

I wasn't sure if she'd hear me, maybe I was too late. But moments later she reappeared at the alleyway in Seventh Street; her face was filled with all the concern of an unvoiced *what?*

Running towards her without dwelling on the implications or awkwardness or embarrassment of what I was about to do, I kissed her on the mouth. And she didn't object. I closed my eyes, while red clouds expanded and burst inside my skull in exciting blooms of scarlet and burgundy. Putting my hand on the back of her head, I held her close, ensuring this time we shared a longer, more meaningful kiss. My arm seared with the red pain of the wolf's bite as I held it aloft, but I didn't care. I was more aware of the blood inside my veins as my heart pumped it more vigorously around my entire body. Relishing the feel of Ginny's lips against mine and the tentative exploration of our tongues, I put my hand on her waist. The feel of her slender shape against my fingers and palm was mind-blowingly thrilling.

When we parted, Ginny looked at me glazed-eyed and

smiled. I think I must have been the happiest boy alive in that exact moment. I don't know where the subsequent cockiness came from, but I actually had the gall to wink at her and say, 'See you later, Ginny Longlegs.'

I walked away then, leaving her to stare after me. I tried my best to swagger, to look cool, when all I really wanted to do was dance. I felt as though I'd crossed over an obscure boundary, entering some threshold of adulthood from which I could never return. Not that I'd want to. I'd metamorphosed from being a gawky, shy boy to a courageous, decisive, more self-assured teen. I might have actually laughed aloud at this thought, I was getting way ahead of myself. But still, I did feel that I'd transitioned. Grown somewhat.

The few minutes it took to walk home was nowhere near as bad as it would have been if I hadn't kissed Ginny. She was the best distraction ever. The house was empty and quiet when I got there; so much so, I could hear the muffled drone of next door's television. I went straight to the bathroom and filled the wash basin with tepid water. Rubbing my hands together in it, I watched as the water turned rusty red. I thought about Martyn Robson. Had I really seen him at the dene? With his broken face and leg.

The wolf did this to me. Now it's coming for you.

I washed the caked blood off my right arm and inspected the bite wound with cautious fingers.

Shit.

It looked bad. Much worse than I'd thought. The underside of my face flashed cold. Would I need to show Dad?

Probably.

I doubted it could be fixed with Savlon and an Elastoplast. In fact, most likely it would need stitches. Pulling the plug, I began to run fresh water in the sink to soak some cotton wool. As I waited for the basin to fill, I was hit by a new thought: The wolf could have caught me and dragged me back into the cundy, so why hadn't it?

I had no idea.

Instinctively, I felt that it must have spared me for its own nefarious reasons. Like maybe it wasn't done toying with me yet. I certainly wasn't deluded enough to think it had let me off the hook.

I dabbed at the raw flesh of my arm with cotton wool and clamped my teeth together. The broken skin and exposed muscle stung with eye-watering sharpness, but a deeper, darker pain had begun to make my entire arm throb.

Lunhart Mohert, motherfucker.

Could the teeth of a land spirit cause an infection? And if so, was that what I could feel? Its badness in my bloodstream?

Would it make me go crazy?

Was I already?

The wolf did this to me. Now it's coming for you.

Once I'd cleaned the wound thoroughly, it looked strangely more disturbing. No longer masked by a superficial layer of dried blood, I could see the grisly extent of damage the wolf's teeth had caused. After such minimal effort on its part too. Was this just a taster of what was to come? Gripping the edge of the wash basin, I squeezed my eyes shut and screamed in my head.

Why the hell had I gone to the cundy again after I'd promised myself that I wouldn't?

Ginny.

Even though I knew it would be dangerous as hell, it was worth it for that first ever kiss.

Would I do it again if she asked me to?

Probably.

You have the strangest looking eyes, you know that, right?

Right.

You're so bloody weird.

I know. I can't help it.

My shirt was ruined with streaks of dried blood and I knew Dad would go mental, but a cunning idea had occurred to me. I could use the bite as an excuse for having skived out of school all afternoon.

Couldn't I?

Yes. Definitely.

My heart accelerated with some small amount of hope, which felt hopeless nonetheless and no doubt served to spread the wolf's badness further round my body. I imagined blackness clogging my veins and arteries. Since when had I become such a liar? I'd lied so much to Dad that week. And the fact it now came so easily to me was discomfiting.

Would one more lie harm in the grand scheme of things though?

Surely not. I was dealing with some messed up shit after all.

Liar, liar, pants on fire.

One more lie. That's it.

I glanced at the mirror and hardly recognised myself in it. I looked older. Not in any physical sense, but in some sort of spiritual way. I was more serious than I thought I'd ever caught myself looking before, perhaps wilier too. Probably because of all the lying and sneaking around I'd been doing while getting to grips with some ancient land spirit who took the form of a wolf and had made me aware that there was something indisputably supernatural going on within the dene. Something which bound life and death together.

I looked like a spirit myself. All pale and ill-looking. My eyes certainly didn't help the cause. Any less melanin would have made them white.

You have the strangest looking eyes, you know that,

right?

I went to the sitting room and sat on the couch like a doomed miscreant, waiting for Dad to come home. I could hear the sound of the Countdown clock through the wall, coming from next door's television. It seemed cruelly apt. Then Carol Vorderman laughing maniacally at something Richard Whiteley said. I heard Dad's car pull up then. He and Colton came into the house at the same time, which made me think Dad must have picked Colton up from school. Which, in turn, made me wonder why. This never happened usually. Yohden Primary School was a two-minute walk along the road, if that.

Dad looked full of hell. I suspected that on top of whatever Colton had done, he'd also received a call from Miss Mawn, my form tutor, telling him of my afternoon absence. My stomach wound itself into tight knots and my body tensed, ready for a verbal onslaught. But Dad's expression sort of slackened when he saw me sitting on the couch. I'm guessing my anaemic glow and bloodstained shirt must have caught him off guard.

'What the hell happened?' he said, stalking over to me, his face filled with what I can only describe as angry concern.

Colton sloped away from the unfolding of the next drama and sat on the bottom stair, watching with interest through the wooden spindles of the bannister.

Lifting my arm, I showed Dad my injury.

'Sorry,' I said, my eyes glazing over with genuine tears of remorse. It had all got too much. Everything spiralling out of control. 'I got bitten and came home. I didn't know what to do.'

The bollocking I'd imagined I was going to get dissipated in an instant and, again, Dad took on an abject look of despair.

'Bitten? How the hell did that happen?' he said. 'The school didn't tell me about that.'

'I popped out at dinner time.' I fiddled with my fingers in my lap. Kept my eyes downcast. 'To go to the shop.'

'You don't have any money,' Dad said matter-of-factly, like he'd already sniffed out the bullshit part of my story.

I shrugged, like it was no big deal. 'I found fifty pence in the yard,' I told him. Ugh. More lies. 'I thought I'd get a packet of crisps or a bottle of pop with it.'

He nodded *okay*. I was back on track with my bullshit story.

'I got chased by a dog on the village green. It was faster than me.' The lie made my insides ache and I hated myself for telling it. But I was in too much trouble and couldn't exactly tell Dad the truth about what was really going on. Hell, I didn't even know what was going on myself.

Dad grabbed my arm and stooped over to inspect it. As he did, his face turned ashen. 'Who did it belong to? And why on earth wasn't it on a leader?'

'I dunno.' I squirmed and tried to pull my arm away in case he might be able to detect that the marks hadn't been made by a dog's teeth after all. 'It was on its own. Probably a stray.'

'It must have been bloody big,' he said, still surveying the serrated edges of broken skin.

'Er, yeah.' I nodded. 'It was a bit.'

Dad bundled me and Colton into his car and we all went to see Dr Chandra, the family's GP. Dr Chandra cleaned the wound properly, then gave me a few stitches and a tetanus jab. If the old man suspected the bite wasn't off a dog, he didn't say. But then, I was being wholly paranoid about it anyway. It's not like Dr Chandra was a zoologist or anything. He was more astute with the diagnoses of water infections, sore throats and B12 deficiencies.

He said to keep a close eye on the wound and to go

back at the first sign of an infection because I might need a course of antibiotics. Then as he bound my forearm with a crisp, white bandage, he asked Dad if he might have a word with me alone. Dad seemed hesitant at first, but nodded then took Colton out into the waiting room.

'I notice your face is a bit bashed up,' Dr Chandra said, once we were alone. He'd finished securing the bandage with a clip, but kept hold of my arm. 'Is there anything you'd like to talk to me about?'

I shook my head. 'No.'

He breathed in slowly through his nose, making a whistling sound as he did, and continued to regard me with his melanin-rich brown eyes. 'How did it happen?'

'Some kids at school.'

'I see.' Pursing his lips, Dr Chandra nodded. 'Change the dressing tomorrow,' he said, handing me a spare roll of bandage. 'Keep it clean.'

'Okay.' I stood up to leave.

'And you know where I am, Sullivan. Should you need to talk.'

'Er, yeah. Cheers.'

When we got home, Dad went over to the couch and flopped down on it. He rested his head against the back cushion and closed his eyes.

Unsure whether to disturb him or not, I decided I couldn't leave things as they were. I walked over and stood before him and said, 'Sorry, Dad.'

His eyes cracked open and he regarded me for a few uneasy moments. Then he wafted a hand, like he didn't want to hear it.

'I mean, for everything,' I persisted. 'I'm sorry about everything that's happened lately.' And I truly was.

Dad remained silent for a while and I didn't think he'd respond, but then he sat forward and tipped his head at me in acknowledgement, as though this time he did accept my apology.

'You're going to your Aunt Julie's on Sunday,' he said, wearily. Then, signalling to Colton who was sitting on the bottom stair, pretending to read, he added, 'So the pair of you better get some stuff packed together to take with you.'

'How long will we be there for?' I asked.

'All of the holidays.'

'Till *September?*' Colton cried. 'That's not fair!' He jumped to his feet and stomped up the stairs, as if he thought throwing a paddy might dissuade Dad.

I simply nodded, willing to accept the punishment. I doubted I could have felt any more miserable anyway, so what difference would a six-week stint at Aunt Julie's make? Besides, being at Aunt Julie's would mean that I'd be far away from the cundy. Was it possible that the wolf might forget about me?

'Tea'll be ready soon,' Dad said, edging forward on the couch. He looked old again that day, I noted. Tired and fraught. 'Go and tell Colton to get his arse back down here and set the table.'

I went upstairs and let myself into Colton's room without knocking. I expected him to kick off, but he didn't. He was lying on his bed looking up at the starry constellations Mam had painted on the ceiling.

'Dad wants you to set the table,' I said.

He grunted some response, but made no effort to get up.

Slipping into the room, I closed the door behind me. 'Did you bunk off school today, shit stain?'

This time he turned his head and looked at me. 'No.'

'So why did Dad pick you up from school?'

'I got detention.'

'What for?'

'Stabbing Ruben Baker in the arm with a compass.'

I wasn't sure I wanted to know why, so I didn't bother asking.

Colton kept looking at me, his dark eyes brewing a storm. 'You went to the cundy today, didn't you?' he said.

Shit.

He was looking at my arm and I knew that he knew damn well what had bitten me. I saw no point in lying. I sat on the edge of his bed and said, 'Yeah. I saw the wolf the other night. The thing from the cundy. It came here. It was right outside the house. It knows where we live.' The wound beneath the dressing on my arm throbbed with a bone-deep ache which tormented all the nerve endings from my fingertips to my elbow. I held up my arm, to help drive the message home. 'It wants to hurt us, Colton. So you need to stay away from the cundy, alright?'

'It's guarding the passageway inside, that's all,' he said. 'Can't you see?'

'If it's guarding something, why did it leave its station to come here?'

'Because it knows that we know. It's scared.'

'Scared of what?'

'I dunno.' Colton looked thoughtful. He looked back up at the ceiling. 'That we'll find Mam?'

'Why would it care?'

'How should I know? You should have tried talking to it.'

Jesus. He sounded like Ginny.

'Are you nuts? Look what it did to me.' I showed him my bandaged arm again.

'Stop being a baby.'

'A baby?' I couldn't believe his nerve. 'I doubt I'd be standing here right now if I'd hung around any longer to try talking to it, you goon. Do you realise how bad it could have been?'

'That's because you're scared of it. And it knows.'

'What's that supposed to mean?'

'If you show an animal that you're scared of it, it goes a bit funny. That's why the wolf acts badly around you. It feeds off your fear.'

'Are you a dog whisperer now or something?'

'It would listen to me,' he chided. 'I'm not scared of it.'

'Well you bloody well should be.'

Colton looked at me again and raised his eyebrows. I could tell he was being obstinate.

'Don't you dare go back down there, mind,' I warned him. 'I mean it. Don't you flipping dare.'

'You can't tell me what to do.'

'Yes I can and I'm warning you, you'd better not.'

'Else what?'

'I'll tell Dad.'

Colton gasped and his face crumpled into a scowl. 'You wouldn't dare.'

'Yes I would.'

'Then you're a bloody big grass.'

This time I gasped. 'No I'm not!' I felt like hitting him, so much so it took all of my effort not to. Instead, I pointed a finger in his face and said, 'I've been covering your arse this whole frigging time. I took the rap the other day for you taking Mam's bracelet, so don't you *dare* say that I'm a grass or that I don't care.'

Colton huffed loudly and his face remained sullen, but I could tell he knew that he'd spoken out of turn.

'I mean it,' I said. 'Stay the hell away from there. Nothing good can ever come of it. It's way bigger than we can handle.'

'But you can't tell me to stay away,' he argued. 'Not when Mam's there.'

'No, Colton, she's not.' I threw both of my arms in the air. 'Mam's not there! She's not anywhere anymore. She's gone. Alright?'

The bedroom door nudged opened a fraction and I

jumped when I saw Dad's head poke round.

'Colton,' he said, his expression unreadable. 'Get down them bloody stairs and get the table set. Now.'

Colton grumbled, but slid off the bed and sloped his way towards the stairs. Dad followed him, but I stayed where I was, sitting on the bed, wondering how long Dad had been standing behind the door.

How much had he heard?

19

Gone

Dad seethed quietly all through tea. It was impossible to tell what he was thinking. There was no television on in the background which was unusual, and it was as though next door had switched theirs off in order to let us stew in their silence too. Every scrape of my knife against my plate and my chewing and swallowing of every mouthful of food seemed uncomfortably loud. I imagined if it was any quieter in the house my thoughts would be audible to everyone.

When we'd all finished eating, nobody moved. Everyone just sat there, awkward. My arm felt like it was on fire beneath the bandage dressing. I wouldn't have been at all surprised to see blood seeping through the white. But there was none. I figured Dr Chandra's stitches must be holding it all together well.

'You two had better start packing your gear together,' Dad said, breaking the silence at last.

'But why do we have to go to Aunt Julie's on Sunday?' Colton whined.

I groaned inwardly. Was he purposefully baiting for an argument?

'Because I said.'

'But you don't work on Sundays,' Colton persisted. 'Why can't we stay here till Monday?'

Dad glared at him.

Colton glared back.

The air of brooding that already existed in the room intensified. Colton, for whatever reason, was pitching his dark side of the moon against Dad's. I had no doubt that Dad's was way darker. In fact, in that moment Dad looked like the embodiment of murder itself. He breathed in deeply, then said through tight lips, 'I'll send you on Saturday if you don't stop whinging.'

'But I don't wanna go on Sunday,' Colton said. All he ever did was add fuel to the fire of any argument lately. He just didn't know when to quit.

Frowning at him across the table, wishing he'd just be quiet, I said, 'Don't be such a dick, Colton.'

Sucking in air to create a dramatic gasp, he cried, 'Dad, he just called me a dick.'

Dad reached out and cuffed us both across the back of the head. 'Get up them stairs, the pair of you. Out of my bloody sight.'

I glowered at Colton. He glowered back.

Instead of going upstairs, I cleared the table and took it upon myself to do the washing up without having been asked. Dad acknowledged my good deed with a nod of his head and I felt in some miniscule way that I was on the right track to mending what had been damaged between us. All I had to do was grin and bear the six-week stint at Aunt Julie's.

What doesn't kill you makes you stronger, right?

The only thing I was overly sad about leaving behind now was Ginny. How could I go all summer without seeing her?

Maybe I could escape on my bike every now and then. Ride to to Horden via Peterlee. It'd probably take less than an hour, I reckoned. I could meet up with her at least once a week. Yes, that could work, I thought. There was something bitter sweet about the idea. Something rebelliously exciting.

I went up to my room and lay on my bed, exhausted by what had turned out to be a more adventurous day than I'd hoped. My arm pulsated with persistent soreness and memories of the wolf's attack and the spirit of Martyn Robson haunted me.

Was I going crazy? Or had I already lost my marbles?

The vision of Martyn Robson could have been a stress-induced temporary glitch, right?

Right.

I had a lot on my plate after all. And besides, Ginny had kissed me just moments before. I'd been in a real tizz.

Also, there was still a very real possibility that the wolf was nothing but a stray dog – a massive one at that, but a dog all the same. The fact that it had turned up outside the house could be a massive coincidence. Hell, how did I even know it was the same animal? I'd never seen the one inside the cundy in order to identify it. So yes, it could absolutely be a vicious stray dog.

And yet, I knew I was lying to myself.

That hellhound in the cundy was no stray dog. The way it smelt. The way its eyes burnt through the dark like pieces of molten rock. The way it had tracked me down. Because just as I knew that Colton was my little brother, I *knew* that the wolf on the yard wall had been the very same creature that resided in the cundy.

So, back to Martyn Robson.

Had I really seen him?

I felt physically sick with dread at the possibility. If I wasn't mad already, I was sure I'd soon make myself so.

I thought about Ginny. The smell of her. The feel of her. If I hadn't pushed her behind me in the cundy, the wolf would have attacked her instead. Strangely, this made me feel as though I'd won some sort of victory against the wolf. In my dream it had stood between me and her, but in reality I'd won. My wound suddenly seemed like a badge of honour. A medal of bravery for having protected the girl with whom I was infatuated.

After lots of ruminating, I got up and collected together some clothes and books; the stuff I planned to take with me to Aunt Julie's house. Then I went downstairs to take an ibuprofen with a glass of tap water, to try and control any swelling and pain I might have during the night. I found Dad on the couch in front of the telly. In his hand, he was nursing an exceptionally large measure of whisky in a glass tumbler. It wasn't typical for Dad to drink alcohol, especially not on a week night. When he was in a good mood he'd sometimes have the odd can of lager or beer, but spirits were never a good sign. The last time I'd seen him on the spirits was right after Mam had died.

Some bloke whose eyebrows didn't coordinate with his hair was on telly rambling on about European governments banning British beef because of the whole Mad Cow Disease outbreak. Apparently anyone who eat the infected flesh was at risk of contracting the disease. No wonder Dad looked depressed. It was like some sort of B-movie in the making. According to kids at school, the cows with Mad Cow Disease, also known as BSE, had developed the disease when the meat from other cows had been put into their feed. Since it's totally unnatural for herbivores to eat meat, let alone that of their own kind, these cannibalistic cows got sick. Mad Cow Disease has a long incubation period, so no one realised the cows were sick till after they'd already been put into the food chain and...ugh, you can guess the rest. It was a sick business. One that saw most meat-eating households in the UK swapping beef burgers for lamb or pork burgers and making their lasagne with turkey mince.

'Do they know when it'll be safe to eat beef burgers again?' I asked.

Dad's eyes didn't leave the television screen. 'Nah, not yet.'

I noticed a bottle of whisky on the coffee table next to him. This was especially bad, I thought. Tonight he meant business. I also suspected that that was about the extent of the conversation I was going to get from him, so I turned and made my way back upstairs.

'Sullivan,' he called after me.

Sullivan. So, I was still in the bad books.

I looked over the bannister and across the living room at him. He took a mouthful of whisky and asked, 'How's your arm doing?'

It was still hurting and sore, but I told him, 'Alright.'

'Good. I'll take a look at it tomorrow.' His eyes were back on the telly. 'Help you redress it.'

Upstairs I got ready for bed and drew my curtains tight against the night, so there was no chance I could see out or the wolf could see in. Then I lay awake wondering how long my arm would take to heal, if it would scar and what I'd do if I was to turn into a werewolf at the next full moon. I had no idea what stage the moon was at in its cycle right now. For all I knew a full moon might be imminent.

You of all people should know, Moon Boy.

I almost laughed out loud.

Yeah well, maybe me and the moon aren't so closely aligned after all, because I bloody well don't.

I fell asleep and awoke some time later to find a chill breeze sweeping through my room. Confused, I sat up and saw that my curtains were billowing inwards. Beyond them the window had been thrown open wide.

Shit!

Scrabbling out of bed, I raced to the window to pull it

shut. Outside, the street was quiet and still, basking in the dusky orange glow from the streetlights at either end. The moon was on its back; a glowing, drowsy eye, hardly paying attention. But I was, I was wide awake, and I could see that there was no wolf. Not in plain sight anyhow. I scanned the street, up and down, several times. Just to be sure. Even watched the dark spaces in our yard and next door's for a minute or two to make sure none of them moved.

When I turned to go back to my bed, my heart almost stopped. The wall above the headboard was hideously bare. Mocking me with its utter starkness.

The dreamcatcher was gone.

I knew right then, could feel it in my core, that something else was in the room with me. Something that had escaped from the hellish realms of dreamscape. As if in answer to this realisation, a floorboard creaked somewhere off to my left. I didn't dare look. Needed to swallow. Couldn't.

I waited.

And waited.

My breathing was quick and shallow, my heartbeat fast and loud.

The floorboards shifted again.

Creeeak.

Creeeak.

Out of the corner of my eye I saw a dark figure looming.

A woman.

Edith.

Oh God.

I closed my eyes and took deep breaths.

1...2...3...4...5...6...7...8...9...10

Slowly, slowly, I turned my head and cracked open my eyes.

And she was right there. Next to me. A black

silhouette. Right there. Next to me. Folds of fabric like bat wings. I could barely catch my breath. Felt my knees buckle. Started to fall. But then her hands were on my upper arms. Holding me upright. Blackness blustered behind my eyes as I begged unconsciousness to take me into its kind oblivion. That she might not follow me there.

'Sully, sweetheart,' she said. 'You have to listen.'

Mam?

The black bluster behind my eyes dissipated in an instant, but my legs still felt weak. Her face came into focus, right in front of me. She held onto me, her fingers tight on my arms. Even in the gloom, in the fuzzy greyscale hues, I could see her clearly.

Mam.

A black-garbed angel.

'The dreamcatcher won't always protect you,' she said. 'It was just a temporary measure, till you're old enough to deal with things yourself.'

'But I'm not old enough yet,' I whimpered.

'You have to be.' She kissed me on the forehead then bundled me into her arms. She was warm. Soft. Very much there. Her skin smelt of freesias and jasmine, which made my eyes fill with tears. I'd missed her so much.

'I always knew you were different, Moon Boy,' she said, her soft yet husky voice like warm milk and cookies. 'You just have to realise it yourself.'

There was a sharp crack on the window pane. Turning my head, I saw a crow sitting on the sill outside. Its black feathers gleamed like oil in the moonlight.

Caw-caw-caw, it said. *Lunhart Mohert.*

'What does that mean?' I asked.

Mam took hold of my chin with her soft, warm fingers and turned my head so I was looking at her again. 'What does what mean, son?'

'Lunhart Mohert.'

She smiled; a sad smile that was filled with both love and concern. 'It doesn't mean a thing.'

'But it must.'

'It doesn't. You're too sensitive, Sully. Your subconscious fills in the blanks sometimes and it isn't always right.'

I felt dejected about this.

'Was Colton right?' I said. 'Should I have listened to him? Are you in the cundy?'

Mam shook her head, her smile turning to a frown. 'No, sweetheart, I'm not in the cundy. It's the wolf that calls to Colton. It beckons to you too.'

'What does it want?'

'For you to go to it.'

'And should I?'

'I don't think you have a choice.' Mam kissed my forehead again, her lips lingering there for a while as she breathed in the smell of my hair. 'You need to wake up.'

'But I am awake.'

'No, you aren't.' She cupped my face with her hands. Her own face glistened with tears. Her eyes were steely, despite her sadness. 'Wake up, Sully. Wake up now. Colton needs you.'

Jolting upwards, I gasped for breath. Disoriented, I looked about.

I was in bed.

The curtains were pulled tight across the window, I saw. And the dreamcatcher was hanging above my headboard.

Mam was nowhere to be seen.

I felt sad and confused and I wanted to cry because of a renewed sense of grief that cut through my heart like a length of razor wire, but Mam's last words made my blood run cold.

Wake up, Sully. Wake up now. Colton needs you.

Scrabbling out of bed I picked yesterday's clothes off the floor and pulled them on, feeling certain that I'd need to be dressed for whatever came next.

It's the wolf that calls to Colton. It beckons to you too.

I dashed out onto the landing and along to Colton's room. His bed was a crumpled mess. Alarmingly empty, as I'd expected.

Ah no, Colton. Please no.

I went to the bathroom, hoping he would be using the loo, but he wasn't. The bathroom was empty. Next I pushed open the door to Dad's room and peered inside. The bed was still made up. Unslept in.

Fuck.

What the hell was going on? Was I still dreaming? In the midst of a nightmare?

Standing on the landing, my bare feet grinding into the carpet, I said, 'Mam?'

I held my breath and waited. Listened to my heart crashing. Imagined my blood racing. Felt my injured arm pulsing. When there was no answer, I sprinted downstairs, using the banister as leverage to get me to the bottom quicker. Dad was on the couch. Passed out in a whisky stupor. I checked in the kitchen, Colton wasn't there.

No, no, no!

That was it then. I knew where he was. Where he'd gone.

'Dad!' I cried, before I could stop myself.

Dad murmured, roused from his inebriated sleep. But I already knew he wasn't in any fit state to help, to deal with a crisis of any kind. I mean, Jesus, it looked like he'd polished off over half a litre of whisky. And to an occasional drinker that was absolutely shit loads.

I went to the cupboard under the stairs to get his spotlight torch, but found that it had already been taken.

Shit, Colton, you stubborn little bastard, why couldn't

you just leave it alone?

Grabbing my jacket from the peg behind the cupboard door, I thrust my feet into my trainers and ran to the front door.

'Sully?' Dad sat up, rubbing his face. In the glow of the television's no-signal fizz he looked like a drunken vagrant. His clothes dishevelled, his hair sticking out at all angles. 'Wha' yer doin'?'

'Colton's gone,' I said, my voice surprisingly calm. I opened the door. Fresh air flooded in. This or my admission seemed to sober Dad up somewhat. He rocked forward and swung his feet to the floor. His eyes were a little more alert, but he lacked overall clarity.

'What?'

'He's gone,' I repeated. I wanted to tell him everything. Wanted more than anything to unload every single thing that had happened since the day Kevin England and his mates had chased us through the dene. But it didn't seem right. Dad was drunk. And I didn't have time. I had to go now. Mam had said so.

Wake up, Sully. Wake up now. Colton needs you.

'Where're you going?' Dad said, staggering to his feet. He stood there swaying on the Chinese rug, as unsteady as a toddler. 'Where's Colton? What d'you mean he's gone?'

'I can't explain, Dad. I need to go and get him. *Now.*'

'Where?'

'The cundy.'

I could see the confusion on his face as he tried to comprehend what I'd said. 'The cun…?'

But I didn't have time. 'I have to go, Dad. I'll fetch him back. I promise.' I rushed out and slammed the door shut behind me and I swear I could hear him calling to me even when I got to the coast road. But I wouldn't go back. I couldn't. The cundy called even louder. I had to get my kid brother back.

I ran as fast as I could. Perhaps fuelled by the light of the moon, which was my only illumination once I'd passed the last of the streetlights on the coast road. Even when I swung through the kissing gate and entered the dene, it peeked between branches, picking out the path enough to show me the way. The dene was a terrifying place at night. There was so much darkness. So many creeping sounds all about. Less than twenty-four hours ago I'd been on the same path, receiving my very first kiss. Now I was plunging headfirst into a nightmare of black arts, faceless voices, land spirits and headless animals. By the time I reached Yggdrasil I had accepted with some sort of instinct that after this night things would never be the same again.

Part of me wondered if I'd even live to see tomorrow.

The odds were stacked against me.

20

The Wolf

I wound my way further and deeper into the dene. Listening. Creeping. The whole place was alive with obscure sounds and smells which seemed to be amplified by the darkness. The moon highlighted the viaduct as a ghostly black leviathan, which towered above the trees like an inescapable nightmare. I imagined Martyn Robson just a few nights ago, standing at the very top of it and looking down on everything. I wondered if he was up there watching me now, or if he was lurking in the trees, tracking my progress.

A scream rang out, sudden and shrill, ripping through the dene's valley like a banshee's wail. I froze to the spot. My heart hammered wildly.

Colton?

No. It had sounded more like a woman. Only, somehow not. Were Mad Bastard and his mates at the cundy, I wondered.

Doing what though?

Torturing someone? Murdering his girlfriend? Sacrificing virgins?

Bloody hell, I hoped not.

Thankfully, logic overrode the terror of my

imagination and I soon decided that it had been a vixen's cry. That was all. A vixen calling out to a mate or her young or whatever it is they get particularly vocal about. She certainly wasn't taunting me.

I carried on walking, sticking to the vague path the moon had picked out for me. My nerves were wound tight. I wished I could close my eyes and wake up in bed. Was this even happening? I was so tense, my shoulders were hunched and the muscles in my arms were aching.

There'd been no rain in days, so the beck was dry and there was no shushing of water channelling towards the beach. I wasn't sure if I could hear the sea's surf in the distance. If I could, it was mostly drowned out by the treetops overhead. There was a constant swishing as the wind ruffled them. Pipistrelle bats dipped and dived all around me, almost too quick to notice, like black floaters in my eyes.

An owl hooted somewhere close by. It was a lonely sound that went unanswered.

As I neared the cundy I realised I couldn't hear any sign of Mad Bastard and his friends. Which could only be a good thing.

A good thing?

I almost laughed. Could any of this be good?

When I came to the clearing, with the cundy straight ahead, the moon's light was more prevalent. This would have been slightly comforting, if not for the fact that I could see the tunnel's mouth gaping at me with all of its deep blackness. My heart sank. There was no torchlight, not that I could see, and the idea of walking into all of that blackness, blackness which forbade daylight never mind pallid moonlight, made my innards tighten and ache.

Would the wolf be waiting inside to finish off what it had started the day before?

A bolt of agony ripped up my arm, a painful reminder of what it had done, making me wince. I crept forward, gaining a better view of the area in front of the cundy, and as I did, my insides relaxed in a flourish of relief. I could see a small figure.

Colton!

He was sitting on the concrete ridge, dangling his feet into the dried up water conduit. I was about to call his name, to tell him to 'get your arse over here', but then I heard him speak.

'I wish you could show me how to do it,' he said, to no one I was able to see.

'Do what?' I asked, edging up behind him.

Colton jumped and swivelled round to look at me. His face flashed with angered embarrassment, as though I'd just caught him talking to Fluffy Lugs his teddy bear. 'What are you doing here?'

'I could ask you the same bloody thing.' I grabbed a fistful of his jacket, ready to yank him to his feet. But as I did so, an almighty growl emanated from the mouth of the cundy. When I looked, I could see two burning eyes within the black. My limbs slackened. If I'd had a full bladder I imagine I'd have wet myself.

'Get off me,' Colton said, shrugging away from my loosened grip, totally unfazed, it would seem, by the wolf.

'We need to go,' I told him, my voice tiny and quivery. I was under no illusion that I could escape the wolf a third time. Even its smell pervaded the air all around us. It was here. Oh God, it was here.

'No,' Colton said, sulkily. 'I'm staying. I want to talk to Mam.'

'Mam's not here.'

'Stop saying that!' He swung round and punched me on the arm.

The wolf snarled; a rich diesel engine sound.

Oh Hell.

This was insane. I wanted to scream. I wanted to cry. I wanted to sit down and admit defeat and let it tear me to shreds because I was all out of fight.

'This isn't a game,' I said, in an urgent whisper. 'That thing's really dangerous. And Mam's not in there.'

The wolf skulked out of its lair. The fur on its gargantuan body was purer than the purest of black and, as the low rumble of threat continued to issue from its throat, it bared its white teeth. Hungry for more violence. It regarded me as though I was its only prize.

'Tell it to back off,' I said, suddenly convinced that Colton could do that if he really wanted to.

Colton clicked his tongue in disdain. 'Tell it to back off yourself.'

'It doesn't like me.'

'Sometimes you're as thick as pig shit, Sully.' He shook his head and huffed.

'What's that supposed to mean?' Had he been right when he'd said that I was showing too much fear? Was that why the wolf was homing in on me?

As if reflecting these thoughts, Colton said, 'I already told you, stop being scared. Just talk to it.'

'Talk to it? About what? It's a *wolf!*'

The wolf lunged forward then, as if to validate this major detail. Its teeth snapped together beneath a furrowed snout and I felt as though its raging eyes might burn a hole in my soul. Colton shuffled his legs round and climbed to his feet. I watched, dumbstruck, as he walked over to the wolf, so casually, so blasé, and touched it. The beast dwarfed him in overall size, to the extent that I felt physically sick. Within seconds he might be dead, I thought. Because if the wolf wanted to, it could kill him in a heartbeat. Thankfully, however, it didn't react at all to the contact; it just stood there, allowing itself to be stroked. Colton's fingers entwined

227

in the coarse, wiry fur of its shoulder and he used gentle, repetitive patting motions, as if to placate it. The wolf looked no less riled by my presence though.

'It's going to kill me,' I said.

Colton's face was white and gravely serious in the moonlight. He seemed to consider this for a moment, then said, 'You need to chill out.'

Chill out?

I felt like I was in a bad dream. That my kid brother, who I'd always stood by and stuck up for, was turning against me. Teaming with the beast from the cundy. I felt like he had some mutual understanding with it, yet he was going to stand by and let it tear me to pieces.

'Why are you doing this?' I said, close to tears.

'*I'm* not doing anything.'

The wolf moved forward, closing the gap between us.

'Just stroke it,' Colton urged. 'Stop being such a chicken and make friends.'

Make friends?

'But…what is it?' I said, my mouth completely dry. 'Do you even know?'

The wolf's head was held low, but if it was standing tall I guessed it would be at chest height to me. On hind legs, I reckoned it'd be way taller than six feet. It was a wonder its jaws hadn't ripped my entire arm off the day before.

'Touch it and see for yourself,' Colton urged. 'Just do it.'

I raised my trembling right arm. The wound pulsed. This was it. Do or die. I had no choice. I couldn't outrun this thing. All I could do was follow the advice of my kid brother.

Make friends.

I edged forward. Swallowed hard. Kept my eyes on the beast as my hand got closer to it. Its eyes were blazing, its teeth were still bared. Somewhere deep in its throat, the lowest of growls grumbled like distant thunder.

I'm not scared. I'm not scared.

Oh God, oh God.

I'm not scared.

I was beginning to hyperventilate. Would it be a quick and relatively pain-free death? Or slow and excruciating?

Time to find out.

As soon as my fingers grazed the fur on the wolf's neck, everything happened so fast. The contact jolted my arm as though I'd been struck by lightning and the wolf lashed out, grabbing my arm between its jaws. Then it pulled me, easily, too easily, into the cundy. Into the dark. Where its claws raked my face and its teeth savaged both of my arms as I fought it.

I screamed.

It hurt.

Oh God, it hurt.

And I fought and fought, lashing out with my fists and kicking with my feet. I could hear Colton's frantic voice, somewhere close, yet miles away, shouting, 'Don't fight it, Sully. Don't fight it.'

How could I even hope to? The idea of fighting this colossal beast was ludicrous. What was the point? I fell still and lay there and waited for death. Tried to zone out from the attack. But then it all stopped. As quickly as it had started, the wolf stopped biting and the blacker-than-the-cundy blackness of it dispersed all around me as though it had combusted into a cloud of ash.

Then death did come to me.

I saw it in the darkness, which was no longer black. More of a murk. All of the lost souls from the dene were right there, lined up along the tunnel. Drawn to me out of curiosity? Or to collect me into their midst?

Martyn Robson was amongst them, his face broken beneath a scowl.

Sully. Sully. Sullivan. Sully.

All of the dead began to chant my name.

Was I supposed to join them? To become part of their forsaken army?

No. I didn't want to.

A man from the deadly line-up stepped forward. He was reedy and grisly, his neck positioned at a funny angle. Dark hair was plastered to his head in a waxy non-style.

'Go back, son,' he said, gesturing with a long bony finger to the night beyond the cundy. 'You don't belong here.'

I made no attempt to go anywhere though. I just lay there hurting and bleeding. Clutching my arms to my torso. My breathing was laboured. I didn't know what to say.

'No, you don't belong here. So get out, you nosy little bastard!' a woman's shrill voice cried. There was jostling amongst the dead spectators, then a thickset woman barged her way to the front of the line-up. She was too young to be old; her curly hair was dark and without grey and there was a litheness about her joints which denied agedness. But she was too old to be young; her clothes were much too old fashioned and her mouth was displaying too many lines. Her eyes, in deep, dark sockets, were wide and glared with madness. She looked as unhinged as any notorious serial killer. Rushing over, she booted me in the side with the toe of her sturdy slip-on shoes. I think I heard ribs crack.

'Go on, fuck off!' she shouted.

From out of nowhere, the wolf reappeared. It roared and sent the woman flailing backwards against the tunnel wall. She held her arms above her head and cowered low.

Gasping for air, I clutched my side, in danger of slipping into the solid black that flittered behind my eyes. The wolf stood over me, as if to guard me from any other assailants.

Beyond fearing what it might do to me next – because why should I care? It may as well finish me off – I said, 'What are you?'

I expected some ancient words in mind-speak, about land spirits and pagan gods and the dene's glacial creation. But that didn't happen. Instead, the wolf merely looked at me and I saw the beginnings of truth in the pits of its fiery eyes.

You need to wake up.

You need to wake up.

You need to wake up!

Mam's voice was stuck on a loop in my head and only now did I begin to understand the true meaning of her words. It wasn't just the dream she'd urged me to wake from, it was real life. She wanted me to wake up and see how things really were. She wanted me to open my eyes, really to *see* what was going on. And the wolf's eyes, with their orange, burning intensity, did just that. Like a bolt of lightning through my senses, the wolf jolted me awake and suddenly I could see everything.

It's the wolf that calls to Colton. It beckons to you too.

What does it want?

For you to go to it.

And should I?

I don't think you have a choice.

And I didn't, I realised that now. This was how it had to be. It made absolutely no sense, yet at the same time it totally did. The wolf's eyes burned brightly, confirming all I'd tried to deny. Relaying the truth; the absolute truth.

It was a mind-blowing revelation.

The wolf, it was me.

Or at least, part of me. Driven by my own angst and despair, the amalgamation of fear and grief had reached an unprecedented pinnacle that day in the cundy when Kevin England and his friends had chased me and Colton. Part of my very own spirit had detached itself from me; some darker, primitive aspect. Which is why Colton realised before I did that the wolf wasn't a threat. He saw in it something familiar. Something protective.

Something…Me.

I clutched my bleeding arms tighter to myself. I was cold. Very cold. The concrete of the cundy beneath me was draining all of my heat. Taking it into itself. My lips trembled. I was close to death. This was how it felt, I thought, to leave life behind. I'd arrived at some enlightenment and none of it made much sense beyond my own newfound self-awareness. I felt surprisingly calm, yet scared out of my wits.

That the wolf had attacked me could only mean that I'd attacked myself. The darker part of me had scared me so much that I'd seen it as a threat. It was all of the badness in me that I hadn't known what to do with. The teeth and claw marks all over my face and body were existential proof of my inner torment. I'd been self-harming for too long, I realised, in an emotional sense. Always making sure everyone else was okay and sacrificing my own happiness. So when I'd attacked myself, so strong was my angst, actual blood had been spilled.

But why had this aspect of me taken on the image of a wolf?

I didn't know.

It was all of the things I was afraid of. That is, all the things I didn't think I could be. Ferocious. Savage. Cunning. Deceptive. Perhaps my subconscious made it that way because of my link with the moon; the wolf being some sort of werewolf. The rogue, untameable part of me. Maybe the wolf charm on Mam's bracelet had lent a subliminal hand in shaping its appearance, or perhaps it was representative of the black dog of depression. It could be that it was symbolic of all of those things. Maybe none.

I didn't know.

I had to consider that Mam had been right all along though. That I had the ability to see through the night sky and into the beyond, because certainly that night I was afforded my very first glimpse into the world of the dead.

And Colton, somehow he knew that I was capable of this.

He was born when the stars were aligned just right for him.

Brotherly intuition? Our water signs swimming the same stretch of sea?

Yes. Perhaps he knew me better than I knew myself.

I felt his small hands on me, his fingers hooking beneath my armpits. He heaved and dragged me out of the cundy, till I was bathed in the soft glow of the moon. The very same moon that had stolen the daylight away at the exact moment I was born. The very same moon that had put extra light in my eyes.

It beckoned to me now.

'Did you see her?' Colton asked.

I knew he meant Mam. I shook my head. Was beyond words. I was hurting and bleeding. Quite possibly dying. My open wounds leaked. My clothes were torn and saturated with the life seeping out of me. I imagined my blood was being drunk by the floor of the dene to feed whatever land spirit might exist there.

Not the wolf though. The wolf was no part of the dene. It belonged in the darkness of the cundy, that was all. And within the darkness of myself. I felt consciousness slipping away from me and wished Mam would come. I needed her arms to soothe me. I needed her wise words to encourage me. She knew all along what I was capable of.

But I'm not old enough yet.

You have to be.

No matter what, she'd always believed in me.

Martyn Robson walked out of the tunnel. Apart from his deathly pale complexion, he looked normal. His face and body weren't broken, except maybe his nose where I'd punched him. Panic stirred as a new thought occurred to me: had the wolf driven Martyn Robson to Gregory's Leap? Had it hunted him down and made him so afraid that he'd thought he had no other choice?

Had *I* killed Robson?

Me?

Oh God.

And was that the reason for my persistent guilt?

'Why did you do it?' I said, as the ghostly figure of Robson stepped over my broken body.

Robson carried on walking, up the embankment, in the direction of the viaduct. I wasn't sure if he'd answer, but he stopped and turned to look at me. Shrugging, he said, 'None of your business, Carter.'

'But…was it the wolf?' I had to know.

'Nah.' Robson shook his head and spat on the floor. 'Couldn't stand the bullshit at home no more. But I'm sure you'll read all about it in the papers soon enough. Nothing like a family scandal, eh?' He started walking again. 'Oh and I was going to return the bracelet you dropped.' He turned and winked at me. 'Honest. Now fuck off out of here, you loser. You're not hanging around with me.'

Selfish relief fell on me in a shroud of black comfort. I closed my eyes.

Colton gripped my shoulders. 'Sully, get up!' He shook me hard, shaking me fully awake. 'Don't go to sleep. Don't! You can't! Don't don't don't. We have to go. Please get up. Get up. *Please!*'

But I couldn't. I hurt too much. Inside and out. The wolf stood at the entrance to the cundy, guarding its portal between life and death. Its orange eyes burnt with decadent knowledge. It regarded me coolly and I wasn't sure if we'd ever *make friends*.

I closed my eyes again, willing to let the darkness take me down into the Earth's soil or up into the night sky.

The beginning of oblivion was interrupted by the sound of Dad's voice though. 'Sully? Colton!'

And I knew then that everything would be alright.

21

The Beginning

I woke up with bright light all around and Dad's sallow, stubbly face right next to me. I would have asked where we were, but I knew already. Nowhere but a hospital has that particular fusion of nauseous smells: disinfectant, bodily emissions and bad food. A quick mental assessment was all it took for me to gather that my body ached in ways I hadn't known was possible. Both arms were bound in bandages and my face was so swollen and sore, my right eye was almost shut. I felt like I'd been hit by a tractor.

Inhaling deeply, which hurt my rib cage, I braced myself for Dad's outpouring of annoyance. Surely I was about to get the biggest bollocking of my life. But as he shuffled his chair a little closer and put his hand on my shoulder, I could see that his dark blue eyes showed no sign of anger.

'Are you gonna tell me what's been going on, son?' His voice was weary but calm.

'It was the wolf,' I said. 'I mean, dog...'

'Yeah, I saw it.' Dad shook his head in disbelief. 'Bloody huge thing it was. Never seen anything like it before. It ran away when I came.'

In a way I was pleased that he'd seen it. It cemented the reality of all that had happened. And yet, it worried me that this other part of me, this angst-ridden depraved spirit guide who had the sun's fire in its eyes, could be seen by others. Did it confirm my sanity? Or did it prove insanity? I didn't know.

'Was it the same dog that bit you on the village green the other day?' Dad wanted to know.

'Maybe.'

He ran a hand over his face. 'Christ, I dread to think what would have happened if I hadn't arrived when I did.'

I wanted to tell him that it would have been fine. That the dog – the wolf – was me. We'd settled our differences. But I didn't say anything. How could I without a psychologist, maybe even social services, becoming involved?

'Why was Colton at the cundy?' Dad's eyes became shrewd and I wondered just how much I could tell him. When I didn't respond immediately, he said, 'I heard you both talking the other day. Why did you lie to me, Sully? Why did you tell me it was you who'd taken your mam's bracelet when it wasn't?'

Sighing, I shrugged. 'Colton's having a rough time. He didn't mean any harm. He just misses her.'

Dad made a strangled sound in his throat and covered his eyes with his hand. He sat like that for a minute or two. I didn't know what to say or do. Dad wasn't one for great displays of emotion and I wasn't sure how to deal with them. Should I squeeze his hand? Pat him on the shoulder? Give him space? He coughed as if to compose himself then looked at me again. I could see his eyes were glazed with tears. His jaw was set tight, as if in resistance of emotional overload. 'We all do, son,' he managed to say. 'We're all having a rough time of it, eh?'

'Yeah, I know. But Colton's only little. He thought Mam was in the cundy.'

This seemed to send Dad over the edge. Tears did fall from his eyes then. He wiped at his cheeks with the heels of his hands and nodded vehemently.

'You're a good 'un, kid, you really are. And I'm so sorry I've not been myself lately. I'm sorry that you've had so much shit to deal with and I've not been there. It's been hard. I know. Really hard. But that's no excuse. It will get better though. It will.'

I hoped he was right.

'Where's Colton now?' I asked.

Dad thumbed over his shoulder towards the door. 'In the waiting room.'

'Is he okay?'

'Yeah. Probably stuffing his face with sweets from the vending machines, truth be told.'

I managed to smile. It hurt like buggery. 'Is he out there on his own?'

'No, Aunt Julie's with him. I had to call her.' Dad looked down into his lap, some element of guilt or embarrassment making him suddenly sheepish. 'I couldn't drive here myself, you know?'

Oh yes, I knew. His whisky bender had rendered him useless.

'Are we going to Aunt Julie's straight after school tomorrow?' I asked, my spirits dying a little more. In fact, *kill me now*, is what I wanted to say.

'School tomorrow?' Dad's eyebrows raised. 'I don't think so, you daft bugger. You're in no fit state to be going to school.'

'Will I be going straight to hers from hospital then?'

'No.' Dad smiled sadly and shook his head. 'You won't be going to stay with Aunt Julie at all.'

'How come?' My spirits perked up.

'I know you don't want to.'

Understatement of the year.

'Aunt Julie's kids are arseholes, I know,' Dad went on, 'and I should have listened to you more. But my hands have been tied, you know? I'm trying to do all of this single-handedly…' I think Dad had a lot more to say but stopped when he realised he was at risk of unburdening himself on his teenage son. 'Anyway,' he said, 'things have changed. A lot. I wasn't actually going to send you to Aunt Julie's, but with the way you've both been, well, sorry, the way Colton's been carrying on lately, I'd had enough. Couldn't take any more. But now, well, I guess I realise he's been wanting my attention. That's all. I should have spent more time with him. And you. I should have spent time with both of you.'

'What'll happen while you're at work though?' I said. 'Will I be keeping an eye on Colton like I offered?'

Dad grinned and there was a strange glint in his eye. 'I know you're not a baby anymore, Sully, and I trust you can look after Colton, especially after all that's been going on, but no. I've been sorting some other stuff out lately. My job's been at risk for the past three months, which I suppose has been putting extra pressure on me. That's why I've been a bit short with you both lately. Anyway, can you remember your mam's Aunt Sheena?'

I vaguely could. Really old lady with hair so white it probably shone in the dark. 'Er, yeah?'

'Well, she got in touch a little while back. She told me she's got a few bob tucked away and that she'd like to help me get back on my feet while at the same time investing in some future security for you and Colton. She's ninety-six and doesn't have any family of her own and your mam was always a bit of a favourite of hers.'

'What kind of investment?'

'She's given us the money to set up a family business. I mean, I argued with her at first, but she insisted. She's pretty stubborn. I mean, scarily stubborn.' Dad made wide eyes. 'Once I put my pride to one side, I could see that it would be a great opportunity not just for me, but for you two as well. So that's what I've been doing for the past few weeks. Securing premises and sorting paperwork, all that sort of stuff.'

'That's really cool, Dad,' I said, happy to see that he could be enthusiastic about something again. I remembered the Saturday afternoon he'd got dressed up and worn aftershave, when I'd thought he was going on a date. How wrong I'd been. 'I'm really pleased. But what will me and Colton be doing over the summer?'

'You can come and help me sort the funeral home. Like redecorating and stuff, so we can get it up and running as soon as possible. You're both pretty handy with a paintbrush and there'll be plenty of wallpaper to scrape off the walls. I want it to be really nice. A proper family business. It's going to be a new start for us all.'

'But I thought you said that sort of business isn't for kids?'

'Maybe not Colton just yet,' he said, nodding. 'But I underestimated you. You don't need to be hidden away from all of that stuff, do you?'

I shook my head. If only he knew.

Dad's smile came back. 'It's gonna be called Carter & Sons Funeral Home,' he told me.

'That sounds great.' And I really meant it. I hadn't had aspirations of becoming a funeral director before, but now I was open to the idea. In fact, I was so pleased that Dad had decided to involve me in his plans, I thought I'd be more than happy to follow in his footsteps.

The door to the side ward we were in swung open. Colton walked in, followed by Aunt Julie. Colton was sucking the end of a straw which was stuck in a carton of a Capri Sun. When he saw me awake, his eyes widened. 'Sully!'

Aunt Julie was less enthusiastic. She must have hauled

herself out of bed when Dad had called her, I reckoned. Her hair was a messy bird's nest on her head and it was the first time I'd seen her out in public without makeup.

'Alright, Sullivan?' she said. The way she said my name always made me feel like she was taking the piss. As if she thought, by default, I was as pretentious as she thought my name to be. 'How's it going?' She stood behind Dad, gripping the back of his chair. Looming over us all like an unkempt yeti.

How do you bloody think? I wanted to say. But, instead, I forced a smile and said, 'Could be better.'

Colton came to stand at the side of the bed, his eyes taking in the bandages and whatever damage he could see on my face. Him being there, knowing the truth about what had happened, made me feel like a freak. I'd caused so much trouble, unknowingly or not. And I was worried about how the whole experience might affect us in the future. Would it serve to bond us even more? Or would it drive a wedge into our previous closeness?

I dunno if Dad sensed the need for me to have some time alone with Colton, but he stood up and said, 'Do you mind if me and your Aunt Julie pop to the café to get a quick cuppa, Sully?'

I shook my head. 'Of course not.'

When they'd gone, Colton slinked closer and sat in the seat Dad had been occupying.

'I hear Dad's not sending us to Aunt Julie's now,' I said.

Colton nodded. If he was relieved, he certainly didn't show it. Frowning, he fiddled with the foil Capri Sun carton.

'How did you do it?' he said after a few awkward minutes had passed.

Puffing out my cheeks, I exhaled loudly. There was only one thing he could be talking about.

'I dunno.' And I genuinely didn't. 'How did you know

it was me?'

'I dreamt about the wolf a lot,' he said. 'It was always nice to me, so I wasn't really scared of it anymore. When I went back to the cundy tonight and saw it there, it just sat watching me and, I dunno, I just sort of knew that it belonged to you. I think even in my dreams I knew. There was something about it.' He shifted in his seat a bit, then said, 'Mam told me before she died, you know.'

'Told you what?'

'That you have the sight. That you'd be able to talk to her someday.'

'Oh.'

'Did you really not see her tonight?'

'In the cundy?'

Colton nodded. 'Uh-huh.'

'No. But I saw her in my dream, just before I came looking for you. She told me I needed to find you.'

'Really?' Colton's eyes widened with something like hope.

'Yeah. She knew where you were.' I coughed and a wave of pain ripped around my ribcage. I closed my eyes, wincing, and waited for the agony to abate. 'Don't tell Dad about any of the crazy shit, mind.'

'I won't.' Colton stretched across and put his empty juice carton on my bedside table. When he turned back to me, he said, 'Are you keeping it?'

'Keeping what?'

'The wolf.'

Despite my broken, hurting ribs, I almost felt like laughing. 'I'm not sure *what* happens now. I mean, it might not even come back.' And I hoped this would be the case. I didn't want to see the wolf ever again. It terrified me.

But Colton assured me, 'It will.'

'How do you know?'

'I just do. It's part of you.'

'Maybe it's back inside me now.'

'Hmmm.' Colton considered this then shook his head. 'I doubt it.'

'Well, we'll see.'

He was quiet for a while, then said, 'You look like you had a fight with Freddy Krueger, you know.'

'Really? How bad is it?'

He pulled his mouth down at both sides, making a wincing face. 'Fairly.'

'Do you think it'll scar?'

Without needing to think on this at all, Colton nodded. 'Definitely.'

'Will I look awful?'

Oblivious to my fragile teen self-consciousness, he shrugged. 'I dunno. Maybe.' He scored his fingers down the right side of his face. 'You can tell people you had a fight with a wolf and survived. That's pretty cool.'

'Except, no one would believe me.'

'I'll back you up.'

'Cheers, but somehow I don't think I'll be telling anyone about what really happened.'

'So what will you say? That Freddy Krueger got you?'

I laughed. 'Hardly. I'll tell them that I got mauled by a stray dog.'

'But that's not true.'

'But it's the story from now on, okay?'

Colton sighed. 'Okay.'

Dad's voice in the corridor marked his return.

'Will you take me to see her, Sully?' Colton said, with a new sense of urgency. As if my answer right then, right that minute, would be immovable and concrete and written in the stars.

'Take you to see who?'

'Mam.' He stood up and gripped my arm. It hurt. A lot. 'Can you? *Will* you?'

'She's not in the cundy if that's what you mean,' I told

him. 'I asked her. She told me.'

'But…can you try talking to her somewhere else? Anywhere.'

I smiled, despite the pain from his nipping fingers, and threw him a wink. 'Yeah. I'll figure something out, shit stain.'

Dad re-entered the room, worn and haggard. He smiled at me. I felt more content than I had done in ages.

Carter & Sons Funeral Home.

I lay back and closed my eyes and wondered if Ginny would think I looked particularly dapper in a black morning suit and tie.

THE CUNDY

Acknowledgements

Thanks to all of my loyal readers who continue to share this journey with me, it's great to have you along for the ride. Your encouragement is always massively appreciated!

A warm welcome to all new readers too. I hope you'll stick around and become part of my clan.

Thanks to Hannah Thompson for editing The Cundy. As ever, you gave some very sound and invaluable advice for making the best of all these words that splurged out of me.

Thanks to my mam and dad, my older brother, Eddie, and all my childhood friends and acquaintances – you all helped to shape this book in some way or another, I'm sure. Especially the Easington Comprehensive School year of '96s. It was good to reminisce those tragic days of shell suits, quiffs, cycling shorts and slouch socks – as well as those popular insults and terminologies of the 90s. Ha!

Thanks to my old maths teacher for sparking the opening idea (pardon the pun). She did indeed fall victim to the electrics in the storage cupboard one rainy afternoon and, subsequently, we all got sent home. My childhood friend, Angie, and I snuck off down the dene instead of going home, however. We didn't go to the cundy, we went in search of the Devil's Rock – but it was a rainy adventure that went on to inspire.

Thanks to Benn Clarkson for listening to me bitch and gripe through the dark days that inevitably come with writing a book. And for sorting my CMYK files again. I owe you, man!

Thanks to Denise Sparrowhawk from Hartlepool

Central Library for the continued support of local authors.

Thanks to my street team members Elizabeth Bage, Kathryn Roebuck, Caroline Howard and Mark Illingworth for their enthusiasm and dedication since the beginning of all this.

Thanks to Kay Deveroux, a lady I've not had the privilege of meeting beyond the realms of the internet, but one whom inspires me greatly with her passion for horror.

Thanks to Marvin and Delilah for the frequent cuddles – whether they wanted them or not.

And last but not least, thanks to my wonderful husband, Derek, for keeping it real, keeping me sane and for the continued support, without which none of this would be possible. You inspire me greatly, mister!

Oh and in case you wondered, Angie and I did find the Devil's Rock that rainy day at the dene. It oozed gunky red stuff, just like legend said. We were pretty sure it wasn't *really* the Devil's blood though...

I think.

About The Author

R. H. Dixon is a horror enthusiast who, when not escaping into the fantastical realms of fiction, lives in the northeast of England with her husband and two whippets.

Visit her website for horror features, short stories, promotions and news of her upcoming books: **www.rhdixon.com**

IF YOU ENJOYED READING THIS BOOK, PLEASE LEAVE A REVIEW ON AMAZON. THANK YOU!

THE CUNDY

Printed in Great Britain
by Amazon